This book is dedicated to Anthony Ian Frazer, who has spent the last forty years guiding me through life and keeping me safe. Thank you so much, Tony.

The Falconer Files
by
Andrea Frazer

The Falconer Files

Death of an Old Git
Choked Off
Inkier than the Sword
Pascal Passion
Murder at the Manse
Music to Die For
Strict and Peculiar
Christmas Mourning
Grave Stones
Death in High Circles
Glass House

Falconer Files – Brief Cases

Love Me To Death
A Sidecar Named Expire
Battered to Death
Toxic Gossip
Driven to It
All Hallows
Death of a Pantomime Cow

CONTENTS

DRAMATIS PERSONAE

<u>The Residents of Steynham St Michael</u>

Buckleigh, Bryony – a widow, retired
Buttery, Noah, and Patience – librarians
Crawford, Craig – accountant and model railway enthusiast
Gifford, Tilly, doctor's receptionist and local gossip
Grayling, Hermione – successful writer
Kerr, Roma – owner of local ladies' fashion shop, married to Rodney
Littlemore, Malcolm, and Amy – own village craft shop
Pounce, Hilda ('Potty') – cleaner for many of the residents
Pryor, Dimity – works part-time in the charity shop
Pryor, Gabriel – bank clerk
Rainbird, Charles – antiques dealer
Raynor, Monica and Quentin– estate agents
Sinden, Elizabeth (Buffy) – dental nurse and local 'bicycle'
Warlock, Vernon – runs the local bookshop

<u>The Officials</u>

Detective Inspector Harry Falconer
Detective Sergeant 'Davey' Carmichael
Sergeant Bob Bryant
PC Merv Green
PC Linda 'Twinkle' Starr
Superintendent Derek 'Jelly' Chivers
Dr Philip Christmas

Introduction
Concerning Geography

Geographically, Steynham St Michael splits easily into four quarters, due to the crossroads consisting of the south to north Market Darley Road, and the east to west road, known simply as the High Street, as it runs through the village.

Its commercial buildings lie mainly along the two sides of the High Street but, after a short run of cottages running north on the eastern side of the Market Darley road, resume again, with one of the two public houses standing on the western side. Slightly further north, Tuppenny Lane leads off to the right, with the fish and chip shop on the corner, then the Strict and Particular Baptist Church (unused now), the library (under threat of funding reductions), a small area of waste ground and, finally, an infants' and primary school, these days seen as a status symbol for any rural community.

To the south west of the High Street are some comparatively recent houses, these having been built when some of the insanitary and tumbledown former farm workers' cottages were demolished. Some of the more sturdy older dwellings, Queen Victoria Terrace and Prince Albert Terrace are good examples of houses built in the nineteenth century, but with a conscience that their fabric should be sound and that the buildings should last.

In the south-east corner of Steynham St Michael is Barleycorn Crescent, built round the edges of the green and occasional cricket pitch and resembling the half-circle of the lower case letter 'b' to the upright of the Market Darley Road, when viewed from above, or from a map. These houses are pure nineteen-thirties, and as out of place as the Victorian terraces, the only advantage to living in them perhaps being direct rear access to the Co-operative Store and the recycling bins.

Old Steynham St Michael is represented by its northern half, containing as it does the church of St Michael and All Angels, the aforementioned Strict and Particular Chapel *(a particular attraction in itself)*, the prettiest and most picturesque cottages, the older and more traditional of the two public houses, and some pretty lanes hiding yet more desirable residences.

Not an obvious tourist trap, and unlikely to become one, but the residents and proprietors of commercial establishments get by as best as they can in this uncertain world, with its precarious local, national, and global finances, and hope that the future has more to offer than today has.

Prologue
Demographic For A New Year

Friday 1st January

The first day of a new year sees few people in their places of work. In Steynham St Michael, however, there was more commercial activity than may have been guessed at.

Charles Rainbird, of Mill Cottage, Dairy Lane, and proprietor of Rainbird's Renaissance *(where beautiful things are given a new lease of life)* was in his stock room at the rear of his establishment, which was situated at the meeting of the Market Darley Road and the High Street, putting it firmly in the bottom right-hand corner of the north-west quarter of the village.

He was sitting in a disreputable-looking old armchair which sprouted horsehair and other components of stuffing at every corner. His upper body was bent over, and right inside an old chest, from which he was steadily removing items and putting them on a table beside him. He had been to a couple of auctions between Christmas and New Year, and had bid for a number of job lots in the hope of finding those things which are overlooked by the general and ignorant public, but are bread and butter – and possibly even jam – to a struggling antiques' dealer.

He had already had quite a few lucky finds, and the proceeds of his fossicking and ferreting in old boxes, crates, and trunks were piling up, leading him to think that, with a bit of elbow-grease, he should have some profits to come from a future auction himself. There were some nice examples of brown furniture, discarded in the general turnout of such items, that would bring a hearty sum if waxed well *(over a bit of judicious*

3

filling here and there) and catalogued properly, and he might even get old Potty Pounce to come and give him a hand. She wasn't such a bad old stick, really, and she certainly knew how to work hard for her pittance.

Potty Pounce, the object of Charles' thoughts, was in fact Mrs Hilda Pounce, widow of this parish, resident at number three Prince Albert Terrace, and 'treasure' of many a resident of the village, both present and past. On this newest day of the new year, she was dressing herself, ready for the low outside temperature, as she had been asked by both the Ox and Plough and the Fox and Hounds to lend a hand clearing up after the celebrations of the night before and, although this meant an early start for her so that the establishments could open again at lunchtime, she set out energetically.

A few extra quid always came in handy, and she needed all she could get to keep up with the rising prices of just about everything. Why, it was getting so that she could hardly afford to heat her cottage, and times hadn't been that bad since she was a child and her father had been out of work; the bitter winter of 1962/3 being a bad time to have a disagreement with your boss and let your mouth run away with you. Ah, the old times, she thought. Not always good times, but always with you, and nothing would ever change them, no matter how hard you wanted to or tried.

Vernon Warlock, who ran the antiquarian and second-hand bookshop in the High Street, sat at his desk in Vine Cottage staring blindly out of his front window overlooking the Market Darley Road and shook his white-haired head in despair, setting free a gentle snow-storm of dandruff which alighted gently on the shoulders of his clean but shabby claret-coloured cardigan. He would have to telephone that chap again and see what he could let him have. Times had never been so difficult, and sometimes he wondered if he shouldn't just sell up and retire, with his beloved books, from commerce, as well as society. No doubt a benevolent and profligate government would look after

4

him, as it seemed to everyone else.

At the cottage known as Chrysanthemums, in Farriers Lane, Roma Kerr looked up from studying the accounts for the ladies' fashions and haberdashery business that she ran with her husband, caught sight of said husband spilling black coffee as he coughed his morning cigarette into the ashtray, lost her temper and shouted. 'Why don't you go back to bed, you drunken, stinking lazy old soak? You're no bloody use to me nor to anyone else! Get out of my sight before I do something drastic, like throw you out with the rubbish where you belong.'

Rodney Kerr put down his nearly empty coffee cup in the fireplace, threw his cigarette butt into the charcoal from the night before's fire, and left the room, trailing an air of cigarette smoke and gloom, mingled with stale whisky. He had no idea why he behaved as he did, except for the fact that he could not see anything to look forward to. Everything before him appeared to be grey, and he didn't see how him stopping drinking and smoking too much was going to inject any colour into the future landscape.

Roma could burble on all she liked about how they would revitalise the business and turn it around, but he didn't see the point. The business was as dead as their future – as dead as their marriage – and nothing he could do could change that.

Immediately opposite the Kerrs' business in the High Street, Buffy Sinden slid open a wary eye, and peered at the pillow next to hers – empty. She might have known that anyone she met at a New Year's Eve do at the Fox and Hounds was bound to be just another 'leg-over' merchant, lacking even the staying power to address breakfast. Oh well, never mind: more bacon for her then, and an extra sausage – the thought of which made her smile as she walked into the bathroom.

Her reflection in the bathroom mirror soon wiped the smug look from her face, as she surveyed what was before her. Eyeshadow, liner, mascara, and lipstick were blurred across her features like old stage make-up. Her hair, bleached beyond conditioning, the ends split from daily back-combing, did not provide an edifying sight. She was thirty-five years old, divorced, had a very chequered past *(the details of which she hugged possessively in the dark side of her heart)*, and a job as a dental nurse in the practice on Market Darley Road.

Apart from these few and uninspiring facts, she did own her own home, Clematis Cottage, or at least as much of it as the building society allowed her to own while she was still in debt to them. She had a job, but not exactly a glamorous and exciting one, and she had a reputation as a good-time girl – the original good time that was 'had' by all. Even the postmen at the local sorting office were aware of her 'social life', and referred to her pretty little hideaway as 'Clitoris Cottage'. It was time she pulled herself together, acted her age, and did something worthwhile with her life. Wasn't it? Or could she really be arsed to make the effort?

Hermione Grayling pursed her over-lipsticked mouth, pulled her eyebrows together with a frown, picked a final full-stop with the index finger of her right hand, and leaned back with a sigh. That was certainly enough for today, she thought, gazing at the sheet of paper in her old-fashioned manual typewriter. It may be very early in the day, but she just wasn't in the mood. At the head of the page was the number '731', and she realised that she was nearly at the end of another of her Victorian family sagas.

With a sigh of satisfaction, she used the fingers of both hands to fluff up the unruly curls of the wig she had habitually worn since her hair had first got a little thin, then stretched her plump arms up in a gesture of relaxation. She would telephone her old school friend Dimity Pryor who lived just down the road in the terrace of ancient cottages on the Market Darley road. They could take afternoon tea together.

That would be nice, and she could tell Dimity all about her ideas for her next nineteenth-century Aga saga. Dimity was always such a help with the little details, and seemed to have such an enthusiastic interest in the development of the lives of the families in the books, that she sometimes sounded

6

proprietorial – as if they were hers instead of Hermione's – though not as proprietorial as Vernon Warlock from the bookshop.

He felt he had an absolute right to tell her what to do with her characters, book after book after book, and also what she should have done with them in those already published. Dear, infuriating old Vernon. She would invite him too.

They should all three of them have toast and caviar, and some of those fresh cream meringues which were so deliciously gooey in the middle, with a pot of Darjeeling. It would serve the interfering little darlings right, for being so special to her, and so dear to her heart. She'd get Hilda to pour it for them, from her dearest great-aunt's silver tea service, and in her very best Rockingham china. Hermione believed in keeping nothing for best, but in using and enjoying things while you had them, instead of keeping them perfect for someone else, after you were dead.

In Pear Tree Cottage, next door to Dimity Pryor, Noah and Patience Buttery were considering their new year's resolutions with earnest zeal. Both of them were descended from the villagers who had, for decades, attended the Strict and Particular Chapel, and they took such a task very seriously. Any attempt to change for the better was to be considered long and hard, and assessed on the chance of its success. If it were to be a case of wasted effort, they would be better looking for something different to make a difference in this world.

Their thirteen-year-old son had decided that he would donate ten per cent *(like a tithe)* of his paper round money to Christian Aid, but that had seemed enough of an effort to him, and he was now happily plugged in to his mixing decks, headphones wagging, lips flapping as, with eyes closed, he got down with the beat.

At the corner of Tuppenny Lane in Forge Cottage, things were similarly lively, and as loud as they were in the Butterys' son's headphones. Amy and Malcolm Littlemore were at it again! Or rather, Amy Littlemore was drunk again *(and so early in the day)*, which was not surprising, as Malcolm brought her her first couple of drinks of the day in bed, so that she could control her shakes enough to leave the bedroom and function, after a fashion. This being a Bank Holiday, she was a little ahead of her usual schedule, and had had more than usual at this time of the morning. Malcolm was trying to pacify her, or at least to turn her wrath upon something other than him if he could not allay it. It was the mention of new stock that had set her off this time.

Malcolm had ordered a smattering of new lines to try to liven up their business. Amy had decided that, in her present mood, the shop was in dire straits and could afford not a penny on new stock, besides which, she personally had chosen their present lines, and why was it she who was always wrong, wrong, wrong?

Neatly ducking a surprisingly accurately lobbed heavy glass ashtray, Malcolm rose to the occasion with a soothing bottle in his hand and, holding it out before him as a peace offering, approached his now silent partner – if only she would remain so! – and tentatively filled her glass. She rewarded him with a glowing smile on a face from which all vestige of malice and hatred had been expunged, and he knew she had forgotten, once more, what had set her off. If he was lucky, she'd be asleep in front of the box by the time the news came on, and he could have a quiet evening with just the gentle susurration of her snores to keep him company.

Tilly Gifford, of Foxes' Run, one of the terrace of old cottages on the Market Darley Road, did not wander downstairs until ten o'clock that morning, and would have stayed in bed longer if she could have ignored Tommy's pig-like snores. She was halfway down the stairs when she saw the envelope lying on the door mat under the letterbox, and her brow furrowed in puzzlement. Today was a Bank Holiday and surely there was no post, so who had pushed a letter through her letterbox?

She could see it was a letter because, even from this

distance, she could identify what was obviously an address. As she got closer she realised that the reason she could see it from such a distance was because it wasn't handwritten, or even typed. It consisted of large letters and numbers, obviously cut from newspaper or magazine article headlines, and was addressed to her.

Knowing that she was bolting the stable door after the horse had bolted, she nevertheless opened the front door and looked both right and left, pulling the folds of her fleecy dressing gown closer round her as she did so, to ward off the cold. No, not a soul in sight, as she'd thought. What exactly had she got here? She'd better keep it to herself and have a look at it later, when Tommy was obviously and noisily in the shower.

Monica Raynor, next door at Badger's Sett, had been up since quite early, and had heard the flap of the letter box as the envelope was pushed through it. Not even thinking that there would be no official post on a Bank Holiday, she nevertheless ambled out to see what it was that had landed on her doormat and, as soon as she had seen the crudely cut and pasted letters on the envelope, shot out through her front door, and looked sharply in both directions.

But there was not a car in sight, let alone a pedestrian with a guilty expression, so she shoved the missive in her dressing-gown pocket, refusing to even look at it until she had at least two cups of hot, strong black coffee inside her. This didn't look like a party invitation, and she wasn't ready for something unpleasant so early in not only the morning, but in the year.

Chapter One
The Physical Aspect of The Occasion

Friday 1st January

Everything was pitch-black, and all Falconer could hear was someone groaning. Something covered his head, he was unable to move, and still the groaning went on. Every muscle in his body ached, and his head throbbed brutally, timing itself to the groans that seemed to be closing in on him. His throat was as dry as dust. What the hell had happened? What the hell was going on? Why was no one coming to his aid? Was he going to die?

Detective Inspector Harry Falconer gradually became aware that the person groaning was himself, and that the reason he was unable to move was that he was wrapped tightly in his own bed linen, the three cats for which he was now responsible adding their weight to his state of immobility. One question, however, still remained. What the hell had happened?

And then it came back: not all of it, but little glimpses, like trailers from a film about hell, glimpses that he knew would grow into great big, explosive, shame-filled, remembered activity, and he rather wished that he *had* been going to die, for he remembered that yesterday he had been best man at Carmichael's wedding!

His cry of 'Aaaaargh! Oh my God! Dear God, no, no, no, no, no! No! Anything but that! Please, God, I don't want to remember!' was as an unanswered prayer, as cats scattered willy-nilly, and he fought his way out of the bedclothes to survey the state in which he had entered his slumber.

New Year's Eve had been the wedding date selected by his no longer acting, but actual, detective sergeant, Ralph 'Davey'

Carmichael, and Carmichael's sweetheart Kerry Long. A truly odd couple who had met during an investigation the previous summer in the village of Castle Farthing, they were as different as chalk and cheese.

Kerry had been first married very young, and was separated from her husband and trying to make ends meet for her and her two sons, when old cow-poke Carmichael had come galloping on to the scene. Carmichael, all nearly six and a half feet of him *(and as daft as a brush, in Falconer's opinion)*, had fallen almost instantly for her, and they had planned their future with no loss of time.

It was just before Christmas that Carmichael had issued his invitation for Falconer to be best man, and asked if he could inspect the contents of his boss's wardrobe. Somewhat perplexed, but too polite to question the request as it involved his colleague's wedding, Falconer had agreed, without demur, to wear the Indian jacket he had picked up on his travels many years before.

The material of said jacket of exotic origins was of alternate threads of orange and brown in Shantung silk, giving a two-tone effect that was muted but eye-catching. It had no collar, but had a fine gold braid which was attached at cuff, neckline, down the front and round the bottom of the garment. Falconer had never had the nerve to actually wear it, but had agreed that if Carmichael wanted him to, he would give it its debut appearance at the Register Office.

Of Carmichael's actual motive for such a request, he was to have no idea until he turned up, half an hour early, as was his habit, for the civil ceremony, only to see the gathering of a clan of bizarrely clad people that he had to assume were members of the Carmichael clan. His outfit, in retrospect, had been a model of modesty and restraint. It was only with the arrival of the bride and groom that realisation of what exactly was happening, had dawned on him.

It was as Cinderella and Prince Charming stepped down from a heavily decorated farm cart that he understood that what Carmichael had been planning was a wedding totally in keeping with the time of year. It was a pantomime wedding! And, as best man, he was going to figure in just about every photograph taken, and may God have mercy on his soul and on his reputation. Moving towards the happy (but surely mad?) couple, there was only time for a, 'Giddy up, Aladdin. We're on in two minutes,' from Carmichael, before he was whisked into the thick of things, and now his life would never be quite the same again.

The ceremony had, in fact, started ten minutes late, which had been enough time for Carmichael's mother to whip a hip flask out of the many layers of her Widow Twankey costume and administer, almost against his will, a couple of hefty belts of brandy. They would have been even heftier if he had not physically moved away, for he didn't think it would be very diplomatic of him to strike the mother of the groom on such an occasion, and therefore, allowed himself to be thus force-fed a couple of what were probably at least doubles.

As the short ceremony ended, Falconer managed to catch sight of the bride's godparents, Alan and Marian Warren-Browne, respectably dressed in matching kimonos and representing God knows what pantomime – possibly innocent bystanders caught up in Aladdin's story – but before he could strike out in their direction, he was, literally, carried off in the bridal party to be transported to the reception, where the photographer was to be given free rein.

How he had ended up in the second bridal car he had no idea, but he had found himself, once again, in the company of the lady now elevated to the position of Mrs Carmichael senior. Like a breast-feeding mother detecting a need for nourishment in her infant, she immediately stuck the neck of a wine bottle into his mouth. Rather than drown, or ruin his exquisite jacket, he drank, and knew that he was being fed by a mother who had had no need of a wet nurse to provide her charge with succour.

By the time everyone was settled at the reception, Falconer knew three things and, if he thought hard enough, he might be able to remember all three. No, that wasn't right! How many things was it he had to remember? The number three came to mind. Now, what had he been thinking about when he had been slightly more coherent? Oh yes, he had been lining things up. What things? And where? And why? Was it a game he was playing, or a competition he had entered?

He really must pull himself together. Now, things in a line – how many was it? With a shake of his head, he took a brief trip back to near-sobriety, and remembered that he knew three things, and had been about to line them up and look at them, examining them as a group.

Taking a mental breath, he considered the first thing he knew, which was that his jacket was still free from stains, creases, tears, burns or other damage.

The second thing he knew, and at which he had to squint slightly to stop it slipping away, was that he had never found himself in a weirder situation, surrounded as he was by Ali Baba and his forty thieves, Wishy-Washy, Jack the Giant Killer, Buttons, Baron Hard-Up, the Ugly Sisters, and just about any other pantomime figure he could imagine.

The third thing he knew, he knew positively and absolutely irrefutably, and this was, that he was drunk, and likely to become drunker as the affair went on. There was no escape for him from Carmichael's lunatic family and friends, and he was just going to have to bite the bullet and let it happen. Even the SAS couldn't rescue him from this benevolent but terrifying captivity.

Yes, examining all three things in a group had been a good idea. Because he now knew for certain that he had been royally and irrefutably shafted by fate, and would have to let the whim of the wind of circumstance carry him where it would. He was powerless in its grasp, and would probably need a damned good tailor to sew his reputation back into one piece after today.

His explosive propulsion from present, to past, and back to the present again, propelled him as far as the kitchen, where his three furry dependents waited, practically tapping their claws with impatience. He was well behind his usual time for feeding them, and they were hungry, after the distinctly meagre *(in their opinion)* scattering of crunchy food they had received for supper the night before. Their person *(for cats are not owned, merely having all their needs catered for)* was definitely not on form, for they were not used to such erratic attention and irresponsible behaviour.

Falconer put on the kettle before attending to his furry charges, remembering the previous January, when it had just been him and Mycroft, his beloved Siamese. Since then, Carmichael had picked up a wife on that case in Castle Farthing last summer. He had picked up a broken heart and two more cats, Ruby and Tar Baby, on the case that followed in the early autumn.

It looked like Carmichael had got the better deal, and he, Falconer, merely a heavier heart and a lighter wallet. Of such things is life made. One just had to get on with it and hope for the best. 'Whye bollocks, man!' he thought in a Geordie accent, pouring his coffee and pulling out a chair at the kitchen table, as he wondered what shit the New Year had in store for him.

He was supposed to be on duty today, having surmised that though attendance at Carmichael's wedding might take up a couple of hours of his time, he would be able to retire with a book at his usual bedtime. As things were, he called the station for a patrol car to pick him up in half an hour, as he was certainly not fit to drive, and had no intention whatsoever of losing his licence as well as his good name.

He started to suffer the flashbacks as he dressed, and by the time the car arrived to pick him up, he was in a cold sweat, imagining that everyone at the station would have had photographs of his humiliation sent to them via mobile phones and the internet, but all was quiet when he arrived at the old redbrick police station in Market Darley, and no one so much as glanced at him as he made his way quietly – almost furtively – to his office.

The criminal element under the jurisdiction of the Market Darley station was either more hungover than he was, or were diligently observing the Bank Holiday, for there were no calls at all on his time, and only a scant number of visitors to the front desk, most of them in search of cars that they had mislaid the night before, and wouldn't mind some help from any officers on patrol in locating their vehicle. Bob Bryant – as usual – fielded them and made the necessary arrangements for any sightings. Truth to tell, Falconer was not aware of anyone else in the building but the two of them, and for this he was grateful – well, sort of, because it gave his mind nothing to occupy itself with, and he could put it into dorm mode.

Sitting at his desk, however, vivid hallucinations – or were they? – troubled him. One was of three strapping lads, each dressed as the Genie of the Lamp, each holding a facsimile of said lamp, smiling benevolently at him. Another was of two strikingly similar Ugly Sisters making up a ghastly trio with Mrs Carmichael senior, all three waving coyly at him. He had a vague recollection that all three of the genies and the two ugly sisters were Carmichael's siblings, but no names came to mind as he tried to banish the ghastly recollections.

During the early afternoon he decided that enough was enough, told Bob Bryant to furnish any callers with the number for his work mobile, and slunk out of the building like a fugitive in search of sanctuary. Carmichael was not taking a honeymoon at such an inclement time of the year and was, instead, just spending the first day of the year – a Friday – and the ensuing weekend, with his new bride and her two sons. No doubt his recollection of the – Falconer was at a loss to know how to regard the events of the previous day – festivities, celebrations, bacchanalian revels – would be better than his own.

He returned home, knowing that he would have a restless weekend until Carmichael could either put him out of his misery, or confirm his awful suppositions, on Monday morning. He should never have agreed to be the best man. He should have known that if left to Carmichael, any event – even his own wedding – would be an absolute shambles and completely bizarre. Who on earth else would arrange, let alone choose to have, a pantomime wedding? It would have been a pantomime even without the costumes, with his DS in charge.

After a meagre snack that he did not really feel like eating, he dry-swallowed two paracetamol and headed for his rumpled bed at seven-thirty, thanking his lucky stars that it was the arse-hole of the year and therefore dark very early, so that he didn't feel too much of a freak turning in at such an unheard-of hour, and grateful that he wasn't rostered for duty again until Monday. It would take him a whole weekend to recover from feeling like this, which was worse than he'd ever felt before. What *had* he been drinking? Meths? Paraffin?

Chapter Two
The Aspirational Side of Things

Monday 4th January

'Davey' Carmichael was a very happy man. He had recently passed his sergeant's exams and been awarded promotion to detective sergeant, and paired permanently with Inspector Harry Falconer, with whom he had already worked two murder cases as an acting detective sergeant.

When they had first been partnered, Carmichael had lived in a somewhat higgledy-piggledy extension at the rear of the family council house, and was involved on a daily basis in the fight for clean clothes that not only fitted, but were intended for the right gender. He led a rather lonely life, as his outlook on things was not exactly normal, but his expectations were high, and he somehow knew that things would come good for him, if he just let life get on with sorting it out for him.

On their very first case together, Carmichael had met and fallen in love with his future wife, and was delighted rather than dismayed, to discover that she had two sons from a previous marriage. In his eyes the boys were a bonus, not a hindrance.

As his relationship with his superior began to take shape, he had proposed to the now Mrs Carmichael but, sticking by the morals and principles that he had been brought up with, but which were perhaps a little old-fashioned, he refused to live with her until they were married, and that was the real reason that the ceremony had been so promptly planned and executed. A couple of his siblings did ask if Kerry was in the Pudding Club, but he had glared balefully at them, and opined that he thought they knew him better than that.

The awarding of his sergeant's stripes *(worn invisibly on*

plain clothes) had been the icing on the cake for him, only to be firmly stood on, on the top of the cake, by him and his bride on New Year's Eve – a date impossible to forget, even for him.

Although he had only taken two days' leave from work – Thursday and Friday, to make sure he wasn't rostered in on the first day of his married life – Carmichael had been busy in that time, making things just that little bit different in his new household. He had woken up on Monday 4th January knowing that, for the first time in his life, he would not have to fight for what he wore today, as his clothes – or those that he could identify as having bought himself – were hanging in the wardrobe in the bedroom of the newlywed couple *(that, physically, he was more like three-quarters than half of)*, waiting for him to take his pick.

He had the wedding photos already downloaded on to a CD, and looked forward to showing them to his boss, and explaining who each member of his family was, as there had been little time for formal introductions on the day itself. It had been a fantastic wedding, in his opinion, and it had been a great idea of Kerry's to have a theme for it. When he suggested pantomime, she had cheered out loud and asked what else they could *possibly* do at that time of year. It was absolutely perfect, and what's more, he was a genius for thinking of it. What a lot could happen in the space of a few months, and he wondered idly where he would be and what he would be doing in a year's time.

Buffy Sinden would not be returning to her work as a dental nurse in the practice on the Market Darley Road until the middle of January, as her employer was, at that very moment, halfway through enjoying his annual thirty nights on a Caribbean cruise. She made her way downstairs on Monday morning at a disgraceful eleven thirty-eight.

Unusually for her, she had spent the night alone, whether as an unconscious sop to a New Year's resolution she had not made, or because her age was beginning to show, and turn off the young men whom she found so attractive and irresistible.

For whatever reason, for once, her face was washed clean of make-up, and her hair sensibly held back with a scrunchie, so she had no difficulty in seeing the envelope lying just inside the front door, as she descended the stairs – no mascara-gummed together eyelashes, no strands of ill-conditioned, bleached hair trailing across her field of vision.

As she picked it up to examine it, the address caught her eye, and she shuddered. The name of her house and road had been made up from letters and syllables cut from some newspaper or magazine, and been glued, in a sufficiently readable way, for it to be delivered, even if 'Clematis Cottage' had suffered a terrible fate.

The postman knew – oh, he knew well enough where to deliver it. Hadn't it been the postman or one of his predecessors who had renamed her home 'Clitoris Cottage' in local parlance? She had not long learnt of this rebaptism of her home, and now blushed furiously as she wondered how widespread the terminology was. Then she noticed there was no stamp, and took a quick peek outside the front door in case whoever had delivered it might still be in sight, but no luck on that front.

Carrying the communication in front of her as if it were an unexploded bomb, she entered the kitchen, and sat down at one of the wheel-backed chairs at the pine table, without altering her position. Once seated, she cut under the flap with the spear of a thumbnail, and carefully removed the one sheet inside, holding it by the tips of her nails only, with the thought that, if this was what she thought it was, then she ought to be careful not to smudge any fingerprints thereon.

As she looked at the crudely cut letters making up the message on the paper, her eyes widened, and she gasped, and continued to hold her breath as the sheet of paper fluttered from her now nerveless fingers onto the table top.

How could anyone be so cruel? she thought; and then: how could anyone actually know?

The craft shop in the High Street wore its 'closed' sign like the pursed lips of an elderly spinster, as if it knew why its door had not been unlocked and the shop not thrown open to the more craft-minded members of the public.

In Forge Cottage, in Tuppenny Lane, Amy Littlemore, one of the co-owners of said establishment, woke to find herself not in bed, but stretched out across the hall floor, at the foot of the open-plan staircase. The shape of her husband Malcolm, the other co-owner of the business, and her husband for longer than either of them cared to remember, was just discernible in the closed-curtained gloom, occupying a wing-backed chair. As she tried to remember what on earth had happened for her to end up in this scenario, she tried to move, and groaned, as various parts of her body cried out in protest. After a few seconds, it was clear to her that she had not chosen to have a little lie down on the carpet before going to bed the previous night, but had obviously reached her present position as the result of a fall.

Although it wasn't unusual for her to wake up with no recollection whatsoever of what had happened the evening before, it was unusual for her not to wake in her own bed. Malcolm usually deposited her there, if she had not been able to make it under her own steam, before he retired to his own room, where he could get a decent night's sleep without her yelling out in her hallucinations, or snoring or urinating while unconscious.

Trying to free her tongue from the roof of her mouth, she raised a hand to her left temple and felt what she surmised was dried blood. What on earth had happened to her? Why wasn't Malcolm on duty to explain things to her, the way he usually was? She raised herself to her knees, clutched at the sofa and rose unsteadily to her feet, then gasped and raised both hands to her mouth before depositing herself on the sofa at the sight that lay before her.

Malcolm looked dead, and it was all she could do not to scream. Reaching out tentatively, she touched his shoulder, then began gently to shake it. Malcolm groaned quietly, opened his eyes, saw his wife standing over him, opened his mouth and began to scream. 'Aaargh!' he yelled. 'Get off of me, you mad cow! If you try that again I'll have you locked up. Get off of me, you mad drunken bitch! You've gone too far this time. Now yer've *got* ter get some 'elp!'

'Malc, what are you talkin' about? What 'appened? Who attacked you? Was it burglars? Talk sense Malc, and tell me what 'appened?' yelled Amy, frightened for both of them now.

'You, yer soppy cow!' he replied as she finally ground to a halt. 'You 'appened. I suppose you don't remember, as per bloody usual. Well, I'll remind you what 'appened, shall I? The way I always do, eh?'

'What are you talking about, Malc?' Amy asked, her voice still shrill with adrenalin-fuelled panic.

'Yer broke a bottle over me bleedin' 'ead this time, didn't yer? And if that wasn't enough for yer, yer gave me a good kickin' as well, while I was down. I managed to get into the chair, but I reckon a few of me ribs is gorn. You're gonner 'ave to get yerself some 'elp, my lady. This can't go on!'

'What am I goin' to do, Malc? What's gonna happen to me?' Amy Littlemore was still confused and panicked, but her face had drained of colour as a little of her memory returned, the dried blood just to the side of one eyebrow standing out as gaudily as stage make-up.

Back at Market Darley Police Headquarters, Inspector Falconer was getting a blow-by-blow account of his sergeant's wedding celebrations, and enjoying every minute of it. It had not taken more than a few minutes from Carmichael catching sight of his boss's wan and embarrassed expression, to the explanation that Harry Falconer, best man and respected inspector with the local CID, had passed out shortly after the celebrations had commenced, had spent the rest of the reception respectfully covered by the cloak of an uncle garbed as a Demon King, and had been sent home in a taxi when things had broken up at an unbelievably respectable hour. The guests had New Year's Eve parties to go to, after all, and didn't want to be delayed by an over-long wedding feast.

The groom himself had escorted Falconer home in a taxi, put some dried food down for the cats, and left him to sleep it off.

23

Most of what Falconer 'remembered' was a product of too much unaccustomed alcohol and an over-active imagination, and on realising this, the inspector came as close to hugging his sergeant as he ever had in their *(purely professional!)* partnership. His reputation was intact, and he would eventually unravel what was real and what was a product of the sordid side of his own imagination.

His sergeant went a good way to assist this process by slotting a CD into a computer, and calling up what seemed like an inordinate number of photographs from the recent nuptials, and Falconer would look at as many as Carmichael was prepared to show him, for he, himself, appeared in very few of them, and in those, he was just an inanely smiling figure, covered to the neck with a voluminous black cloak.

As relief flooded through him, Falconer was able to relax for the first time in nearly four days. Relief made him benevolent. He really began to see the amusing side to the idea of a themed wedding, and actually enjoyed meeting Carmichael's family for the first time, twice, as it were.

Chapter Three
Insult to Injury

Monday 4th January – continuation

The first call came as the two detectives were admiring a delightful shot of Mrs Carmichael senior, showing off her frilly garter from the depths of her very heavily petticoated Widow Twankey pantomime dress.

'Detective Inspector Falconer speaking. How may I help you?'

An explosion of high-pitched noise burst from the handset, as he held it away from his ear defensively. 'Please calm down. I can't understand a word you're saying. Calm down and speak slowly!' You've received a what? It actually said that, did it? I agree, very nasty. Just stay at home, and we'll be there as soon as we can. 'No, I don't know if the use of language implies a threat to your safety either, and I shall need to see it before I get involved in any conjecture. Keep it safe, and handle it as little as possible. We'll be as quick as we can.'

As he put the receiver down, he noticed that Carmichael had also been answering a call. 'I've got a poison pen letter. What've you got?' he asked, feeling almost flippant.

'Don't know whether it's a case of wife- or husband-bashing,' the sergeant replied, looking perplexed. 'That was one of them house-officers, young doctor whatsits from the A & E Unit. He's just had a couple in – married, like – and either they're both bloody clumsy, if you'll excuse my French, sir, or they've been at it hammer and tongs. He's got a head wound needing stitching and three cracked ribs, and she's got a black eye and bruises from here to kingdom come. At the moment, they're as high as kites on painkillers.

'He said he didn't know what to do, not having seen anything like it before, and having heard that domestic violence is difficult to deal with, so he phoned us in the hope that we might just take a look in on them at home, to let them know that their situation is recognised officially, so that if one of them feels they need help, we're already on the alert. What do you think, sir?'

'Interfering little arse-licker!' Falconer replied, then, remembering where he was, apologised briefly and asked where the couple lived.

'Steynham St Michael,' he was informed, and nodded slowly.

'We'll take a look in, then. My poison pen's in the same village, so we might as well kill two birds with one stone, and respond to both calls. The poison pen could spread, and that insufferably self-righteous little prick at A & E could follow up his 'so concerned' call via his consultant, who might just be best buddies with Superintendent Chivers, and mention it in passing. Sometimes you have to be devious back, first, before they're devious to you. That way, sometimes, you win.'

'As you will, sir,' answered a puzzled Carmichael. 'Does that mean that we're going to follow up both calls, then?'

'Indeed it does, my newly married DS, so let's shoot off into action.' Relief had left Falconer in a very facetious mood and, although he realised he was acting rather strangely, he decided to enjoy it for a while, and stop being such a worry-guts.

Steynham St Michael was a drive of less than four miles, but the weather conditions had become atrocious since earlier that morning, when a watery sun had dripped a pallid light across the frost-bound countryside. Rime coated the bare branches of the trees and hedgerows, and the grass twinkled with hoar frost, and crunched underfoot. Above, a watery sky with just a tinge of pale blue prevailed.

In the last hour or so, however, a covering of cloud had appeared, tentatively at first, but now built into a solid dome over everything, and the temperature had risen just enough to allow mist to rise in wraiths and swirls from the frost-bound ground, reducing visibility for the traveller of rural lanes, but not melting the frozen dew enough to allow him safe passage. Black ice was still a hazard that had to be taken into account too, if one did not want to finish the morning in a ditch or, worse, in either the hands of the inexperienced SHO at A & E, or being measured for a wooden overcoat by the final tailor of one's life.

Falconer drove, putting his faith not only in his belief in his own mortality, but in the mechanical soundness of his own vehicle, and Carmichael, as head of a new household, did not demur as his priorities and philosophies of life had changed considerably during his few days away from work.

In the town, conditions were tolerable, but when they left the shelter of huddling buildings, Falconer found that it was like driving through cotton wool on an ice rink. Junctions suddenly loomed up at them, surely too quickly, as did trees and telegraph poles, menacingly bearing down on them with murderous intent. All sense of time and distance became lost in this cloud-haunted frozen dome and, even in second gear it was difficult to see more than a few metres ahead.

They stopped twice to check on cars that had skated off the road – losers in today's battle with the elements – and, having checked that no one was injured and that help was on the way where necessary, they continued their trek through suddenly hostile territory, if just a little more tentatively than before.

They arrived outside the post office in Steynham St Michael a little under an hour and a half after they had left the police station, and stopped to ask for directions to their first destination, both silently thanking their maker that double yellow lines had not yet reached this rural outpost, for they would never have found a place to park in these conditions.

'First left at the end of the terrace on our left, and Clematis Cottage is the only dwelling on the left before Farriers Lane bears off to the left. Got that, Carmichael? It seems to be everything left.'

'Yes, sir.'

'Good, because in this weather, I'm liable to forget how to drive, let alone how to find Ms Sinden's address. Correct me if I go wrong.' But there was little likelihood of that as the instructions were so simple, and the cottage so easy to find, standing alone as it did and, in only a couple of minutes, they were drawing to a halt in front of a stone garden wall with a little hat of thatch running along its top, broken only by a metal gate with a semi-circular top, standing about two feet higher than the wall.

'Well, I suppose it's behind there somewhere,' surmised Falconer, rubbing the windscreen with his sleeve and peering through the mist. 'Best get on with what Her Majesty's government pays us to do.'

Once out of the car they could make out the shape of the building at the end of the short garden path. Although Clematis Cottage was not large, such were the weather conditions that its proportions were exaggerated, and it appeared to loom out at them, as they approached it. 'Ooh-er, sir. It looks a bit creepy doesn't it?' Carmichael commented and Falconer, although he had no intention whatsoever of agreeing with his sergeant out loud, mentally concurred that it did, indeed , look a little creepy.

'But only on the outside, Carmichael,' he said aloud. 'And only because of the weather. Agreed?'

'Agreed, sir.'

The door was opened almost instantly, as if Ms Sinden had been sitting at the foot of the stairs waiting for them, which indeed she had. She ushered them in hurriedly, as if they were enemy agents, and herded them into the kitchen where she had cups, teapot, and biscuits all laid out. 'Please, please sit down and take tea with me. I really can't talk about this without trying to dilute how I feel with a little cosy domesticity,' she explained, ushering them both to sit down.

'We can get the introductions over with, have tea and biscuits, then I'll show you … it. I can be washing up while you look at it. I really don't think I can bear to look at it again, even though I know what it says by heart.' At this, tears began to track slowly down her unmade-up cheeks, and Carmichael took the chair next to her, patting her shoulder and making soothing noises.

He really did have his uses, Falconer thought. He, himself, was no good at this 'there, there, don't worry, it's going to be all right, we'll catch the bad man *(or woman, these days)* for you' stuff, but Carmichael had it down to a T.

As Carmichael soothed and poured the tea, Falconer rose and wandered round the kitchen, trying to absorb anything he could about the woman who lived here. That she lived alone, he had already gathered from her telephone call earlier. That she either did not enjoy the services of a cleaner or was totally disinterested in the domestic arts, he was learning now.

The dresser and shelves sported a good smattering of dust, and there were stains on the floor in front of the cooker, the sink, and where she obviously made tea and coffee. The lid of the pedal bin was proud of its usual position, and had obviously not been emptied for some time. A small vase on the windowsill behind the sink held dead flowers, and its rank water added to the undertone of neglect about the place.

Retaking his place at the table, he swallowed his tea in one gulp, making his eyes water, as it was hotter than he had expected, then asked Ms Sinden if they could see the letter that she had phoned about. 'Oh, do call me Buffy,' she cooed, now restored to near-normality, now that Carmichael had paid her some attention, and she had the company of two strong men in the house.

Falconer smiled noncommittally, while thinking that an error of judgement on his part that large would have her tripping him up, and appearing underneath him like greased lightning before he had even landed. Ms Sinden she would remain to him. Who in their right mind would hand a cannibal a knife and fork, and a cruet set? It was all right for Carmichael – he was married! Oh, dear God, surely he wasn't *jealous* of Carmichael now? Turning his mind firmly back to the here and now, he reached out for the piece of paper that was being offered to him.

Even though it had been read to him over the phone, he was still shocked by the wording and the hatred it contained – the sheer spite of such a thing; the hurt it had been intended to inflict in so few words:

How many more babies are you going to slaughter before you learn to keep your legs together, whore?

Carmichael's inhalation of shock was an audible groan, as he read what had been passed to him, and his whole countenance fell, as if the insult were directed at him. 'How do people do it, sir? How do they sink to these depths? No wonder you were so upset, Ms Sinden.'

'Buffy, please!'

'Er, Buffy. No wonder you called us, and quite right too.'

Shock and horror now over for this visit, Falconer wanted to get down to business, and asked if she had any idea who might have sent such a poisonous message, and if there was any link between the contents and reality; a harsh but necessary question, given the circumstances.

'It has been necessary for me to terminate the odd pregnancy, due entirely to circumstances beyond my control, you understand. I was driven to it,' she answered, wary now.

'Can you tell me exactly how many, Ms Sinden – no, I won't call you Buffy: it wouldn't be professional. How many terminations have you, in fact, been – er – driven to, in the past?'

Falconer had to ask her to speak up, as her answer was inaudible, and was staggered to hear her say, 'Five.'

A hiatus of silence was broken, as he cleared his throat to repeat, 'Five?'

'Yes, Inspector.'

'And have you any idea who might know this, and try to use it against you in this way?'

Carmichael had slid his notebook out of his pocket and was scribbling away in his own version of shorthand. As Buffy Sinden slipped into a brown study, the sergeant thanked God it wasn't something more comfortable she had slipped into. He began to suck his pen, as was his wont, and glanced across at the inspector, but all he received in return to his incredulous gaze was a mouthed, 'Get your pen out of your mouth – you know it stains.'

Carmichael was quite blasé about which end he sucked and had often interviewed members of the public with a black tongue and stained lips, which gave him a look of the living dead, and usually frightened the living daylights out of elderly ladies.

But the silent advice made no impression on him, however, as he imagined the enormity of five terminations. Most women found it hard enough to agree to one, and then found themselves haunted by what might have been for years. And here was this woman, blithely saying that she had been driven to commit this difficult and morally muddy act five times! He was stupefied, and it took a good, long throat clearing from his boss to return him to his notes, and the case in hand.

'... there's only Tilly Gifford who works at the doctor's surgery that I can think of. Even then, it's only because she works there. I wouldn't have thought anyone hated me enough to send that horrible letter.'

'Let's leave it there for today, Ms Sinden. I have the letter – thank goodness you had enough forethought to keep the envelope too – in an evidence bag, and I'll get it straight off to forensics when we get back to the station. Now, if you will excuse us, we have another call to make in the vicinity.'

Once back in the car, Falconer sighed gustily and explained as if to a simpleton, 'Well, if you've never met one before, Sergeant, THAT was a man-eater and a half,' and barely noticed when he received no reply. Carmichael merely sat in the passenger seat staring into the middle distance through the dirt-besmeared windscreen of the car, lost in his own thoughts. Five babbies!

After further directions from the obliging lady in the post office, they made their way back down Market Darley Road the way they had arrived, turned right at Tuppenny Lane, finding Forge Cottage at a junction where Farriers Lane joined it. The mist was beginning to disperse now, and the cloud cover was following suit, allowing the sun to peer myopically at the landscape below.

Amy Littlemore answered the door to them, and bade them enter and take a seat in their over-furnished living room, where Malcolm was ensconced in a chair, a bulky pad and bandage covering the top of his head, and evidence of neat stitching on both of his hands. He sat very still, conscious of how painful movement would prove to be, given the state of his ribs.

Amy sported a magnificent black eye and a dressing at her left temple. Her lower legs, visible beneath the just-below-the-knee skirt she wore, were decorated with a number of bruises in various stages of colouring, varying from purple-blue, through black and crimson, to the yellow-green of the almost disappeared.

For the first minute or two they were the perfect, if damaged, host and hostess, acting airily as if there were nothing incongruous in their appearance – for what could be more normal than Mr and Mrs Littlemore from the craft shop?

At the first intimation that Falconer and Carmichael might want to enquire into the state of their physical health, and how they had obtained their injuries, they changed, quick as a flash, into snarling and spitting cobras, both as protective of their privacy as an animal is to its young.

'What do you fink you're up to, then? There's nuffin' gone on in this 'ouse that ain't perfickly legal. There might've been a little scuffle, but no charges are bein' brought, are they?'

Falconer agreed that he was perfectly correct in that no charges had even been mentioned. Malcolm Littlemore was a big chap – in more than one way – and Falconer agreed that he, Malcolm Littlemore, had a perfect right to live his life as he saw fit, without any interference from the police, or any other namby-pamby, busy-bodying organisation, and he looked him fairly and squarely in the navel as he agreed with his host.

Carmichael concentrated more on looking his height-equal in the eye, and couldn't resist the temptation to offer a little advice from the heart. 'I don't think it's very fair to hit a woman, do you, Mr Littlemore?' he asked, leaning forward just a little. Malcolm Littlemore matched him look for look, and answered, 'No, neither do I, son. And I mean that most sincerely. Now, git orffa my property before I 'elps yer on yer way – no offence intended, squire.'

'And none taken, sir.' Falconer's voice was like a ricochet in its immediacy, and by the time the words had left his mouth, he was already pulling Carmichael by the arm towards the front door. 'We'll see ourselves out, if that's all right with you, Mr Littlemore?'

Back in the car, neither of them spoke, and it wasn't until they were halfway back to Market Darley that communication resumed. 'Carmichael, do you mind if I ask you something?'

'Ask away, sir.'

'Well, now you're married, how …? Has there been any change …? Who …?'

'Spit it out, sir. It might be solid gold.'

Falconer spat. And it was. 'That's a very nice outfit you're wearing today, DS Carmichael. Did you choose it to wear today, yourself?'

'No way, sir. It's a bit staid and middle-aged – no offence intended – for me, but now we're married, Kerry leaves out my clothes for me the night before. She says it saves me five minutes in the morning, which gives me five more minutes to snuggle up in bed – beggin' your pardon, sir.'

She'd cured him! The clever little thing had cured Carmichael of his chronic colour-blindness and disastrous dress-sense, and without a word of criticism ever passing her lips. All she had to do was to offer to leave out his clothes for the next day the night before, and the promise of five more minutes in bed was enough of an incentive to rouse no suspicion in his mind, that there had been anything wrong with the way he dressed before.

'She's a very special lady, is your Kerry,' he congratulated his sergeant, while smugly hugging to himself the thought that he would never have to start the day again with a rainbow Carmichael in his view (or in his company – and in public, at that!).

'I know, sir. That she is,' replied Carmichael, without the

hint of a grin or a spark of understanding of the subtext. 'And to change the subject completely, sir, do you think it would be a good idea if we got the area car to make a little loop that passed Forge Cottage whenever its beat took it through Steynham St Michael?'

'Excellent idea, Sergeant,' replied Falconer, pleasantly surprised at his partner's joined-up thinking. 'And I'll get this letter off to forensics, to see if our spiteful little pen-pal left behind any clues to his or her identity. If not, we'll just have to wait to see if anyone else owns up to receiving one. It's unlikely to be a one-off, but you know how shy people can be about anything iffy in their past. It may take a bit of digging to bring a letter or two to the surface.'

Chapter Four
Clubs Are Trumps

Tuesday 5th January

'Hello, Vernon darling,' Hermione Grayling trilled into the mouthpiece of her telephone. 'Will you be joining us tonight, to avoid the contemptible bitch? What do you mean, that's physically impossible for you, if I'm going to be there? Naughty, naughty Vernon. I shall have to slap you on the wrist for outrageous bitchery – pardon the pun, ha ha,' she cooed.

It was the following day, and the two branches of the Steynham St Michael card club were due to meet that evening, to hone their skills for the inter-club tournament at the end of the month. Hermione was a founding member of the branch that played at the Ox and Plough, just across Crowhanger Lane from her house.

The other members, whom she was just about to remind of tonight's meeting by telephone, were Vernon Warlock, her first call; Charles Rainbird, who answered in the middle of a possible transaction in his shop and was, therefore, rather short with her; and Dimity Pryor, who was sorting bags of goods donated over the festive and new year seasons, for she worked voluntarily in the charity shop opposite the bank in the High Street.

Monica and Quentin Raynor were next, situated almost directly opposite her house on the Market Darley Road in their estate agency, and as Hermione made her gentle reminder over the telephone about the planned soirée, she waved to Monica from the bow window of her drawing room, Monica acknowledging her salute with a rapid wiggle of the fingers of her left hand.

The two younger single gentlemen members were the last on her list, and Craig Crawford answered the phone on the first ring. As an accountant, he was also an accurate and cunning card player, and a respected member of the team, despite his tender age, which was estimated to be somewhere in the late thirties by those ladies who lived to gossip and gossiped to live. Craig was never difficult to track down, as he was self-employed and worked from home, home being a large, detached residence with considerable grounds, situated on the other side of the Ox and Plough.

Hermione's final phone call for that session was to Gabriel Pryor who worked at the bank, and lived rather out-of-things in Barleycorn Crescent, but good with money, meant good with counting, meant good with cards, and he had been allowed to join their select group because of his loyalty to figures, numbers, and amounts, even though he was not exactly one of them. 'N-O-S' was the opinion of most of the others in the group – Not Our Sort, but many a 'needs must' had been uttered, as they had justified his inclusion in their number.

Hermione left a message on his answering service, as she knew she would have to, because Gabriel would be at the bank now, totting up his columns of figures and balancing somebody or others books or accounts, or whatever clerks did behind closed doors in banks. Miss Grayling was a snob of the first order, and made no bones about the fact, but she was so over-the-top with her prejudices and dislikes, that her snobbery lent her a humour of which she was not aware, and even someone pierced by the barb of her tongue always laughed about it afterwards, because it was not them who had ended up looking ridiculous. Everybody loved Hermione Grayling.

There had originally been only one cards club in Steynham St Michael, and the club's game had been bridge. After five years, however, old faces had left, and new ones had joined, swelling numbers to an uncomfortable level, and enthusiasm for the game itself had palled. About eighteen months ago, during the long summer break that allowed everyone to enjoy a decent holiday, the club had amicably split itself into two separate branches to admit yet more new members, and the breakaway branch now met in the village's trendier pub, the Fox and Hounds, the current game for both groups being Black Bitch, played with two packs of cards, to add spice and danger to any flamboyant tactics.

Bryony Buckleigh, an elegant and still pretty widow of sixty-two, was currently stretched out on her chaise longue in Honeysuckle, a des-res must for anybody with chocolate box leanings, also on the telephone, rallying the players of the now rival cards club branch to play, that evening. She had two less calls to make than Hermione because her group boasted three couples. Tilly Gifford was easy to reach as she was receptionist at the doctor's surgery in the High Street, next to the church of St Michael and All Angels, and confirmed that she and her husband Tommy would be in attendance.

Roma and Rodney Kerr – Chrysanthemums, Farriers Lane – were also a cinch, as their premises for the sale of ladies' fashions and haberdashery items, tucked up next to Vernon Warlock's bookshop in the High Street, was currently open for business, and Bryony's second call lasted less than a minute. Her penultimate call was equally as short, as Amy and Malcolm's craft shop had returned to normal hours, now that the December silly season was over, and the last name on her list was that of Buffy Sinden.

The phone rang unanswered for quite a long time, and she was just about to hang up and try again a little later, when a nasal voice gave the number and announced that it was, in fact, Buffy Sinden speaking. 'Whatever's wrong with you, my dear?' asked Bryony. 'You sound like death. Are you ill or something?'

'No,' croaked Buffy, whose voice was hoarse from crying. 'It's nothing!' The anonymous letter she had received had affected her much more than she would have considered possible, and she had had a wretched time of it since showing the epistle to the policemen the day before. Events that had merely been a convenience in her hectic past social life had suddenly been made real, with all the emotions and what-might-have-beens that that involved, and she felt as if she had been mentally shredded, held up for judgment, and been found seriously wanting.

'It's obviously NOT nothing,' replied Bryony, knowing how happy-go-lucky Buffy usually was; how she shrugged off any overt or implied criticism of her man-filled lifestyle. She sounded positively crushed. 'I'm coming round right away, whether you want me to or not. There's something wrong, and even if I can just make you a good strong cup of tea and lend a shoulder to cry on, it'll make you AND me feel better. I'll be there in a couple of minutes,' she concluded, put down the phone, and headed for the hall for her coat and her house keys. A short walk down Farriers Lane would take her to Buffy's cottage, so she had no need of the car.

Both card groups were a member down that night, which rather complicated matters for the seven remaining members of their card-playing octets. The game of Black Bitch has many names, such as Find the Lady and Black Queen, but the game remains the same whatever its name.

It is usually played by four people, all of the cards in the pack, with the exception of the jokers, being dealt out. The game is played in five rounds like whist, the first four having one of the four suits as trumps *(hearts, clubs, diamond, spades is the usual order)*, the last round having no trumps. The art in the game is to win no tricks with hearts in them, as these count, numerically, against you in the finally tally. Two to ten score at face value, the picture cards scoring ten, and the ace, eleven points.

But, one must also avoid winning the trick which contains the queen of spades, which adds twenty-five points to your total. The game is evil, not only in the hearts and spades trumps rounds, but in the fact that, before play is begun, and when everyone has sorted his or her hand, they must then pass on three cards to the player on their left. The queen of spades may not be passed on. But it doesn't stop a player with an initially bad hand from passing, say the king, queen, and ace of trumps to their unlucky neighbour, or the king and ace of spades and perhaps the ace of trumps, to them.

This is the part of the game that throws everyone's initial strategy. These two groups had long ago abandoned this game, which had become childishly easy with familiarity, but played it still, unchanged in quartets of players in fours, but with *two* packs of cards, and passing on *four* if it was a 'friendly' game, *six* if it was a needle match.

It will now become obvious what difficulties the loss of just one player to each club presented. Each player normally had to hold twenty-six cards in his hand, not an easy feat in itself. With a quartet down to a trio in each pub, the inter-club rules decreed that the two of diamonds from one pack be discarded, along with the two of clubs from the second pack, thus leaving a number of cards divisible by three, to be dealt. The consequence was that each of the now three players had to control thirty-four cards, without dropping the unwieldy mass on the floor.

This situation arose rarely, but when it did, three players usually volunteered to sit-out of a game, three different players taking their place for the next game and so on. This not only relieved the pressure on those who would have had the well-nigh impossible task of holding so many cards, but allowed the various members of the groups to leave the small function rooms in which their meeting invariably took place, and go to the bar for a very welcome drink and a bit of a gossip – a sop to the dummy, in a four at bridge.

At the Ox and Plough the absent player was Gabriel Pryor, and Hermione Grayling was holding forth, defending her position as club 'reminder'. 'Of course I phoned him. I did it when I called all of you. But you know as well as I do that he's at work at that time of day, and I always leave a message on his answering service, and he calls me if he can't make it for some reason. I don't know why he's not here, but I *did* leave a message.'

She was most indignant at the implied criticism that she had forgotten to call him, and broke off to take her mobile from her handbag, along with a little notebook. 'His number's in here. I'm going to call him now, and ask him what he thinks he's playing at, leaving us a player short, and without a word of warning,' and she proceeded to dial, pressing the button for speaker phone, so that they should all hear his excuse.

Three times she tried to get through, and each time, after ten rings, the call went to his answering service. 'There, I told you it wasn't my fault. Something's obviously come up, and he hasn't even given us a thought.'

'But that's not like him at all,' interjected Craig Crawford, one of his regular team-mates.

'Well, like him or not, it can't be helped, unless someone wants to waste even more time going down to Barleycorn Crescent to knock on his door, and see if he's just not answering his phone.'

But this suggestion bagged no takers. They all lived close enough to the Ox and Plough to leave their cars at home, so that they need not pay too much attention to their blood/alcohol levels. The temperature, although not bitter, was cold enough to be slippery underfoot, and a heavy sky promised snow in the not too distant future. A walk in the dark was not an inviting prospect.

Hermione, Vernon Warlock, and Charles Rainbird charitably volunteered to sit-out the first game, as befitted their status as founding members of the club, and headed a little too enthusiastically to the bar, while the other players watched them leave rather wistfully.

In the trendier Fox and Hounds *(lower lighting, no open log fire or horse-brasses)* the other group of card players found themselves in an identical situation, as Buffy Sinden had not turned up to play. In the case of her absence, however, they had an explanation of sorts from Bryony Buckleigh, although it was not a very satisfactory one.

'I did remind her earlier, but she didn't sound too well, so I went round to see her. There's just no way that she can be with us tonight, and we'll just have to live with that.'

'What's wrong with her, then? Man trouble?' called Roma Kerr from the rear of the room, then sniggered into her hand and winked at her husband Rodney.

'I wouldn't be so indiscreet as to disclose the details of someone's illness.' Here, Bryony gave a brief but pointed frown in the direction of Tilly Gifford, who must have understood the discreet implication, because she blushed, and blew her nose to cover her surprise and flushed countenance.

Bryony cleared her throat and continued, 'I can assure you all, however, that she is in no state to join us this evening, and we shall just have to manage, as we always do, when we are missing a player. Unless three of you fancy playing with an unwieldy fistful of cards, you'd better sort yourselves out into players and non-players for the first game, and let's get this evening going before last orders, please, ladies and gentlemen.'

Roma Kerr hastened away in search of a drink to calm herself down, after another furious exchange of insults with Rodney, and Amy and Malcolm Littlemore (*quelle surprise!*) volunteered to join her, much to Bryony's disgust. Amy was a bad player at best, but when she'd had a few she couldn't even remember the rules of Black Bitch, and made a real shambles of any game she was involved in. Heaven help them if she came back at half-time determined to join in for the second half.

Maybe when they took a five minute break between games to refresh glasses, she might be able to persuade her not to play at all tonight. After all, it wasn't really the cards she was here for, was it? It was the convivial atmosphere and the demon drink, as anyone who knew her a little more than superficially understood. She must also ask about their somewhat injured appearance too, before the end of the evening. They certainly appeared as if they had been in the wars. Surmising that their appearance was probably the result of a drunken fall, she dismissed the subject from her mind, and picked up her first hand of cards.

Perched on bar stools in the only bar *(ah, modernisation!)*, Amy, Malcolm and Tilly got down to some dirt digging, each in his or her own inimitable way. Malcolm was the most direct of the three. 'What do yer think 'as 'appened to the old Bicycle tonight, then? 'Ot date? 'Angover? Shortness of breath?' This last amused him so much, that he indulged in a little chuckle before taking another enthusiastic slug from what was already his second pint.

'Don't be so 'orrible, Malc. Maybe she's really ill. You've no idea what she said to Bryony, so why speculate?'

'She's probably got 'erself a dose of the clap,' he retorted, making himself cough with the speed with which he swallowed his mouthful of beer. 'What d'yer reckon, Tilly? You work down the doctor's don't yer? She been in there for a dose of penicillin?'

Instead of her usual gushing response to the invitation to indulge in a little character assassination and gossip, Tilly Gifford positively bridled, fixed Malcolm with a beady eye, and exclaimed. 'How on earth should I know? And you know that anything I learn at the surgery is not to be bandied about in general conversation. Anything like that is covered by medical confidentiality, and I should be putting my job in jeopardy if I treated it as anything else!'

''Old yer 'orses, Till! I was only askin'. No need to bite me bleedin' 'ead off, is there?'

'Sorry, Malc. Just a bit jumpy tonight, that's all. Must be the weather. And anyway, what about you two? You look like you've both gone a couple of rounds with Mike Tyson and come off the worse for it. Going in for a bit of wife-bashing are you, Malc? I should watch him, Amy. If he tries it again, I should go for him with the poker.'

Made bold with a combination of strong analgesics and alcohol – they'd had a few before they went out, of course – Malcolm, minus his rather alarming bandage of the day before, and sporting only a small plaster now over his stiches, commented, 'Well, you and everyone else would know all the details by now, if we'd sought treatment via the surgery. Your sticky beak would've been covered in tasty little morsels about how we got like this, wouldn't it? Gawd! My ribs don't 'alf 'urt. I fink I'm gonna need a few more nippie-sweeties before

42

I'll be able to get any kip ternight!'

'You mind yer own business, you gossipin' old witch,' Amy cut in, from behind her dark glasses, in guilty defence. 'What you 'aven't talked about, that's gone on down that doctor's surgery, is nobody's business. And now you're playin' the innocent and trying to pry into me and Malc's personal business. Why don't yer wind yer neck in and keep yer great big neb out of other people's business for a change?'

'All right, all right, Amy. Sorry I spoke, I'm sure!'

'And why did Bryony look in your direction when she was talkin' about Buffy? If that wasn't an accusation, I don't know what is!'

'How dare you! I've got no idea what you're talking about.' Tilly Gifford had got a bit more than she bargained for when she had ordered a double gin and tonic, and sat at the bar for a nice chat with a couple whose company she usually enjoyed. 'I'm not staying here to be insulted like that!'

'Where d'yer usually go then, love?' called Malcolm towards her retreating back as she grabbed her coat from the coat rack and left the pub. They finished their drinks in silence and waited for the first game to be over, although neither of them felt like playing cards any more.

In the saloon bar of the comfortably old-fashioned Ox and Plough, a fine fire crackled in the over-sized grate and, at a table just to the right of it, sat Hermione, Vernon Warlock, and Charles Rainbird. They had volunteered to sit-out for the first round, their situation being identical to the one at the Fox and Hounds.

'I've nearly finished my current little offering, and, as we're surplus to requirements at the moment, I wonder if you had any teensy weensy little idea-lets for what I could get my teeth into next?' Hermione asked with an innocent expression.

'Nice one, Hermione, but you must be joking. If I had even an inkling of an idea, I'd lock it away in my safe, to keep it away from you. You're a shameless baggage who has grown worse over the years,' Vernon stated with somewhat more vehemence than seemed necessary in the circumstances.

'What?' Charles Rainbird hadn't been listening, and had just tuned in to the conversation as Vernon had uttered his final sentence. 'Shameless baggage? Hermione? I'd trust that woman with my life, Warlock. Utterly trustworthy, and of impeccable character.'

'Bollocks!' retorted Vernon, as if that was an end to the subject, and lifted his glass up in offering to his companions. 'Anyone fancy another one? I'm in the chair.'

'Oh, I suppose so,' said Hermione a little ungratefully, 'but I was so enjoying listening to you two squabble over me.'

'Squabble over you?' queried Vernon, and with a cheeky half-grin, made his way over to the bar to place their order. 'I should coco!'

In his absence, Hermione leaned over the table and asked Charles in a hushed voice, 'Have you any idea where Gabriel's got to tonight?'

'How dare you, Hermione. You promised you'd never utter a word on the subject again, and yet whenever you identify an opportunity, you always say something. Why can't you just leave the subject alone as you promised you would do?'

'I'm not bringing up any subject. Anyway, you're a bit touchy tonight, aren't you? I only asked if you had any idea where he was. Sounds like a guilty conscience to me!'

'Will you leave it alone, woman! I've got enough to worry about without you inventing things to torture me with.' And on that cryptic comment, he snapped his mouth shut, rather like a turtle's, and turned his gaze away from her and towards the flames of the fire.

At that point Vernon arrived back at the table with a tray laden with glasses and packets of crisps. 'Here we go, me hearties!' he carolled.

'Oh, sod off!' Charles exploded at him, breaking his reverie and returning to his recent acid mood. 'I'm going home!'

As the pub door closed behind him, Vernon put the tray on the table and started to offload its contents. 'What's eating him?' he asked, as he shared Charles' gin and tonic between their two glasses.

'Haven't a clue!' answered Hermione, innocently and untruthfully. 'Now, Vernon, do you know why young Pryor hasn't turned up tonight?'

'Absolutely no idea, but I don't like to see you rag Charles so.' Vernon replied.

'Oh, poo! Charlie-boy shouldn't be such a shrinking little violet. And I really did ring Gabriel, you know,' she continued. 'I can't think why he didn't have the courtesy, at least, to ring me back, or even to let me know in advance, if he was tied up with something else.

'Now, I'm just going to have this little drink, and then go through to get my quota of games. Wouldn't do for me to slide down the league, as it was me that set it up, now would it, Vernon my dearest?'

And she was not joking, as the cards club did, indeed, keep scores and a league table. This had been Hermione's idea when the actual playing had palled with the bridge, and since they had commenced their current and horribly devious game, Craig Crawford the accountant had kept the scores.

At the end of the playing year – 1st June, so that they could fit in their holidays, traditionally taken in the summer months by all the members – the figures were totalled, and a Victorian silver-plated cup was presented to the winner *(donated by Hermione!)*, to be kept by them until 1st June the following year. Most of the players took their cards seriously, and considered that it must have been something extremely galling that evening for Charles to have walked out like that, denying himself the opportunity to score when it was his turn to play.

Chapter Five
Spades Are Trumps

Wednesday 6th January

A number of households received spiteful poison pen letters the next morning, two of whom were Vernon Warlock and Charles Rainbird and, had they but known it at the time, the letters were of very similar wording.

Charles, always an early riser, had picked his post up almost before it had hit the floor, and whisked it off to the kitchen, to open it with his breakfast.

Q. What do you call a businessman with more than one set of books?

A. About to be arrested. Be sure your sins will find you out, as I have, and you will pay, he read, and whistled in surprise and amusement. Somebody thought they were a right little know-it-all, didn't they? Well, someone was about to find out that his displeasure was not something to be summoned lightly. He would be having more than a word about this missive.

At the other end of Dairy Lane, in Vine Cottage, Vernon Warlock wandered into his hall at a little after nine-thirty to collect his post, even though he was supposed to open the shop at that exact hour. 'What on earth was this?' he thought as he glanced at the envelope with the address formed from cut-out letters. Was it some new form of advertising, trying to part hard-working folk from their money in yet another way?

The envelope's contents soon put a stop to such thoughts as he read:

Q. What do you call a fencer of stolen antiquarian books?

A. A convict doing a stretch. Beware the wrath of the law.

'Good God!' he exclaimed out loud. 'Who on earth can have

sent this?'

Hilda Pounce, known locally as Potty Pounce purely because her antecedents had attended the Strict and Particular Baptist Chapel in the village, and were particularly rabid about the somewhat peculiar rituals it indulged in, left her home in Prince Albert Terrace, the last of the village housing on the Market Darley Road, and cycled carefully northwards, over the crossroads that contained the commercial heart of the community, then turned right into Dairy Lane, to make a shortcut to the library to return her books.

The snow, threatened the night before, hadn't materialised, but the going was treacherous, and there was little tread left on the tyres of her old bicycle. Still, she'd promised Miss Grayling *(my lady author, as she thought of her employer)* that she'd have a thorough turn out in the kitchen this morning, then, after lunch she'd have to pop into Barleycorn Crescent and give old slimy Pryor a quick once-over. She was due to clean for him on New Year's Day, but the promise of a couple of hours at double time clearing up at the pubs had been a more attractive proposition, and she had changed her arrangements accordingly.

When she handed her books in at the library, she was surprised when Patience Buttery, one of the library assistants, announced that they were overdue by a day, and she would have to pay a ten pence fine on each book.

'How can they be overdue? I know when I got them out, and I marked it in my diary to bring them back today.'

'I'm sorry, Mrs Pounce, but if you'd care to look here, and here, you can see that the date for return is the fifth of January.'

'But it is the fifth!' Hilda almost shouted.

'I'm very much afraid you're mistaken. Today's the sixth, isn't it Noah?' she called to her husband who also worked there, and was preparing to return a trolley-load of returned books to their proper places on the shelves.

'That's right. It's the sixth. So easy to lose track of what day it is, when there are so many Bank Holidays, isn't it, Mrs Pounce?' he called over cheerfully, before returning to steering his chariot of knowledge and entertainment.

Hilda Pounce merely stood with her mouth open, gaping after him. How could it be the sixth? She was so sure of herself that she even glanced over at a copy of the Times that had been left carelessly across the returns counter. It confirmed her worst fears. Today *was* the sixth, and she must pay a fine for the late return of her library books, something that had never happened before, in her narrow and convention-bound world.

Reaching into her grubby string bag, she extracted her purse and carefully counted out the pennies into Patience's hand.

A few minutes later, Hilda parked her bicycle at the side of The Spinney and let herself in through the back door, her face still grim at the thought of her confusion over the date, went to the kitchen cupboard that held her cleaning materials and surveyed the state of the kitchen, opening cupboard doors and drawers as she assessed her task for that morning.

'Coo-ee, Hilda dear. Is that you?' A voice trilled from the direction of the little room that Hermione referred to as her 'author-torium', and Hilda put down a nest of dusters she was holding, and set off to see what her employer Miss Grayling wanted.

'Hello, my dear. I thought I heard you come in. Happy New Year to you, and I hope you had a lovely Christmas. Now,' she continued, not allowing her cleaning lady to get a word in edgeways, so determined was she to state her own plan for that good woman's toil, this morning.

'I know we decided that you could turn out the kitchen, for I really can't find anything at all these days. Oh, I know it's my own fault for not putting things back where they belong.' Once more she ignored the opening of Hilda's mouth to make a comment. 'And I'm afraid I'm just as careless with things that go into sideboards and drawers, so I wondered, when you've finished in the kitchen, and I'm sure it won't take you long, as you're so terribly efficient, if you'd just whizz through the sideboards in the drawing room and the dining room – not in here, of course, because it may look very muddly to you, but I know exactly where every scrap of paper is, and what's on it.

'Now, I won't keep you from your work, because that's very naughty of me, but if you could just do me a cafetière of coffee, and bring it in here when it's ready, I'll let you get on. Thank you so much, Hilda, my dear.'

Hilda Pounce didn't even try opening her mouth this time, but turned her steps back to the kitchen where she put the kettle on, ground a sufficient amount of Hermione's favourite blend of beans, and laid a tray ready to take in when the water was hot. Usually she enjoyed her work here, feeling honoured that she worked for a famous writer, but today hadn't started to the expected pattern. And now she'd been lumbered with the sideboards, as well as the kitchen: there were two of these in the drawing room, and four in the dining room – two pairs along the wall that flanked the long mahogany table – and she winced as she remembered the jumbled mess that inhabited each one. She'd never get all that finished in one morning, and she still had Mr Pryor's place to go through this afternoon.

Walking carefully, so that she didn't slop any milk from the small jug, she made her way down the hall, two cups and saucers on the tray, recalling with pleasure that Miss Grayling usually invited her to join her for morning coffee and a nice chat – such a kind and civilised lady. Momentarily forgetting her ire at the sideboards, she knocked and entered the holy of holies, where Hermione composed her long-winded Victorian family sagas, only to find her employer gathering up keys, gloves, and handbag, in preparation for going out.

'I'm so sorry, Hilda, but I completely forgot that I promised to pop over to Spinning Wheel Cottage for coffee this morning. Dimity made a point of asking me last night, but I can hardly keep track of the days, when there are all these ghastly Bank Holidays, and people taking days in lieu, and everywhere closing down for two weeks at Christmas. I'm so sorry we can't have our usual lovely chat, but *c'est la vie*, eh? *C'est la vie*. If I'm not back before you finish, I'll see you on Friday at the usual time. Toodle-oo! Pip pip!'

Hilda Pounce's day was going to wrack and ruin, and yet she had not the slightest inkling that the worst was yet to come.

Tommy Gifford had left Foxes' Run for work about an hour earlier, but Tilly still sat at the kitchen table, still not dressed, and sunk deeply in thought. There was no surgery in Steynham St Michael, as this morning was home visits only, and the answerphone would take care of it if she was a bit late arriving.

She'd not felt herself since the arrival of that dreadful letter and, as she remembered it, her hand moved unconsciously to the pocket of her dressing gown, where it still resided. Pulling it out and smoothing it out on the table top, she read it again, her expression puckered in distaste and with just a hint of fear:

'Anyone would think you had never heard of medical confidentiality the way you gossip to your cronies. You are going to end up in court one of these days if you do not learn to control your tongue,' she read.

Who on earth would send something like that to her? She never talked about anything that went on at the surgery, or anything that she learned from her work there – except for a few very close friends who wouldn't breathe a word, knowing that what she said had been told in confidence.

And it couldn't be one of them, surely. She thought that they treasured their position as confidante to someone 'in the know'. If she hadn't believed this, she would never have said anything to anyone. None of them would behave like this, would they? And what if they did something about it? What if they identified one another, and made a complaint of breach of confidence. She'd lose her job, and that would be a catastrophe, as belts were being pulled in where Tommy worked, and he couldn't be certain of a job for more than six months, when the management would review the situation again.

Placing the letter back in her dressing gown pocket, as unconsciously as she had removed it, she rose slowly from her chair, her mind given furiously to think. Had she fallen out with anyone lately? Had she said anything that might be considered censorious or hurtful to any of her inner circle? She couldn't remember doing so, but she'd have to have a good long think, to see if this might be a spiteful little prank, to pay her back for some ill-advised remark.

51

She'd have to get a move on to get to the surgery and man the phone for anyone requiring an appointment, but there would be little else to do apart from a little filing, and she would have plenty of time to mull over her recent conversations while she worked.

Next door, at Badger's Sett, an almost identical scene was taking place. Quentin Raynor had left the house to open the estate agency that he ran with his wife, leaving Monica behind to tidy up a little. Household chores had got rather neglected over the festive season, but Quentin was sure his wife would get things sorted out and back to normal, lickety-split.

Unfortunately, his wife lacked her husband's confidence in her domestic abilities, and looked about her in despair. Every surface in the kitchen was covered in dirty plates, pots, and pans. There was dirty crockery and cutlery still left on the dining table from a couple of nights ago, and she knew that there were numerous dirty glasses and nibbles dishes in the sitting room from last night, waiting to be collected, washed, and put away.

Their bedroom was a sea of clothes that had been discarded, either worn and needing laundering, or tried on and considered not suitable for whatever occasion was being considered. The bathroom was also unfit to be seen by an outsider, there being soap and toothpaste stains all over the basin, and a veritable brown ring round the bath where it had not even been wiped out after use, let alone cleaned, for some considerable time.

She just couldn't manage with the business and their busy social life, *and* keep the house immaculate as well. It was far too much for one person, but Quentin just said it would get done in its own time, and not to worry – she just needed to put her mind to it, and everything would be show-home tidy in no time at all.

Snarling out loud at the stupidity of the man, she went over to her handbag and took out a packet of cigarettes and a lighter. She had promised to give up at New Year, but then Quentin had promised over Christmas that he would help her get the house back to normal before they went back to the office. And he hadn't. And what was sauce for the goose was sauce for the gander, she thought, as she inhaled hungrily then blew the smoke out through her nostrils with an expression of pure enjoyment.

It had been all right when old Potty Pounce came round three times a week. Everything had run like clockwork, then. And then they'd had that silly little disagreement at her going to Hermione's for a few hours a week and changing her hours here slightly, and off she'd flounced. And Monica had just stood there, smug that she would not notice her absence – and the effort she put in – three days a week, and had blithely let her go, over a silly point of principle about the hours she worked.

She'd be willing to pay her twice the money she was on before, now, for half the hours. She needed the woman's services, and she'd have to go crawling back on her hands and knees to her, and be ever so nice and smiley and ingratiating, and suck up to her sickeningly. Damn it!

And now this! Removing the letter from her dressing gown pocket, where it had remained since she opened it, she read it one more time. How could anyone know about that property deal that was just the teensiest bit iffy – well, *very* iffy – in fact, probably illegal? They'd been living in the West Country until three years ago, and that deal had been done nearly a decade ago. There was no one here who could possibly have the slightest idea of what they'd done. But someone *did* know, and she was just going to have to find out who that person was, and deal with them.

Viciously stubbing out her cigarette in her saucer, she steeled herself for speaking to Potty Pounce – begging for the favours that she had once taken for granted. Life was an absolute shit sometimes.

Leaving the kitchen in the same condition that she had found it upon waking, she went back upstairs to get dressed. If she couldn't talk old Hilda round, then Quentin would either have to clean the place himself, or get in touch with an agency who supplied domestics. She simply couldn't carry on living like this.

She knew she'd get a lot more done in the house if she wasn't so worried about the business all the time, what with every sale needing so much time, so much chasing, and for such a small return in these difficult financial times that it hardly seemed worth it. If things went on the way they had been going, estate agents would soon become a thing of the past.

House prices had plummeted so low over the last couple of years, and banks and building societies were reluctant to lend to those without a huge deposit, so there was absolutely no money in property sales because no one was buying. The whole wretched situation was down to the first-time buyers, and as nobody would lend them any money, the property market was practically at gridlock. It was a stalemate with knobs on, in her opinion. They'd already laid off their receptionist, and stood down those they used to conduct viewings. That only left the two of them, and so much leg work to do just to clinch one sale.

But a few people *were* still moving, weren't they? They had to move for all sorts of reasons – work, family, deaths. Work was the biggest motivator. If people got a new job, or were transferred to another area, they were more likely to rent now, and to let their old house, until things got moving again.

Perhaps they could develop a lettings agency to boost their income, and keep their business afloat until better times returned, as they surely would. She'd have to have a word with Quentin about it: see what he thought of the idea when she got to the office. It could be an absolute lifesaver for them.

Hilda Pounce pedalled her bicycle down the Market Darley Road in the teeth of the easterly wind, which buffeted her sideways and chilled her to the bone, especially her knees, which were fair game, as they led the advance, as it were. She gritted her teeth at the cold and tried not to shiver too hard lest she lose her balance and fall. That would be just about the last straw, after the morning she'd had.

Nobody would believe the amount of old tat and absolute rubbish that that Grayling woman had shoved in to her sideboards over time, and Hilda's patience had been tried to its limit when she had opened the last one to find it full of newspaper and magazine articles, cut out and paper-clipped or stapled together.

God alone knew what she was to do with them. Were they things that the author had hoarded for their content, for possible inclusion in some future book, or were they just a whim of hers, stuffed in there without a thought and then forgotten? She'd had one small job to do for herself before she left, and she was already late. Now she would have no time for lunch before going to Mr Pryor's, so in the end, unable to come to a satisfactory decision about whether to throw them out or not, she had just stacked the yellowing paperwork in little piles on the dining room table, and left a note explaining that she thought Miss Grayling should make the final decision on whether they stayed or were discarded.

As she battled her way across the crossroads with the High Street, she was seething with self-pity at how put upon she was and how tired she felt after just half a day, with, no doubt, another New Year clear-out in the offing in Barleycorn Crescent. Her life had always been hard work and challenging, but today was particularly bad, and she would be glad when it was over, and she could sink down into an armchair in front of the television, and put her feet up with a nice comforting glass of gin.

Wind-battered and chilled to the bone, Hilda Pounce arrived at Barleycorn Crescent, dismounted from her bicycle outside number three, and opened the over-fussy wrought iron gate to park her machine at the side of the house, as she had done scores of times before. She knew Mr Pryor would be at work in the bank, so she headed for the back door, pulling at the string attached to the inside of her battered handbag, where she kept his key for safety.

Once inside, she took off her ancient tweed coat and hung it on the hook on the back door as she always did, and looked around her at the kitchen. A sink full of dirty dishes was the first thing that caught her eye, then the pile of dirty clothes –

shirts, socks, and underpants mainly, that sat in a heap on the floor, in front of the washing machine.

She'd have thought he'd at least have had the decency to stick the soiled garments into the machine, instead of leaving them sitting there for anyone to see, and for her to have to handle. She gave a little grimace of distaste at the thought of the underpants. It simply wasn't decent, leaving them for her to pick up, and him so well brought up in the ways of the Chapel. He ought to know better.

Pushing the pile of dirty laundry through the open door of the washing machine, her nose wrinkling again in distaste, she decided to get the washing-up out of the way before she investigated the state of the rest of the house. He probably needed the bed linen and towels changing, but the machine was over half-full now, so she might as well let that get on with being washed, while she put the kitchen in order and, collecting a pile of plates and mugs from the kitchen table, she emptied the sink of its contents onto a working surface, and began to fill the bowl with hot sudsy water.

The bed linen and towels would have to wait for later, until the washing machine was free again, because they constituted a full load by themselves and there simply wasn't room. It might help if he managed to do the odd load of washing himself. It wasn't as if his time was taken up with a brood of family or anything. He lived alone, but never seemed to lift a finger to keep his house in order, leaving it all for her when she came round. Value for money, she expected he called it – not having a dog and barking himself. The bloody cheek of it!

It took her about half an hour to restore order in what was one of the smallest rooms in the house and, wiping her hands dry, she opened the cupboard under the sink to collect dusters, spray polish and glass cleaner. The last sane thing that Hilda Pounce did that day was to open the door to the hall and step through into the main body of the house, at which point she went completely astray of her wits.

Hermione and Dimity had spent a very pleasant couple of hours over several cups of coffee, holding a post- mortem on the various hands of cards played the previous evening. Hermione had joined the players after the first game, when Quentin had very graciously volunteered to stand down. His real motive was to get to the bar and have a couple of pints, but he thought he might as well pick up a couple of house-points for chivalry at the same time.

When he'd been served with his pint of best bitter (in his own pewter tankard that lived behind the bar, of course) he found that Charles had already left and gone home, but he was quite happy to sit and chew the fat with good old Vernon. With all the worries about the business on his mind, he didn't feel up to the complicated mathematics and tactics necessary to tackle their regular game tonight, and was happy just to pass the time in idle conversation.

Hermione had triumphed in her four, having very few points at the end of the first game, and having foiled Craig Crawford's plot of going misère in the no trumps hand, leaving him with nearly all the points in that round to his discredit. She had never played so well, but had been gracious enough to congratulate him on his daring at such a brave manoeuvre at such a late point in proceedings, changing his mood from black despair to not-quite-triumphant heroism.

Autopsy over, the corpse of the previous evening metaphorically before them, cut with sharp tongues and wits into neatly incised pieces, Dimity asked Hermione if she would care to stay for lunch. It was only cold salmon and salad, but if she didn't mind taking pot luck, she was more than welcome.

Hermione was loath to deprive herself of such a delicious treat, the price of salmon being what it was *(she might be relatively wealthy, but that didn't stop her being mean about petty things)*, and Dimity was adamant. 'It's not like you haven't snatched an even tastier morsel from my grasp before, is it?' she asked, but she twinkled as she said it, and winked at her old friend before leaving the room, now suffused with a miasma of old, unhappy memories, which Hermione had rather hadn't been brought up so casually and so unexpectedly.

There was little time for her to dwell on this, however, for at that moment she became aware of a sort of siren wail coming along the Market Darley Road in the direction of Spinning Wheel Cottage, and then of a furious banging on the front door, while the siren wail resolved itself into a scream, and continued to sound, as the knocking continued without break.

Everything got rather louder as Dimity pulled the door open to see what dreadful banshee had landed on her doorstep, only to find Hilda Pounce, her face pallid and shocked, her hair blown to kingdom come. As the door reached the fully open stage, Hilda ceased to scream and had only the breath left to mouth at Dimity, 'It's your cousin. It's your cousin. Dead! You've got to come.'

Hermione arrived behind Dimity at that moment, which was lucky as Dimity's knees showed signs of giving way. 'Which one?' she asked, panic in her voice. 'Patience or Noah? Which one, woman? For God's sake tell me!' But Hilda Pounce had still not recovered sufficiently from her madcap dash from Barleycorn Crescent, for speech, and just continued to mouth at them, in ironic mockery of the piscatorial treat that now lay neglected on their plates on the dining room table.

Dimity was so frustrated with anxiety that she grabbed the cleaning woman by the shoulders and began to shake her, shouting, 'Which one, damn you? Which one, woman?' Hermione gently pulled her away and escorted Mrs Pounce into the house, so that they could question her in a more civilised manner. Shouting and shaking on the doorstep was no example to set to the neighbours, after all.

After being pushed down into an armchair in the sitting room and given a glass of water, Hilda managed to gasp out, 'Neither of them. It's Mr Gabriel.'

'Gabriel?' queried Dimity, shocked that he should not be at his place of work on a weekday. 'Whatever's happened to him?'

Draining her water glass, Hilda held it out for a refill and continued, as if in a trance, 'He seems to have hanged himself from the top of the staircase, Miss Pryor. Found him about ten minutes ago when I'd done the washing-up.'

'You didn't just leave him there, did you?' Dimity shouted in disbelief. 'Surely you can't have calmly got on with the washing up while he was … just hanging there?'

'Of course I didn't Miss Pryor. I did the kitchen first. It was when I went through the door to look at the rest of the house that I found him.'

'Have you called the police or an ambulance?' Hermione was feeling a little left out of the drama.

'No, I haven't. I got straight back on my bike and high-tailed it up here to tell you. I didn't know what to do, but I knew you would.'

Dimity's knees were in danger of withdrawing from the field of action again, and Hermione led her gently to a sofa and sat her down. 'Both of you stay here while I phone for help, then I'll make the two of you a nice cup of hot, strong tea. We'll get this sorted out, don't you worry.' Command was Hermione's forte, and she rushed eagerly into the hall to dial 999.

Chapter Six
Mis-Deal

DI Harry Falconer and DS Davey Carmichael sat on opposite sides of the inspector's desk looking at a fresh selection of photographs from Carmichael's New Year's Eve wedding, Falconer now at ease, because he realised he had not disgraced himself in any way, and was, in any case, fascinated at the size and number of the members of his sergeant's family, now revealed before him.

There were three brothers, all named after Shakespearian characters, as was Carmichael himself, and all of almost identical build to their policeman sibling. There were also two sisters, only slightly smaller in build, and a gargantuan mountain of a woman who proved to be the mother of the brood.

Falconer had always assumed that Carmichael's mother was a widow, and was therefore puzzled by the presence in so many of the photographs of a tiny, wizened man, dressed as a gnome or dwarf or something similar. He must be a close relative to appear in so many of the photographs. Rather than risk a badly worded question, he just pointed to the little fellow and raised his eyebrows at his colleague, hoping that his face conveyed the convivial interrogative conjecture he had attempted.

Carmichael's laugh boomed round the office. 'Him? That's my dad, that is!'

Falconer's careful check on his diplomacy vanished, like the demon king in a puff of smoke and, before he could stop himself, the question was asked. 'Your father? But he's so tiny and old,' and then he winced, as if expecting a slap *(which he was, really)*.

'That's what my mum says, sir. He used to be a bit taller when they met, but she says she saw the quality stock in him. That's why she married him, even if he has got a glass back, and she's had to look after him for years now. He's hardly been able to work a day since the last of us kids was born, almost as if the effort were too much for him after that.'

To Falconer's eternal gratitude, this conversation was abruptly terminated before it could get even more intimate and embarrassing by the ringing of the telephone, and he lifted the receiver to his ear with an inward sigh of relief. This sudden good mood didn't last for long, however, for, as he terminated the call, he had the look of a child who is being sent to his room for misbehaviour.

'Whatever's wrong, sir?' Carmichael asked with concern in his voice.

'There's feuding again in banjo country. I'm going home to get my wellies,' he replied sulkily.

'What? What are you talking about, sir?' Carmichael was now running after the inspector, none the wiser to what was going on, but knowing that something had upset him. 'What are you talking about, sir?'

'Death – looks like suicide – in one of those God-forsaken villages again. What do they put in the water there?'

'Which village, sir?'

'Steynham St Michael, where we went the other day about that poison pen letter and the Fisticuffs Twins. You can drive, Carmichael, because I simply can't be arsed to do another rural run in this ghastly weather in my sophisticated lady, and we're going via my place, so I can pick up my wellingtons and change into something a little less expensive!'

When Carmichael drew up outside number three Barleycorn Crescent there were already two other cars present, one parked on the drive and the other on the road outside. Recognising the one on the road as that of Dr Philip Christmas, newly appointed police surgeon, they approached the front door, assuming the car on the drive to be that of the deceased occupier.

Wrong, wrong, wrong! They could not have been more wrong if they had thought about it with great intent. Dr Christmas opened the door, but his face bore a look of panic, masking fury, and from behind him wafted the babble of women's voices, raised in excitement to the excited chatter of starlings. Looking Falconer firmly in the eye, Dr Christmas took a step over the threshold and hissed, 'Get them out. For God's sake use your authority as a representative of the law, and get them out. They won't listen to a word I say, and they're trampling all over the locus like a herd of elephants.'

The inspector's reaction was instant, drawing inspiration from the authority he had wielded in his army days, and he stepped into the hall, took in the situation at a glance, and announced, 'Ladies, I am Detective Inspector Falconer, and I wish to inform you that this could be a crime scene, and interference with a crime scene is viewed in a very censorious light by the police authorities: in fact it is a criminal offence.

'Please give your names and addresses to Detective Sergeant Carmichael here on your way out.' At this point he dipped his head in the direction of the looming bulk of his partner. 'I shall be calling on you all later to take your fingerprints, to eliminate them from any enquiry that ensues from this sad event, but I must insist that you leave immediately, and without laying a further finger on anything. Thank you for your co-operation in this matter, and good day to you all.'

At the mention of fingerprints, Hermione, Dimity, and Hilda Pounce, who had all rushed to the scene of action – or rather inaction, seeing as the householder was not up to much at the moment – to see what pickings there were for the gossip vultures, prepared to take their leave, in anticipation of an exciting visit from the forces of law and order, later in the day.

The women departed as they had left; in Hermione's car, headed back, this time, to her house, so that they could have a good chew on the fat they had harvested, and enjoy a good old session of conjecture. Even the fact that Gabriel Pryor had been related to Dimity did not dim their anticipation, as the two of them had never been close, and maybe the other two were about to find out why.

Within just over five minutes, only the three men remained in the hall of three Barleycorn Crescent, all eyes looking upwards at the dead weight that was suspended from the newel post at the top of the stairs. With a ghost of a sigh, Falconer made a decision and asked if Dr Christmas would be so good as to declare life extinct, and draw any conclusions that were waiting around. In a moment of quiet rebellion, he struck a discreet but dramatic pose, in hope that Christmas had a pencil. If there were any drawing to be done, he wanted it to be of him, Falconer, chief investigating officer.

Abandoning that thought as rapidly as he had adopted it, he charged Carmichael with the job of summoning a SOCO team, in case this was not what it looked like, while he, as the senior officer in attendance, went to look for a note.

His instinct did not go unrewarded, as there were two envelopes propped up on the mantelpiece in the sitting room, one addressed very properly to the coroner, the other simply addressed 'To whom it may concern'. This, Falconer assumed, would be him, and he unstuck the flap, making as little contact with the paper as possible, in case any complications occurred which proved this to be other than a case of suicide.

The contents of the note were pathetic in the extreme, merely asking whoever had taken charge of the letter, to let Mr Carstairs, the manager of the local bank in the High Street, that 'it' had been an aberration on the part of Pryor, and that all the funds had been returned to the relevant account within a matter of weeks, and that it had all been a long time ago, now.

'Stupid man!' Falconer muttered under his breath, 'Stupid, stupid man!' wondering what had prompted this overwhelming attack of conscience, if the matter – obviously a case of 'borrowing' – had taken place sometime in the past, and the funds had all been replaced. There had obviously been no suspicion of what had taken place at the time, so why kill himself now? For Falconer was absolutely convinced that this was a case of suicide.

64

A casual examination of the contents of the room's wastepaper bin had provided the answer to that one as, screwed into a tiny ball, was a note similar to the one that he had been shown by Buffy Sinden, and this connection immediately returned his mind to that woman's pathetic face. Ms Sinden obviously thought of herself as a wild child, a free spirit. Well, he supposed that was as pretty a way as any of describing someone whom others may consider a whore or a slapper. Women like her were particularly pathetic in the mornings, when they had started to lose their looks and the wrinkles were setting in.

Hauling his mind back to the matter in hand, he finished smoothing out the sheet of paper and read:

'Flee! All is discovered. Be sure your sins will find you out.'

A general letter hinting at nothing in particular, but it had proved effective in this case, as Gabriel Pryor obviously had a guilty secret, and his reaction had been extreme, but there was no accounting for people's reactions in any given circumstances.

He had worked on a case once where a man had been diagnosed as HIV positive, and rather than own up to his wife that he was bisexual, he had cut her throat and that of his two-year-old son as they slept, then slit his own wrists and sat in the bathtub to die so that he wouldn't make a mess of the bathroom floor: a final act of irrationality that had been confirmed by the note he had left behind, apologising for any mess.

A bit of undiscovered embezzlement that had been regularised wasn't a strong motive for suicide. Perhaps, even in death, Gabriel Pryor had hidden another guilty secret. He'd have to do some digging, more for his own peace of mind than for any other reason, for the requirements of the law were satisfied by the note he had held by his fingertips, and if the note to the coroner confirmed what the first note had said, then it was case closed, and on to the next merry dance of death. But there was more here than met the eye: of that he was sure.

And at least he had another of those beastly notes to work on. If there were more than one, and this was evidence that there were, there would probably be more, and he would conduct some judicious questioning himself, to find out who the other recipients were, and if they were still being received. A poisoned mind, like the one that produced letters like that, could cause any amount of damage to the recipient – it could even wreck lives, as it had this one, or split asunder marriages that had seemed solid as a rock on the surface.

A ring of the doorbell returned him to the here and now, and he exited the sitting room to greet the SOCO team, advising them of what he had found, and he and Carmichael left them to it, Dr Christmas only a few steps behind them.

As they approached Carmichael's car, Philip Christmas caught them up and reached out his hand to shake Carmichael's. 'I heard about the wedding,' he said, smiling up at the detective sergeant. Congratulations, and what a fantastic thing to do. There ought to be more people around like you. The world would be a better place for it.'

With a nod at Falconer, the doctor strode off to his own car and drove away. 'What was all that about, Carmichael?' Falconer asked, puzzled about the thought that the world would be a better place if there were more Carmichaels in it – more colourful, maybe, but better? Whatever was the man talking about? Must've been sniffing his own ether, or something!

'It's nothing, sir. He's probably just happy that Kerry and me got wed. Just ignore it.'

'OK,' agreed the inspector, still left intrigued, but it probably didn't matter in the great scheme of things, he thought, and they had three twittering old women to interview.

If Hermione had been able to tune into this thought, she would have been furious at being lumped in with the others in such a category, as she was seven years younger than Hilda Pounce, and Dimity's junior by nearly a year. At fifty-six, she considered herself still young, having fallen for the myth that fifty is the new forty, and with copious make-up and her youthful wig to fortify her opinion of herself, she would not be shaken in this belief.

He and Carmichael found said 'twittering old women' cosily ensconced in Hermione's drawing room, sipping tea from delicate bone china cups, and nibbling delicious, crumbly, hand-made biscuits. The only concession to the fact that the three woman weren't equal socially was made by Hilda Pounce, who didn't feel it was right that she should sit at ease in one of Hermione's comfy leather armchairs, and had perched herself on a wooden Windsor chair that usually lived in a corner by the bow window.

The arrival of the two policemen silenced their avid chatter and supposition, and they listened with mounting disbelief, and a shared look of disgust, at the thought that the poor man they had found dead earlier had, in Hermione's words later, when recounting it to countless friends and acquaintances, been hounded to his death. Her telephone was fated to be red hot for the whole of that evening, loving as she did, to be first with the news on anything, especially something as sensational as this.

Announcing his intention to interview them, as they had been first on the scene, Hilda Pounce stuttered her excuses, and said that she had to get away and inform her other employers that she would not be at work for a day or two. Claiming that the discovery had 'really taken it out of her', she scurried from the room, muttering that they could call on her at home if they wanted to.

She had explained to the nice tall gentleman that she had no telephone, and she would have to call on the others she was scheduled to work for over the next day or two, or drop them a note through the door. Someone in her position in life couldn't afford luxuries such as a telephone, working her fingers to the bone as she did both before and after her Bert died, just to keep body and soul together, pay the rent, and put food in her belly. The last words they heard from her as she went out of the door were, 'Well, he won't be any loss to anybody. Used to interfere with little boys, and I don't approve of that. And him coming from a Christian God-fearing family.'

Falconer could believe her impoverished existence, for her appearance confirmed what she had just told them. Her shoes were scuffed and down at heel, there were ladders in her thick stockings, and her skirt and jumper were much-washed and misshapen. She wore no make-up, and what thin, grey hair she had left, was scrunched into a mean bun at the back of her neck, barely kept in place with an elastic band and two hair grips. Her final remark, however, looked as good a springboard as any from which to launch his dive into what he hoped would be a very short investigation.

'What did Mrs Pounce mean about Mr Pryor interfering with little boys, and why make a point of how pious his family was?' Falconer never let anything get past him if he could help it, and wanted to examine both strands of Hilda's parting remark.

To his surprise, it was Dimity that took the lead in answering him, but then that was only logical, when she explained that she and Gabriel Pryor were cousins, although no close social relationship existed. 'He was always a loner – a strange secretive child who grew into a strange and secretive man,' she said. 'Oh, there were rumours about him, especially when he was a teenager. I'm only a few years older than him, so I heard what never got to the ears of the grown-ups.'

'And what was said?' prompted Falconer, as she stopped speaking and gazed into the distance, obviously remembering.

'Oh, they said he tried to touch younger boys. Enticed them with sweeties to go into the churchyard with him, and then tried to touch them – on their private parts,' she added, getting red in the face at the very thought.

'And were the rumours true?'

'Who knows?' Dimity exclaimed, shaking her head a little to clear it of old, forgotten, far-off events, now grown indistinct with age. 'It hardly matters now, does it? The man's dead, and we shouldn't pursue him beyond the grave, over silly things that children said about him forty years and more ago, should we?'

Hilda Pounce had not cycled straight home when she had left The Spinney, but had gone a few yards in the opposite direction to her own home, to take a long-cut via Tuppenny Lane, stopping opposite where Farriers Lane pared off to the right, and leaning her bicycle against the wall of the building opposite this junction. Her day had started badly in the library, and this was her last port of call before going home, to see if she couldn't reverse her fortunes at least a little bit.

Once inside, she approached the returns desk where Patience Buttery stood, exactly as she had done six hours earlier, when Hilda had discovered that she had committed an offence for the first time in her life. 'Hello again, Mrs Pounce. How may I help you?' Patience greeted her return visitor, and was surprised to see that the old woman had tears in her eyes. 'Why whatever's the matter?' she asked, unable to conceal her natural concern.

'It's them books, my dear. I've never done it before, and I still can't believe I've done it now. It'll be on record, and I'll be marked down officially as dishonest and untrustworthy, and I just don't know what to do about it. I've never done anything wrong before.' Hilda's pathetic voice straggled to a halt, and she just stared at Patience pathetically.

'I'm sorry. Mrs Pounce, but I'm not really sure what you're talking about.'

'It's them library books. I got the date muddled, and they was late back, and now there's a black mark against me somewhere, and there's nothin' I can do about it, I suppose?'

Patience gave a sigh of disbelief, and tried to comfort the elderly cleaner, as the tears rolled unchecked down her cheeks. 'Please don't worry yourself about it. It's not marked down in a book or anything like that. The money just goes into the fund for general fines, and nobody's name is specifically mentioned. Please don't distress yourself like this. It simply isn't worth it. Nobody can find out that you returned your books late. It's totally anonymous when it goes into the account, so don't give it another thought.'

Patience put her arm briefly around Hilda's shoulder, and then patted her on the back. What a fuss to make over a piddling little library fine. She knew that Hilda's family had been very religious, as had hers, and her husband Noah's, but to get herself distressed and in such a state just for bringing a couple of books back a day late was ridiculous. With a final smile at what proved to be her penultimate customer for the day, Patience took herself over to the counter where someone was waiting to take out some volumes.

Hilda Pounce, cleaner, general dogsbody, potty and, in some people's eyes, less than human, was given furiously to think. The words and gestures of comfort from Patience had strangely moved her, and made her think in a way she never had before. What a nice young lady, and such a pity her cousin had committed suicide. But that wasn't really the point, was it? She'd made herself clear, and there was a price.

It was a wonder Hilda hadn't thought to mention Mr Gabriel's suicide to her – but then, that wasn't her job, was it? She was a cleaner of houses and pubs, and a scrubber of floors. But those biscuits she'd had at Miss Grayling's had been lovely, she thought as she remounted her bicycle at the bottom of the library steps and set off, finally, for home, at the end of what had seemed a very long day indeed.

Falconer had also found it a very long day, still not quite recovered as he was, from his unremembered and heavily assisted bender of the previous Thursday. He was looking forward to spending a quiet evening in front of the television and an early night, following his evening meal. That morning he had left out a meaty salmon steak between two plates, to defrost on the work surface, and he was looking forward to that, with some new potatoes boiled in their jackets and a green salad. Washed down with a glass of crisp, flinty, well-chilled white wine, he would be a happy man when he took his seat in front of the television set.

As he entered his house and hung up his coat, he called out to the cats, and was surprised when there was no response. Unless they were out in the garden, they usually greeted him with great enthusiasm, but he could hear noises from the kitchen, so they couldn't be out hunting. What on earth were they up to, to keep them away from welcoming him home?

What they were up to involved two broken plates, a salmon steak considerably depleted in size, and a very messy kitchen floor. As Falconer entered the kitchen, Tar Baby and Ruby sat under the kitchen table watching a criminal action happening right in front of their eyes. On the floor in front of the sink sat Mycroft, hunched over what was left of the salmon and chewing enthusiastically, his jaws ceasing only when he heard his master shout very loudly.

'You little sod! That was my supper!' he greeted his beloved seal-point Siamese, now exposed as a thief.

Chapter Seven
New Cards

Thursday 7th January

Although the cards club had been Gabriel Pryor's only real interaction with the social life of the village, his death, nevertheless, had repercussions that sent out ripples further than he would ever have imagined, had he been alive to observe them.

Buffy Sinden woke up early that morning, alone in bed, and, if not exactly happy with that, at least reconciled that her previous way of life had not been the way to a stable and happy future. Although the letter had truly upset and frightened her, to think that someone had been observing her behaviour and knew her medical history, which she had believed was strictly between her doctor and herself, she was aware of what an empty existence she had been leading.

It was nearly a week into the New Year, but, even if a little late for resolutions, she determined to change, and find some self-respect. She had, in effect, been pimping her own body in the vacuum that her life had become, since her first termination at the age of seventeen, and it was time that she came to terms with what had happened in the past. She needed to move on and start leading some sort of life. Her emotional development had been halted after that first destructive relationship, and she could see, now, that it had coloured her view of men, and of life in general, ever since.

It may be a bit late in the day to stop acting like a cheap tart and throwing herself at whoever signalled that they were available, but better late than never. She wasn't too old to meet Mr Right. In fact, she thought she had, at one point, but that relationship had bitten the dust like all the others, only this time there was a divorce involved but, fortunately, no children.

At the thought of children, she stuck out her lower jaw in determination. She may have been around the block a few times, but she was, in fact, only thirty-five. She had time yet to meet the right man and have a family: perhaps lead a more conventional life, and even find that so-far-elusive Holy Grail, happiness.

All in all, Buffy decided, on reflection, that letter, although cutting, cruel, and censorious, had been a wake-up call for her, and had maybe even done her a favour. She didn't want to end up like Monica Raynor, still chasing eternal youth at fifty-two, and directing all her energies to keeping her many assignations and flings secret from her husband, Quentin.

Buffy determined to engage in no further physical relationship until she really knew the other person involved. Her new goal would be real contentment, not the casual buzz she had sought previously in her disastrous short-lived liaisons and one-night stands.

Feeling buoyed-up with this new goal, she thought she would treat herself to a little visit to Monica this lunchtime, and see what the older woman thought of her new grand plan. In fact she'd give her a ring at home now, before she left for work. Even if she were cynical enough to pooh-pooh her new outlook on life, at least Buffy would have the moral high-ground, and she felt she could do with a bit of that at the moment. It had been a long time since she had been in that position, and she looked forward to it, as eagerly as a child looks forward to a bag of sweets.

Monica Raynor had no idea that Buffy had plans to make her feel tawdry and cheap about her little affairs, but was concerned, at the moment, with changes in her own life. Gabriel Pryor's demise, although not directly affecting her day-to-day existence, had made her think. Life really was too short to let little irritants sap your energy, she thought, as, once more, she looked around her messy and dirt-encrusted kitchen.

The rest of the house was in a similar state, as neither she nor Quentin had managed to muster the necessary enthusiasm and energy to do anything about it. As she stubbed out her cigarette – supposedly forbidden since the first of the month, but she had had a lot on her plate, and that poisonous letter hadn't helped – she thought back to the days when old Potty Pounce had come round three times a week to 'do' for them.

In those days, everything had been spick and span. All the wooden furniture sparkled with polishing, carpets were vacuumed, work surfaces were spotless, and no washing-up spilled out from an already full sink. As well as cleaning, dear old Potty had tackled the clothes washing on Monday mornings, the ironing on Wednesdays, and the bed linen and towels on Fridays.

How silly she had been to fall out with her over a bit of adjustment to her hours. Although business was abysmal, Potty's wages had been a bargain when one considered how much time she saved them, not only in trying to keep the house in order, but also in looking for things that had got mislaid, or buried under the mess and squalor.

She'd made her mind up! She was going to go and see Potty – Hilda – smarm, schmooze and, if necessary, beg her to come back. She was sure Quentin would agree that if she could get the Pounce woman to come in on, perhaps just Tuesday and Thursday mornings, for she now went to Hermione's on Monday, Wednesday, and Friday, it would be worth it financially, just to restore some order to their lives.

Gabriel's death would be a lesson to her, not to be petty in the future, and not to hold grudges or cut off her nose to spite her face. It was Thursday and she knew that Hilda cleaned for Tilly Gifford on a Thursday afternoon. She'd take a little stroll down to Foxes' Run at about two-thirty – God knows, they were hardly likely to be snowed under with clients – and throw herself on the old woman's mercy. She might not be good for anything else, but by thunder could she clean!

Decision made, Monica Raynor's mind returned to the here and now, and she was surprised to find that she had another lit cigarette in her hand, and there were five butts stubbed out in the ashtray. Well, what could anyone expect, with the pressure she'd been under lately?

And she had lunch with Buffy Sinden to look forward to. She could confide in her about the difficulties of meeting Rodney Kerr, without either Quentin or Roma getting a whiff of suspicion. They had only managed to meet once or twice, what with Christmas and everything else at this time of year, but she had hopes of at least a couple of months of extra-marital high jinks, before caution forced their trysts to cease.

If she managed to restore the services of old Ma Pounce, it would give her more time to arrange and attend liaisons, and to savour the possibilities of the situation, without being haunted by the thought of floors to mop, lavatories to clean, and all the other sordid jobs that running a household encompassed.

It would appear that Hilda Pounce was in for a windfall of extra cleaning work and a useful addition to her meagre wages, for when Charles Rainbird opened his shop for the first time that year – it hadn't seemed worth the effort before today, as nobody would be out scouring for antiques so soon after the festive season – he looked around him at the accumulated dust of weeks, and his heart sank.

He just wasn't the kind of man to knuckle down and enjoy cleaning his stock. OK, so he wasn't as masculine as old Vernon, but he had enough trouble keeping standards up to scratch in Mill Cottage, without the burden of all this wood and glass. And then there was the silver; and the brass and copper. Auctions might like things 'fresh to the market' – in other words, filthy – but his customers expected everything to be immaculate, or they demanded a heavy discount, and that wasn't the way to make a fortune in this game, now was it?

His thoughts turned to Gabriel Pryor, and how he had been found hanging from the bannisters, but everything in his house usually beautifully tidy, and all the chores up to date. It was no good! He was going to have to remedy his situation, so that he could concentrate on the accumulation of lots of lovely money, before he, too, hanged himself in despair.

In the past, he had employed old Potty Pounce, and he had to admit that she did a marvellous job of making everything look as if it had been lovingly cared for for the whole of its life. They hadn't parted on such bad terms, with him claiming that the financial climate was forcing him to rein in his expenses, and he saw no reason why he couldn't approach her to return, claiming, quite truthfully, that he couldn't manage without her, because her work was an asset to his business, because it had been. He just hadn't realised it in his ire at her snooping.

In fact, there was nothing stopping him just turning the 'open' sign to 'closed', and slipping down to Prince Albert Terrace now, to plead his case to her. He knew that several people had dispensed with her services in these harsh 'credit crunched' times: had he not used, somewhat dishonestly, the same excuse himself when he told her he would not be requiring her services again? Well, he had been wrong. He needed her back, and he would just have to be more careful in the future, wouldn't he?

Hermione Grayling typed the words 'THE END' on her ancient manual typewriter, pulled the sheet of paper out with a sigh of contentment, and added it to the other eight hundred and nine piled up on the table beside her. That was another saga to go off to her typist, before the whole thing went to her publisher for editing and proofreading. She already had an inkling of what the next enormous tome would be about, and had been making preliminary notes for the last day or so. She could safely leave the idea to simmer as she had now finished this lengthy and complicated family story, and take a few days of well-earned rest, to relax and revel in her success at the completion of another money-spinning string to her bow.

Patting the ancient Underwood, she smiled fondly at it. It was the machine she had used since her first book had been accepted, and she now looked on it as an old friend, as well as a good luck charm: not that she needed good luck. She had enjoyed an unexpected level of success with her writing, and felt, as she always had, that the fates smiled upon her and her chosen occupation.

She certainly earned enough to justify still writing her stories on Old Faithful, for she could easily afford the services of someone to present them in whatever format was required now, and if she was a little slapdash here and there with her spelling or her grammar, Mrs Who's-it – she could never remember her name, even though she had worked for Hermione for over twenty years – would sort it all out for her, and put it into an immaculate state, before her editor got her hands on it.

Even this lady's name escaped her in her euphoria at reaching the end of another book, and she had edited Hermione's books since her fifth or sixth volume, and always kept an eagle eye on the plot, in case Hermione had made any little continuity errors, or got her names or dates in a muddle. Really, she was another treasure. Lifting her hands to her head and running her fingers through the wild mass of curls that was her wig, she shouted out loud for joy at a job well done.

And thinking of treasures, her mind turned to the thorough job that Hilda had done yesterday with her sideboards, even if she'd left her a load of rubbishy old papers to burn on her return from Dimity's. That, of course, led her mind to what had happened when her cleaning lady had gone down to Barleycorn Crescent. Poor Gabriel!

When they had been playing cards the other evening, nobody had the slightest inkling that he might be contemplating suicide, or that he might, even then, be dead, hanging in his own hall, life extinguished by his own hand. With a quick thought of how fleeting life really was, she decided that her next book could go hang – an unfortunate choice of words, but she ignored it, lest it ruin her good mood. With the realisation of mortality in the back of her mind, she came to a decision. She was going to book a flight, and high-tail it off to her house in Barbados. It was January, it was cold, and it was miserable, and she wanted some sunshine to warm her bones.

January really was the pits, and she was very happy with her new property investment. Previously she had owned a house in

Morocco, but she soon found out that it simply wasn't easy being a woman in an Arab country, and had sold it in favour of a Caribbean hideaway. And she still had the condo in Florida and the villa just outside Nice, if she fancied a change. She really was a very lucky woman.

As minds do, hers immediately returned to someone who had not been very lucky, and whose fate she had been distracted from by her decision to spend a few weeks in the Caribbean. Whatever could have made Gabriel so desperate that he took his own life? She had not known him very well, as a card player, more than a friend or acquaintance, but there must be others who had had a bit more to do with him than her. Her curiosity was definitely aroused.

The possibilities for speculation and gossip were endless, and she went into the drawing room to make a few phone calls, maybe get some of the card club together in the Ox and Plough for a jolly good gossip. Nothing as gruesome or exciting as this had happened in Steynham St Michael in all the years she had lived here, and it seemed such a waste not to make the most of it. Removing her address and telephone number book from its usual resting place in the drawer of the telephone table, she lifted the receiver and began to dial.

Within an hour, she had gathered a respectable crowd, for what she hoped would be a convivial evening, replaced her book in its customary place, and rubbed her rather chubby hands together with glee at the prospect of what was to come, later that day.

Buffy Sinden and Monica Raynor met at one o'clock in Goldfinches, the little restaurant next to the interior design shop in the High Street. Although Monica had had to make her way from the estate agency at the north end of the Market Darley Road, it was a more private place to meet than either of the pubs, because each table was situated in an oak booth, giving both visual anonymity, and, by the very thickness of the wood and the general background noise of muzak, made it impossible for any of the other diners to eavesdrop on what was being discussed in an adjacent booth.

Their meal started well, with Buffy confiding in Monica about the anonymous letter she had received, without actually divulging its contents, for that would be too shaming, even for Monica to envisage. So caught up in her own 'road to Damascus' moment was she, that she didn't notice a blush darken Monica's cheeks at the mention of the letter.

'Well, I should just ignore it if I were you, Buffy. I mean, whatever it said, whoever sent it wouldn't have the guts to prove it and make it public, would they? Otherwise they would have signed the letter, or challenged you with it face-to-face. Anyway, who do you think sent it? Have you any idea at all? What did the police say?'

'The police just put it in an evidence bag and took it away. I think they rather hoped that there might be others, to give them a bit more of an idea who sent them,' Buffy answered, again missing the colour that rose in her companion's cheeks. 'And as for who sent it, well, considering its contents, which I'd rather not discuss if you don't mind, then the only person I can possibly think of is Tilly Gifford, and I'd always rather liked her,' she concluded, finally looking up at Monica.

'Tilly Gifford?' Monica queried. 'I wouldn't have said she had a poisonous bone in her body, would you? I mean, she's so friendly, and she's always either laughing or smiling.'

'Oh, I agree, but I simply can't think who else it could possibly be.'

'Just ignore it, then,' was Monica's advice, and was surprised to see her companion's face glow as if from an inner light.

'I'm not going to do anything of the sort, Monica. It was only the truth, and it's made me look it in the face for the first time ever. Whoever sent that letter has done me a favour, not a disservice. I'm going to change. I'm never going to cheapen myself again for short-term happiness – although it wasn't even happiness when I look back on it. From now on, I'm going to live my life with self-respect, with the hopes and dreams of a normal woman, and not those of an ageing slapper. And I'm going to clean up my living space too. Clean house, clean life.'

'I say, Buffy. That's a bit harsh, isn't it, calling yourself a slapper? Don't put yourself down so much. Remember: to thine own self be true.'

'That's exactly what I'm going to start to do. My life wasn't a mad whirl of fun: it was a desperate whirl of disappointment and self-loathing,' Buffy admitted, fully committed to the cause of being absolutely honest.

Monica pulled a wry face and enquired, 'Does that mean you're not going to be interested in my latest exploits with my new conquest?'

Buffy looked shocked, although she knew Monica wasn't exactly faithful to Quentin, and never had been. 'I don't understand how you can do it, I really don't,' she hissed, lowering her voice as a waiter approached the table to see if everything was all right. 'You've got what I always wanted, and you go risking it all for a stupid little roll in the hay.'

'What do you mean, I've got what you always wanted? I thought you wanted lots of men and an exciting life.'

'Yes.' Buffy nodded sadly. 'That's what everyone thinks, but all I've ever wanted is what you've got. You've been married to the same man for, like, forever, and you've got your son Adrian. I know he's grown up now and left home, but you still had him to play with and bring up and – oh, I don't know – just to love.'

'That sponging little twerp? It was him coming along that put me in the shackles of motherhood at the tender age of twenty. And as for how long I've been married – the answer to that one is too long, honey, too bloody long.'

With a sigh at Monica's refusal to appreciate what she had, Buffy retorted, 'I think you ought to sit back and count your blessings and not your curses. At least, when you get home from work you've got someone to spend the evening with. At least on Mother's Day you've got someone to send you a card.'

'Sentimental crap,' Monica responded, thinking of the letter she had received, and what might have been in it, had she not been so discreet in the past. 'Now, let's change the subject before I lose my appetite completely. Are you sure you haven't been abducted by aliens or something?'

Hilda Pounce started, as was her habit, with the kitchen, when she arrived at Foxes' Run. If everything was ship-shape in the kitchen, then anything else she found in the rest of the house that needed to be washed and put away, at least had somewhere to await her attentions, instead of being stacked on top of an already full sink.

She smiled as her hands plunged into the hot soapy water, thinking that her luck might have turned a bit. It had not really sunk in yesterday that, with Gabriel Pryor dead, she would lose the hours she usually worked for him on Monday and Friday afternoons. She had already lost other hours over the last few months, and when she finally realised the consequence of poor Mr Pryor's suicide this morning, a dark mood had settled on her.

She had always worked her fingers to the bone, just to get by. It hadn't been easy raising a family on a farm labourer's wage, and what she could bring in from a bit of cleaning here and there. She had thought that things would get easier when the children left home, but her Bert had decided that that was when what he referred to as 'me glarse back' was going to stop him having to go to work, permanently.

Although he had been paid some sickness benefit, and had done the odd bit of gardening for Mr Warlock, who had no time for plants himself, and just wanted the lawn mown and the weeds kept down for him, it was still down to her to work whatever hours God sent, to pay the bills.

Then her Bert had died. There had been no long illness to warn her of how different life was about to become. She just found him dead in front of the television one day when she got back from work, and that was that. What meagre savings they had went to pay for the funeral, and the kids were no help at all, feeling nothing more than a mild inconvenience at having to come back to Steynham St Michael for his funeral.

And then, this morning, as she was screwing up sheets of

newspaper to lay the fire and relight the kitchen boiler, which had unaccountably gone out overnight, Mr Rainbird had come round and asked her if she would be willing to go back and clean his shop for him, and all the lovely things in it.

Pleased? She'd be delighted, and the money would make up for what she would lose by not going down to Barleycorn Crescent twice a week, for he paid well for her to take extra care of his precious old things – a load of old junk, in her opinion, but if he was willing to pay well, that was just her good fortune, and about time a bit of it came her way.

As she rinsed the suds out of the sink and off the draining board, preparatory to drying them, there was a brief tattoo on the back door, and Mrs Raynor put her head round it, with a very winning smile on her face. If Mr Rainbird was willing to let bygones be bygones, maybe Mrs Raynor's arrival heralded yet another recovery in her fortunes. Returning the smile whole-heartedly, Hilda Pounce bade her previous employer enter.

'Hello, Mrs Pounce. I'm so sorry to disturb you at work, but I felt I couldn't wait any longer to speak to you. I know we've had our little differences in the past, but do you think you could see your way to letting bygones be bygones, and coming back and 'doing' for me again. I'd be most awfully grateful, and it could be whatever hours suited you. And there'd be an enhancement to your hourly rate. What do you think, Mrs Pounce, dear? I'm completely drowning in household chores and mess and stuff, and I desperately need your help.'

Hilda Pounce could hardly believe her luck!

And when she got home, she was even more amazed to find a note from that woman of easy virtue at Clematis Cottage, asking her if she would come and clean for her once a week. What with her hours at Miss Grayling's, her hours at Mrs Gifford's, her work at the two pubs, and her reinstatement at two of her previous employers, she had never had it so good. Mr Pryor may have considered his life not worth living, when he had such an easy time of it, all things considered, but his passing seemed to have definitely changed Hilda's luck for the better.

She was a restless woman, who found it almost impossible to sit and do nothing, and knitted furiously as she watched the television of an evening, so that her viewing time was productive and not wasted. Her life-style had made sure that she wasn't afraid of hard work, and if that hard work was the paying sort, then she was more than glad to do it. She could do with a few new clothes, and that old sofa of hers was leaking stuffing all over the place. Maybe things were about to get a lot better.

Hermione was a little late arriving for the gathering that she had initiated in the Ox and Plough that evening, as she had spent some time on the telephone arranging her little break in the sunshine. But with her tardiness also came her generosity. Before she swept over to the group that awaited her, she paused at the bar and asked for half a dozen bottles of champagne on ice to be delivered to her friends' tables: an unusual order in a rural pub, but the landlord was used to her extravagance, kept the bottles chilled and at the ready, and just assumed that she had finished another of her wildly popular Victorian sagas.

Her arrival, closely followed by her bubbly offering, was greeted with grateful enthusiasm, and the favoured few metaphorically licked their lips at the treats, both alcoholic and verbal, to come.

Even though some of the men from the usual cards' gathering had demurred, they still made quite a crowd. At one table, still maintaining a separated identity as the Fox and Hounds players, sat Tilly Gifford, Roma Kerr, Bryony Buckleigh, Buffy Sinden, and Malcolm and Amy Littlemore.

At an adjacent table sat Vernon Warlock, Charles Rainbird, Dimity Pryor, Monica Raynor, and Craig Crawford. Laying claim to a Windsor chair from beside the roaring fire, Hermione dragged it over, and placed it equidistantly between the two tables, mistress of all whom she surveyed.

'Well, that's another one finished. I'll be off in a couple of days for a few weeks' well-earned rest in Barbados,' she declared, holding the glass that Charles had gallantly charged for her as soon as the delicious sound of the cork popping had assailed their ears and tantalised their taste-buds.

'It'll probably take you a few weeks to find a new plot to filch from some unsuspecting stranger, eh, Hermione?' Vernon was a very old friend, and, if not able to get away with actual murder, could commit verbal manslaughter in Hermione's eyes, and not merit punishment.

'You always say that, you old pseud, but you know you can't string two words together when it comes to writing,' retorted Hermione, after a pause to drink deeply from her glass.

'Touché!' Vernon replied, flashing a rare smile to all in attendance.

'Now!' Hermione rubbed her plump little hands together with glee. 'What news of our very own village tragedy?'

Her eagerness was bluntly expressed, and because Hermione was facing away from the bar, she didn't catch sight of Hilda Pounce wincing as she heard her employer's words. Hilda had had another piece of luck in that she had been asked to come in this evening to give the cellar a good clear out. It was lucky she had so much energy, the hours she put in, for a very modest hourly rate, all things considered.

'When we were at Gabriel's house, I thought I saw that inspector reading a letter, and the paper was all screwed up, then smoothed out again, as if it had been thrown away, then retrieved,' offered Dimity who, with Hermione and Hilda, had been part of the cavalry trio that had so surprised Falconer when he arrived. 'Do you think it might have been an anonymous letter? I mean, you wouldn't write a suicide note, then throw it away, would you?'

'Good point, Dimity,' Hermione concurred. 'I thought you might have been a little more upset, him being a relation and all.'

'We never had very much to do with each other: well, not since all that gossip when he was a teenager. My parents told me to stay well away from him, even though I was a girl. They said there was no telling what he might do.'

'I didn't realise it was such a scandal,' interjected Bryony

85

Buckleigh, who had received an update on the situation from Tilly Gifford, the fount of all knowledge in Steynham St Michael.

'Oh, it was all hushed up, you know. It might have been common knowledge, but we kept it to ourselves,' Dimity explained. 'Not like today, when it would be all over the papers, and a huge fuss made. In those days we dealt with our own problems in private.'

'How?' asked Bryony, definitely intrigued to discover how things had changed.

'Well, to my certain knowledge, his father gave him a fearful thrashing, and told him that if there was any more talk, he'd thrash him again, and to within an inch of his life if not to the other side of it.'

'But I thought you lot used to be Strict and Particular,' Tilly queried, on the scent, once more, of a good tale probably worth repeating to anyone who wasn't present here tonight.

'We were. And that was how things were dealt with, and with the blessing of the pastor. Any deviation, criminality, homosexuality, that sort of thing, was to be thrashed out of the perpetrator. 'Driving the Devil out' it was referred to. Thank God people are rather more enlightened now.'

'And what about Noah and Patience? He was their cousin too, wasn't he? And I noticed that the library was closed today, when I went to change my books. Very inconvenient, if you ask me. They shouldn't have husband and wife working there together. It stands to reason that, if something like this happens, or they get ill together, there's no one to cover for them, and people like me have a needless walk for nothing,' Craig Crawford complained.

'Don't be so damned self-centred, you young whipper-snapper,' barked Vernon Warlock, with a glare in the young man's direction. 'They're both very knowledgeable about books, and have the most impeccable manners, which is more than I can say for you, young man.'

'Sorry, Granddad,' Craig replied in a sarcastic tone, but his face belied his public embarrassment and glowed a warm red, much to his discomfort.

Charles Rainbird thought that he would not have been so harsh on the young man, for just saying what he thought, but then Charles was Charles, and rather a different kettle of fish from Vernon.

There was a long moment of silence, as the door on that particular subject was discerned to close, and Buffy broke it by saying meekly, 'I had a letter too.'

'You did?' Hermione was on to her like a shot, and Charles Rainbird smiled to himself as he imagined her new book, based round a series of poison pen letters, culminating in suicide, and family feuds lasting decades.

'Yes. It was absolutely horrible, and I don't want to talk about it, but I just thought I'd mention it.'

Anyone closely observing the convivial group would have noticed a shadow pass over several of the faces there present, but, unfortunately, no one was.

Chapter Eight
The Black Bitch Is Played

Friday 8th January

When Dimity Pryor returned from her morning duty at the charity shop in the High Street *(for she only worked there part-time)*, she noticed that the curtains next door at Pear Tree Cottage were still closed, indicating that Noah and Patience had either gone into mourning or gone away after Gabriel's demise. And that would mean that they had again failed to turn up to open the library, and that was very unlike them, because they were a very conscientious young couple.

Being a somewhat shy person herself, she didn't like to intrude on what she saw as their grief, but was nevertheless concerned, and decided to slip along to Hermione's to see what she thought or knew, about the situation. She might even get invited to stay for lunch, if Hermione was feeling as full of the joys of life as she had been the previous evening.

Spurning the front door as unfitting for so old a friend, Dimity walked round to the rear of the property, and let herself in through the kitchen door, which Hermione habitually left unlocked throughout daylight hours, so that unexpected visitors would not disturb her train of thought if she were writing.

Once inside Dimity called 'coo-ee' but, receiving no answer, began to check the rooms to locate her friend. Had she been out, the back door would definitely have been locked. No one in the drawing room, no one in the dining room. That was odd. Hermione had said she'd finished her book, and there was no way she would start another one so soon, especially as she had booked a holiday.

An embarrassing thought occurred to Dimity, and she stood outside the downstairs lavatory, listening carefully at the door, but there was no sound from within, and opening the door confirmed that Hermione was not in the middle of conducting any 'business' – how embarrassing if she had been, thought Dimity, horrified at her unsuspected ability to pry like that.

That only left her writing room her author-torium, as she would insist on calling it. With no other choice, Dimity walked down the hall, knocked discreetly, in case her friend didn't want to be disturbed then, receiving no shouted instructions to the contrary, opened the door and went in.

Dimity gave a little moan at what she saw, and slipped to the floor, unconscious.

In the CID office at the Police Headquarters in Market Darley, Detective Inspector Falconer and Detective Sergeant Carmichael were engaged in a discussion of word usage and derivations: in other words, a little discussion concerning etymology was in progress. Or rather, Harry Falconer was holding forth on the current lax use of English, and Carmichael was trying to look like he was listening, and realising that this was all his own fault. If only he'd kept his mouth shut.

It had started with Carmichael bowling in, bubbling over with bonhomie because today was what he declared, his first week 'anniversary'.

This of course was like a red rag to a bull to Falconer, and he dived in, word mis-use antennae waving so fast they were a blur. 'Do you have any idea of the root of the word 'anniversary', Carmichael?'

'No, sir. Does it matter?'

'Does it matter? Of course it matters, Carmichael. When mis-use becomes common usage the whole language goes to pot, communication becomes ineffective, and we might as well communicate in a series of grunts, which the younger generation seem to have degenerated to already anyway.' Falconer was beginning to get red in the face, and was in danger of falling off his soap box.

'But you knew what I meant, didn't you, sir?' Carmichael was feeling bemused at such a vehement response to such a simple statement, and began to tune-out the sound of his superior's voice, while maintaining an attentive and interested facial expression.

'… so it can only be used when referring to years, not days, weeks, or even months. Years, Carmichael! Only years! And why are you dressed like that? I thought the new Mrs Carmichael was leaving out your work clothes the night before! You look like a clown!'

'Kerry said that I was being so good about her choosing my outfits, that I could have 'dress down Fridays', so that my personality and natural exuberance would not be stifled for one day of the working week,' he explained, as if he had learnt this by rote, for whenever he was asked about his present garb.

'And did she say anything about not stifling your congenital lunacy and complete lack of colour co-ordination?'

'Not that I remember, sir.' Carmichael was getting used to Falconer's little ways, and just humoured him whenever necessary.

'Well, she should have done. Just look at you! Lime green jogging bottoms! Why?'

'Because it's minus five outside, sir, and they're fleecy-lined.'

'Bright yellow fleece, 'Don't worry' written on it, and a smiley face. Again, why?'

'Same reason, sir. Also, the colour makes me feel happy.'

Falconer sighed deeply and addressed himself to the most elevated garment in the ensemble, the hat, which was multi-coloured striped, South American in style, with a bobble on the top, and ear-flaps from which appended long strings, should his sergeant wish to tie said garment under his chin to keep him even more cosy.

'And that thing?'

'The boys gave it to me for Christmas, sir.'

Well, there was no answer to that, not without accusing Carmichael's young stepsons of having the most appalling taste in presents, so that was the end of that conversation. And it was just as well, as at that moment of 'where do we go from here?'

the telephone rang.

Falconer was only a few minutes on the phone, mostly listening and scribbling on a scrap of paper. As the call ended, he sprang up from his desk and headed towards the coat stand, calling over his shoulder, 'That place we went to about that anonymous letter, the domestic violence, and the suicide – what was it called?'

'Steynham St Michael, sir. Why?' Carmichael asked, getting to his feet quickly in reaction to the inspector's movements.

'Because it just got even busier, and we're going there again. And this time it sounds like murder! At least, if it's not, it'll be the weirdest case of suicide I've ever come across. Now do your hat up like a good detective sergeant, so that you don't catch cold, and let's get on the road.'

Carmichael couldn't be bothered to point out to Falconer that one didn't catch a cold from getting cold: that a virus was involved, for he knew the inspector knew that, and was just teasing him about his attractive and unusual headgear. As he left the office, he pulled the ear-flaps down a little bit, for extra protection against the temperature outside, thinking how well Kerry's boys knew his taste and just accepted it as part of him.

They took Falconer's Boxster this time, and didn't bother making a call at his home for a change of clothes, as he had been to this particular village recently, and knew that there were no muddy tracks and rutted, puddled pathways for the unwary. It was a well-maintained village that he could visit in his usual immaculate garb, with complete peace of mind.

On the journey there, not a long one in distance, but made longer in time by the presence of black ice on the roads, the conversation turned from the resemblance between Kerry and her boys, to physical traits in general, leading Falconer to tell of the Roman nose which, although missing him out, on his swim through the gene pool, haunted nearly every member of his father's family, including the women. He concluded, somewhat unfortunately, 'Noses run in my father's family,' and then, realising what he had uttered, waited for Carmichael to come up with some smart-alec answer.

But there was just a short silence, before Carmichael made his contribution to this discussion on genetics. 'Whippets run in my Uncle Pete's family – but they never win!'

They left the car in the drive of The Spinney, and went round to the back door, as instructed. Dimity had said that she'd wait there, as she really didn't want to go anywhere else in the house, and that's where they found her, a half-drunk cup of very strong tea in front of her, as she sat at the kitchen table, an empty brandy glass just to the right of the cup.

Apart from two small red patches on her cheeks, evidence of the spirit she had consumed, her face was pale, and her hands shook as she took another sip of tea, before rising to greet them.

Introductions were made, and both detectives noticed how cold her hand was, and how it fluttered like a frightened bird in their grasp. Her knees shook at the effort of standing too. The shock had affected her badly, and Falconer bade her sit again, and leave everything to them.

He had alerted Dr Christmas, thinking this was home territory for him, but were informed that things had changed. He would attend in his role as police surgeon, but his two sessions a week in Steynham St Michael were now history, as a permanent doctor had been appointed – Pierce, his name was, if Philip Christmas remembered aright – and they'd better give him a buzz too, for the sake of protocol.

Thus updated, he alerted a SOCO team, as well, as they were leaving the station, knowing that at least he couldn't get that one wrong, but now they were here, they'd better take a look at Steynham St Michael's latest effort to make his job more difficult.

For all he knew, there were dozens of poisoned pen letters out there, people committing suicide like it was a new dance-craze and a whole clan of Littlemores beating each other senseless in the throes of alcoholic rages. And now he had a murder to deal with as well. So much for a happy and peaceful New Year!

Dimity Pryor had given them directions to Hermione's

writing room – what she occasionally referred to whimsically as her 'bookery nook'; more often as her 'author-torium' – and Falconer was first through the door, using a clean handkerchief so that he did not disturb any fingerprints that might prove important during the investigation.

Both men entered the room, their immediate reactions differing hugely. Falconer took a huge intake of breath, making a noise that would probably be spelled 'huuuh'. Carmichael hooted with laughter, which bordered on the hysterical, then clapped both hands over his mouth to stop the noise, that was obviously involuntary in its inappropriateness.

Hermione Grayling, or at least the shell that had been Hermione, sat in front of the ancient Underwood, which was placed in its usual position for typing, but her proportions were skewed by the presence of a tea towel *(clean!)* over something which protruded from the top of her head, making her look as if she had a severe case of antlers.

Dragging his eyes away from the whiteness of the tea cloth and the red streaks that had run down Hermione's face, Falconer turned his gaze to the typewriter, while Carmichael fought to regain control of his behaviour. The sergeant had rapidly exited the room, and now stood in the hall, taking deep breaths to calm himself, after his brief demonstration of hysteria.

There was a sheet of paper in the machine, sadly decorated with its author's blood, but it was still readable, and Falconer read:

How many more stories, not to mention men, are you going to steal, to fill the void that you foist on the reading public as your storytelling gift? And give the Victorian period a rest, will you? The whole era didn't last as long as your interminable books about it.

And having read, straightened up with a start. The woman had been writing a poison pen letter to herself! Only this one was typed! Did that mean that she was responsible for the other letters? He briefly wondered how many of them had been received: no doubt a much greater number than had been admitted to. And why was this one typed? Was it just a writer's instinct to make a note of what they wanted to use, so as not to lose the flavour before, in this case, tracking down the letters necessary to actually construct the letter?

He'd have to get the keys of the machine tested for fingerprints, of course, before he drew any hasty conclusions, but it might be a good idea, in the meantime, to discover who else had received anonymous missives. This might mean case closed, as far as the letters went, but if somebody had found out that it was Hermione sending them, then that gave them a splendid motive for murder, especially if their letter had hinted at something shameful or illegal in their past that they still couldn't risk being bandied about as common knowledge.

Carmichael re-entered the room at this point in Falconer's conjecture and, as always, went straight to the nub of the matter. 'What's that thing sticking out of her head, sir?'

'No idea, Carmichael. I haven't got close enough to take a good look yet. We'll have to leave the cloth in place until after it's been photographed, but it you want to see if you can peek under the edge, be my guest.'

Fully in control again, Carmichael worked his way from one side of the body, round behind it and to the other side, bent double and, skewed his neck to one side, his face pointing upwards. He then repeated this short inspection in reverse order and, standing straight once more, announced, 'I'm not sure, sir, but I think it's a billhook. Very nasty!'

'A billhook!' Falconer repeated, aghast.

Taking this for ignorance of the implement, his sergeant began to give a physical description of the tool and its uses, only to be cut short.

'I know what a billhook is, Carmichael, but I'd have lumped it in with machetes and the like, as more likely to be used by drug dealers in gang warfare. This cannot, by any stretch of the imagination, be gang warfare.'

'It's not, sir. It's village warfare, that's what it is. This place is surrounded by agricultural land, so there are likely to be no end of murder weapons disguised as farming implements, with respect, sir.'

'By god, you're right, Sergeant. I just hope we're not looking for a psychotic farmer for this one! Combine harvester beats patrol car any day of the week, never mind paper, scissors, stone.'

Chapter Nine
New Game

Friday 8th January

News travels fast in a village, and the first ears to hear of the tragedy were Tilly Gifford's. It was just her good fortune to be on duty at the doctor's surgery, when Dr Philip Christmas called to keep Hermione's GP abreast with events. It may have been a private telephone call, but that didn't stop Tilly listening in on the reception area extension. That extension was one of her major gossip-gathering tools, and she was very fond of it.

Hanging up a second or two after Dr Pierce, she was just in time to catch him as he headed for the exit, calling that he had to make a quick visit to a patient, and may be gone some time. The latter part of this information mattered nought to Tilly, as there was no more surgery that day, and she was due to finish at four o'clock; and the former piece of information imparted was easily interpreted as Dr Pierce going off to The Spinney to have a good old nose at the murder scene and, no doubt, a good old gossip with Dr Christmas.

It must be very lonely for him in a one-man rural practice like this one, she thought, as she sorted out her telephone chat-list for that evening of those unable to spare the time for a good old gossip at this time of day.

Tilly was glad of the privacy now that he was gone, and with such a valuable and rare nugget of news to share, she immediately removed her mobile phone from her handbag and began to dial. Without there being any danger of Dr Pierce interrupting her, she could enjoy the reactions to her news bulletin from several of her friends, giving them only the bare bones now, and promising to dish the dirt in more detail when she got home and could enjoy the much lower tariff of her landline.

There was a welter of activity at The Spinney when Dimity eventually left to go home. There was a plethora of evidence bags, photographs were being taken, fingerprints checked for, Hermione's hands were encased in plastic bags – just in case she had managed to take a swipe at her executioner – as was her beloved old Underwood. Philip Christmas had pronounced life extinct, and was discussing the bizarre choice of weapon with Dr Pierce, when the mortuary vehicle arrived to remove Hermione, feet first, from her home, for the last time.

It was at this moment that Dimity, who had waited patiently to give her statement, but had been unsuccessful as yet due to all the said activity, decided that she could stand it no longer, and had to get out of that house of death and back to her own home. By now she was feeling decidedly ill, and wanted nothing more than to have a mug of cocoa with a goodly shot of Baileys in it, and go to bed and sleep till the morning. She had had enough of today for today and she just couldn't deal with any more of it.

Carmichael, noticing her severe discomfort, offered to walk her to her own door, but she declined his kind offer, as it was only about a hundred yards away, and she was unlikely to come to grief in such a short distance. He did, however, tell her that he would watch her down the road to Spinning Wheel Cottage, in case she came over faint again, and for this she was grateful.

As she passed the junction with Dairy Lane, however, she met with Vernon Warlock, who was approaching from the opposite direction, obviously on his way home. Seeing them meet and stop to talk outside Vine Cottage, Carmichael called it a day for little-old-lady sitting *(Dimity would have slapped his face for him, if she'd known that was how he thought of her. She was only fifty-seven, and that wasn't anywhere near little-old-lady status, not these days)*, and went back into the residence of the late, and hopefully to be lamented, Hermione Grayling.

As Dimity had crossed the Market Darley Road towards

home, she had considered calling into Pear Tree Cottage, the occupants of which had been the subject about which she had gone over to The Spinney in the first place, but without the chance to chat to Hermione *(and that there never would be again, she thought, her eyes blurring with tears)*, she made a snap decision to give it a miss.

They had obviously taken Gabriel Pryor's suicide to heart – she had not realised they had been so close – but that was probably because she had avoided contact with him, originally on advice from her parents, but of later years from long established habit. They would probably not welcome what they would consider was her interference and she could hardly call there without saying something of the afternoon's events. She found that she didn't really want to burden them with any more bad news at the moment, and discovered that tears were pricking at her eyes again.

Vernon, on the other hand, was a very old friend, and had been part of the same circle as her for years. The sight of him affected her like the breaching of a dam, and as he greeted her, she burst into floods of tears, and held out her arms to him like a child seeking comfort from its mother.

Vernon was not a large man, but Dimity was of a tiny build, and his hug, in response to her pleading arms, engulfed her. 'Whatever's wrong, Dim? It can't be as bad as all that, can it?'

'Oh Vernon,' she spoke through her sobs. 'It is! Hermione's dead!'

Pulling away suddenly from the embrace, Vernon stared at her incredulously and ushered her through his front door and into the kitchen, where the old-fashioned wood boiler pulsed heat into the room. He ushered her to one of a pair of chairs either side of the source of heat and comfort, and drew out his silence a little more, by taking the time to fill and put on the kettle, before he took the chair opposite her.

Dimity's eyes were drying, now that she'd actually said the words, and she looked to Vernon for guidance as to what happened next. 'What do you mean, Hermione's dead? She can't be. I spoke to her on the phone, only this morning. Was it a heart attack or something?' he asked, sceptical as to the veracity of her two word statement.

'Or something,' Dimity answered somewhat cryptically.

'What sort of something? A stroke? A brain haemorrhage?' Vernon wracked his brain, but could think of no other medical event that could cause so quick a demise.

'A billhook,' Dimity stated, two words again, plain and unadorned. The shock was having a quite different effect, now that she was out of The Spinney.

'Did you say a *billhook*?' Vernon looked aghast at her, sitting there calmly now, and uttering such madness. Had she lost her mind?

'I did indeed, Vernon. She's been murdered.'

'It can't be true. That sort of thing only happens on the television and in books, not in quiet, normal villages like Steynham St Michael. Have you had a blow to the head or something, Dimity?'

'I assure you I'm speaking the absolute truth. If you don't believe me, you can go over to her house now, and speak to the police who are still there. Her body's been taken away, but I'm sure that, if you ask nicely, they'll let you have a peek at where it happened.'

Dimity was beginning to feel a little light-headed now, and reached out gratefully for the mug of strong coffee that a still-unbelieving Vernon handed across to her.

'I can assure you that I wouldn't be so crass as to do anything of the sort, but for God's sake tell me what happened, Dim. First you tell me that someone I've known for most of my life is dead, then you imply there was a billhook involved somewhere, and I don't know what to think.'

Dimity sipped at her reviving drink, and began to explain. 'I don't know exactly what happened, Vernon. All I know is that there was something that I wanted to discuss with Hermione: something I wanted a bit of advice about – oh, nothing very important – just the usual everyday stuff. And I went over to the house and let myself in through the back door, the way we all do when she's at home.' Vernon nodded for her to go on, as she momentarily hesitated.

'I called out, the way one does if she's not actually in the kitchen, and then I tried all the other rooms: I even stood outside the downstairs lavatory to see if I could hear her in there ...' As this memory occurred to her, she gave a hoot of hysterical laughter, after which her face crumpled into a mask of disgust, and she plunged her face once more into her mug, in search of comfort.

'She was in her writing room, Vernon. I went there last, just in case she was working and didn't want to be disturbed. Oh, I knew she's finished her latest, but she may have been making notes for something else. I even tapped on the door, to see if she'd tell me to "sod off" or something – you know how she was when she was caught up in the throes of an idea.'

Not waiting for a reply, she continued, 'Well, she didn't tell me to sod off, and she didn't ask me to come in either, so I went in anyway, thinking that she might actually be out, and had forgotten to lock the back door. And there she was! There she was, Vernon, with a bloody great billhook sticking out of the top of her head, and I couldn't believe it was happening. And I closed my eyes to see if it would go away, but it wouldn't, and I didn't know what to do, so I got a tea cloth – a *clean* tea cloth, not a used one – and I threw it over the billhook, because it looked so awful, sticking out of her head like that, her wig all split and ...'

Dimity's voice trailed away to nothing, as Vernon came over and, leaning down, wrapped his arms around her. 'There there, old thing: don't take on so. It'll be all right!'

Rallying briefly, she lifted her head to look him in the eye, said, 'Don't you "platitude" me, you pompous old bag of testosterone!' then dropped her gaze again, as the weeping returned. 'Nothing's ever going to be all right again, is it?' she asked haltingly through her tears. 'How can my best friend be dead? It's not real! It's all a dream! It just can't be! I shall go mad! Vernon, what am I going to do without her?'

Vernon did the only thing possible in response. He knew Dimity well, and he knew her habits, so he half-lifted her to her feet, led here two doors down to her own cottage, and saw her safely inside. Leaving her in an armchair in the sitting room, he popped up to her bedroom and fetched a hot water bottle from the bottom of her bed.

After filling that and placing it where her feet would rest when she retired, he returned to the kitchen, warmed some milk for cocoa, and added a drop of her favourite tipple, Irish cream. 'Now, come on, old girl. I closed early today to get a bit of time to myself, and I've played nursemaid for enough of that free time. I've put a hot water bottle in your bed, I've got your favourite bedtime drink here, and I'm going to see you to your room now, and trust you to get yourself undressed and off to sleep. There's nothing else for it, after the shock you've had, and if you need any more specific help, ring the emergency doctor, and see if he can give you something to help you sleep.'

'Oh, Vernon,' she almost moaned, as he was about to go downstairs.

'What is it, Dim?'

'It was Hermione who wrote that poison pen letter to Gabriel Pryor. There was another one in her typewriter, when she was killed.'

'Let's just leave that for another day, shall we?' Vernon advised, hiding his shock at this accusatory statement. 'I think you've had enough to deal with today. Now, get that drink down you, and get off to sleep. There's nothing that looks so bad after a good long sleep.'

Five minutes later Vernon Warlock was walking briskly down Market Darley Road towards the High Street, his original plan when closing early for the day now abandoned. With what he had just learned, he was off to have a chat with good old Charlie Rainbird. They were birds of a feather, those two, and maybe they could flock together for an hour or so that evening at Charlie's place. Mill Cottage was a little more off the beaten track than Vine Cottage, and their consultation therefore less likely to attract notice.

Dimity's last statement still echoed round his mind, however, and he found it difficult to take it in: Hermione the

102

writer of those beastly letters? Why, that meant that she was morally responsible for Gabriel Pryor's suicide, and he just couldn't imagine his old friend indulging in anything so sordid or cruel. But, if there was physical evidence, and Dimity had said she had actually seen a letter in Hermione's faithful old typewriter, then he may have to believe it in the end, but he would never understand how, or why she would do such a thing.

Monica Raynor had been glued to the window of her estate agency for a little over five minutes, before Quentin noticed her, and asked what there was out there that was so fascinating that she couldn't take her eyes off it.

Without even a hint of losing her temper at the sarcastic tone in which he had phrased his question, she answered, 'There's something going on at The Spinney, but I can't work out what it is.'

'What do you mean, something going on? What could possibly be going on over there?'

'I don't know, but there're a lot of cars outside, including a police patrol car, and a uniformed constable has just placed himself in the middle of the drive, down by the gates.'

'Here, let me see!' Quentin didn't have a bone in his body that would have recognised embarrassment, and he gaped through the glass like a kid at an aquarium.

'You could at least have the decency to stand back a little bit. If you stand any closer to the window, the nice policeman will be able to see your tongue hanging out,' she admonished her husband for his blatant nosiness.

But her embarrassment meter was about to register dangerous levels before exploding, for Quentin actually left the office, crossed the road, and engaged the policeman in conversation. How he had the nerve she did not know, but her suddenly ruddy complexion cleared a little, as she realised that he might come back with all the gen about what was going on over there, and she would know as much as he had found out, without looking like a complete arse-hole and nosy parker.

Although they didn't often occur, there were definite, if infrequent, benefits to being married to a veritable 'sticky beak', as she believed the Australians termed it.

Of course, he made her beg for it when he returned, success written all over his smug, smirking face, and he spent some time telling her how helpful and polite PC Green had been, when approached for information, and how forthcoming he had been with said information, because he knew that it would be common knowledge very soon, so there was no reason at all why he couldn't tell the concerned gentleman, what had occurred at The Spinney.

'Come on, Quentin! You've made such a meal out of it that you must be on to the brandy and cigars by now. Just tell me before my head blows up with pent-up curiosity. What the hell's going on over there?'

'All right, I give in. I might as well tell you, before that bloody old gossip Tilly Gifford phones up and steals my thunder.'

'And?' she prompted him, as he had taken a rather protracted pause, and she had found herself holding her breath. 'Tell me, you unspeakably smug git!'

'Old Grayling's dead!'

'She can't be!'

'Oh yes she can. And she is. Apparently Dimity Pryor found her when she nipped over for a quick chat. The old girl was as dead as a dodo at her writing desk, with the best part of a poison pen letter in front of her, in that wreck of an old typewriter of hers.'

'No!?'

'True!' Quentin was loving being the bearer of dramatic tidings, and he determined to string it out as long as possible. It wasn't often his wife actually listened to anything he said, so he would enjoy it while he could.

'What was it? Heart attack?'

'Nope! Try again.'

'Massive stroke?'

'Nope! Try again.'

'Quentin, if you don't tell me immediately, I shall phone Tilly Gifford, and have it hand-fed to me, *and* covered in chocolate.' She would phone Tilly anyway, to see if she had any more details, working as she did at the surgery, but Tilly wouldn't be home just yet, and Monica wanted to know *now*. 'Brain haemorrhage? There you are, that's three guesses. You have to tell me now.'

'Well, it wasn't *exactly* a brain haemorrhage …'

'Don't tease, or I'll kick you in the nuts; I really will, and you'd better believe me.' The suspense was really getting to his wife now, and he knew she would prove as good as her word, so he gave in and provided the last of the information he had managed to elicit from PC Green.

'Billhook in the head!'

'No!?'

'Really! I'm not joking,' he reassured her. 'And I'm sure that nice constable wouldn't lie to me. It would be more than his job's worth if he did, and I complained. Oh, and get this – she was the author of the poison pen letters. And Pervy Pryor only went and committed suicide because of one of them, didn't he?' Without waiting for an answer from her, he continued, 'And if she hadn't been murdered, they'd have done her for the letters *and* being the cause of a suicide, and our wonderful, famous authoress would've ended up in clink.'

'And it *really was* her that wrote all those letters? Those *two* letters, I mean, although these things usually occur in bunches or whatever, don't they?' She had nearly dropped the ball there. She should have shut up straight away, without saying anything daft about there being just the two letters. She'd almost mentioned the one she'd received, and given herself away. She'd have to watch her mouth in future. Whoever had killed Hermione Grayling had probably received such a communication, and it had sent them over the edge. Hadn't Gabriel Pryor killed himself after getting one?

'Looks like it, my sweet. But don't worry about an alibi. I'll tell the police you were here with me all day.'

'What do you mean? Why should I need an alibi?'

'Because I've been hunting around for your secret stash of fags, my little duckling, and one of the places I looked was in the pockets of your dressing gown. But don't let it worry you. We were both involved in that little deal, so I'm not about to cut my own throat, am I?'

For once, Monica was speechless. So he'd already known about the letter! She hoped he wouldn't get any ideas about trying to pin this murder on her, or even hint to the police that she had received a letter. He would know it was all nonsense, of course, but he'd have a good old laugh up his sleeve watching her squirm, and trying to talk herself out of the frame, while he denied all knowledge of the contents of her dressing gown pocket with the sweetest of smiles on his dishonest little face.

Taking a key from her handbag, she unlocked a drawer in her desk, and withdrew a half-empty packet of cigarettes and a lighter. If she'd ever needed a cigarette in her life, she needed one now.

As she lit up, Quentin, who had returned to his observation post at the window, called over his shoulder, 'I think they're taking the body away now.'

'Well, don't you get any fancy ideas about not giving me an alibi, buddy, because I could do exactly the same to you. And it was you who pointed out that the letter referred to a deal that both of us were involved in. Instead of threatening me, you should be taking care of me: making sure I don't go shooting off at the mouth.'

'That piece of string's got two ends, Mon, and we both nipped out for a few minutes earlier. Let's just call a truce, and keep out of each other's way till this whole distasteful situation blows over, eh?'

'Done!' agreed Monica, knowing it was the best deal she was likely to get in the circumstances.

As Quentin was having a good goggle at the mortuary van, Craig Crawford turned the corner from Tuppenny Lane into the Market Darley Road. He had tried again, in vain, to change his library books, but he had found the building locked up and in darkness for the second day in a row. Being a rather cowardly young man, he had decided not to confront Noah and Patience, and maybe engender bad feeling between them, but he was determined to phone the County Council, as a concerned, and not a little disgruntled, library user, to find out what the hell was going on, if they even knew themselves what the situation was.

His angry and self-centred thoughts completely left his mind, however, when he saw the plethora of vehicles outside The Spinney, and the policeman on duty at the road end of the drive. He had to cross the road at some point, as his house was the other side of the Ox and Plough, so he might as well cross it now, and have a word with the policeman outside, about what was going on.

Nothing much ever happened in Steynham St Michael, and after the suicide of his comrade-in-cards, it looked like there was something else afoot now. What fun, he thought, with the callousness of the young, and mentally rubbed his hands together.

PC Green greeted him courteously, understanding perfectly well that his function this afternoon was to repel all boarders, whether members of the public or – heaven help him! – representatives of the press. He had been instructed in how much information he was allowed to give, and passed this on, now to a second eager seeker-of-knowledge. He didn't give a hoot how many people came to question him, so long as they didn't try to enter the premises. He had his orders, after all.

Five minutes later, curiosity satisfied, Craig Crawford headed towards Cedars and home, his mind now totally distracted from his unchanged library books. They were all murder mysteries, his favourite genre, and here was a real life murder mystery, practically on his own doorstep. Whoever could be responsible?

As he went indoors and headed for the kitchen to make himself a pot of tea, he felt an involuntary tingle of excitement, and then felt ashamed, as it concerned the death of another. But, then, what the hell! Frissons of excitement didn't exactly come his way every day of the week, and he might as well enjoy the puzzle of who was responsible while he could. It wasn't as if they had been bosom buddies, or anything like that: he'd just played cards in the same group as her and, to be quite honest, he found her rather intimidating.

Monica Raynor, assessing all the implications of Hermione's demise, and never one to look a gift horse in the mouth, waited until Quentin was 'washing his hands' and then slipped out of the office and round to her car in the tarmacked area at the rear of the building, its access being from Tuppenny Lane and invisible from the office windows.

Before Quentin could come out looking for her, she put the car into gear and sped off in the direction of Prince Albert Terrace. If she remembered right, old Potty Pounce always 'did' for Hermione in shifts that had crossed over the ones she had originally done for Monica. Well, she'd already bagged back her services, maybe she could bag back her old hours as well, which had always suited perfectly.

As she drove, she wondered how she could have been so dull-witted as not to react immediately after hearing about Hermione's death. Their house also needed a damned good spring clean, that would take days rather than hours, and she wanted to inveigle Hilda to take it on: get it all shipshape again before resuming her regular sessions, that they had arranged the other day when she (Monica) had 'got in quick' after Gabriel's suicide. She'd be happy to pay double-time for this extra service, which she was sure would attract old Potty.

Even though this would be only a temporary rush of work for Hilda, it would leave her with a reasonable number of her hours replaced for now, some of them on a regular basis, and surely it didn't matter who she cleaned for, as long as she earned a crust

The old dear was probably worried sick, with two of her regular clients gone beyond the great divide, and her income dwindling by the day. In fact, she thought, as she parked her car outside the house in Prince Albert Terrace, she ought to be jolly grateful to get the work. There was only so much cleaning to be done in a village the size of Steynham St Michael.

Although Monica realised she was kidding herself, and that Mrs Pounce's services were like gold dust, she continued to present a brave and positive front, as she knocked at the door, surprised to find herself nervous, even though she had no idea that Charles Rainbird and Buffy Sinden had already pipped her at the post. The old dear didn't have a telephone, and probably didn't even know that Hermione had been killed.

But of course she did! The village grapevine is as intangible as mist, and saturates at about the same rate, and equally as thoroughly. Hilda was, of course, very pleased to be offered more hours, but she'd have to see what she could do, what with her new hours at the antiques shop and Clematis Cottage. She magnanimously agreed to consult her work schedule and let Monica know if she could fit in the extra time for her proposed 'blitz' when she was next at that end of the village. The change in time for her visits to the Raynors' was agreed without demur.

In some ways it would be nice to get back to the way things were before she'd been snaffled by that author-woman. Although Hilda had been proud to work for such a famous writer, Hermione could be a bloody nuisance, with her every 'could you just do this', 'would you mind just doing that,' and 'would it be too much trouble to stay on and finish …' At least with Mrs Raynor she finished on time, and there was no discussion about it.

And she didn't have to worry about breaking or damaging any valuable ornaments, the way she would have to again at Mr Rainbird's, but then he did pay extra for her vigilance in this matter.

On her way back to the office, Monica didn't know whether she was pleased or seething. She'd gone there, like Lady Bountiful, to make the old dear's day, and Hilda had trumped her ace, graciously checking to see if she could fit the Raynor residence into her busy new schedule. How callous the residents of Steynham St Michael were, she thought, conveniently forgetting her own selfish motives in hoping that she had got in first.

While Monica Raynor was humbling herself on Hilda Pounce's immaculately clean doorstep, Malcolm Littlemore took a stroll from his craft shop to Charles Rainbird's antiques emporium for a little chat. He had taken a fancy for a Wellington chest and, after a few sessions of fruitlessly looking for one that didn't cost a king's ransom, he had decided that Charlie might just be his darling in respect of achieving this goal.

He found Charles vigorously cleaning a few pieces of very fine silver, and brimming with the feeling of bonhomie that having news to impart engenders. And Malcolm was all ears. Although Vernon had wandered down to apprise Charles of the stunning events at the top end of the Market Darley Road, Malcolm had been helping Amy with the end of the year stock-take, as well as keeping an eye on the shop.

They hadn't gone home for lunch, but had got the restaurant to make them up some sandwiches, locked the shop doors, and eaten while they worked. As it happened, they had had not a sniff of a customer the whole day, and it was with absolute horror *(and a little shiver of excitement, that such a thing could happen almost on their doorstep)*, that Malcolm listened to Charles' tale of murderous mayhem – exaggeration and embroidery were a couple of his unacknowledged hobbies which he wasn't even aware he enjoyed.

Malcolm, of course, rushed back to his own establishment, so that he too should have the enjoyment of imparting such blood-thirsty tales, and with thoughts of local murder in their minds, both he and Amy were of the shared opinion that they should close up shop for the day and go home for a little drink, to steady their nerves.

Using the illogical excuse that they'd be safer in their own homes – Hermione hadn't been, after all – they locked up, drove at an unnecessarily fast pace back to Forge Cottage, and poured a large one each, in order to deal with the shock from which they were obviously suffering. They then had another large one, to toast the soul of their dear departed friend, and another even larger one, to toast the future apprehension of the murderer, and that was them set for a good old session that evening.

Well, it didn't matter really. Tomorrow was Saturday, and they probably wouldn't even bother opening the shop, the way business had been, and they had plenty of savings. The shop was more of a hobby than anything else, and it was beginning to feel that it was time for a new and less time-consuming pastime.

Tilly Gifford had a thoroughly enjoyable evening, both disseminating information and collecting it where possible. Hermione's murder, although shocking, wasn't the only subject discussed. Tilly had lain full-length on her sofa, the handset of her telephone, if not red hot, then at least very warm to the touch, sipping Chardonnay to keep her throat from getting too dry.

When she finally hung up on her final call and tried to get to her feet, she was surprised to find that her balance was not what it was when she had first lain down and, what was even more surprising, was that the bottle of wine, that she had newly opened before she had begun her marathon session, was now completely empty. It had been a long evening, though, as witnessed also by her throat, which was sore from talking.

It was no wonder she felt a little wobbly after all that alcohol, she thought, and began to have a little sympathy for Amy Littlemore and her bruises. If the poor woman constantly felt like this, no wonder she kept falling down and bumping into things.

Still, it had been a good old gossip, and after her seventy-five centilitre nightcap, she knew she would sleep well, and there was no surgery on a Saturday for her to get up for. Saturday's were covered by a locum service, and Tilly, therefore, had her weekends to herself – apart from Tommy, of course, but then they'd never lived in each other's pockets.

Vernon Warlock scuttled furtively round to Mill Cottage for the little chat that the two men had arranged earlier that afternoon, when the news of Hermione's murder had broken. After his hostly duties of sorting out refreshments, Charles settled himself on a leather Chesterfield and asked Vernon what it was he had the wind up about, as something was obviously bothering, and he hoped it wasn't a guilty conscience.

'It's this poison pen letter business,' he began. 'When Dim told me that Hermione was responsible for them, I don't know how I managed not to blurt out that I'd had one myself – and I tell you this in the strictest confidence, Charles. I don't want this knowledge bandied about all over Steynham St Michael, you understand?'

'Fair enough, old thing,' Charles replied, adding, 'Got one myself too, if truth be told. Didn't mention it before, because it was no other bugger's business but my own, but we're both men of the world, Vernon, and we know how to keep a confidence, don't we?'

'We certainly do, Charles. What was yours about?'

'No, you go first, old man. After all, it was you who raised the subject in the first place.'

'Fair enough! Mine was some nonsense about selling books that were a bit dodgy – memory's not what it was – can't remember any more than that. Threw it on the fire, as a matter of a fact. What about yours?'

'Some accusation that my books may not be all they seem. I didn't really take it in. Saw what it was immediately, and decided to ignore it. Burnt mine too. Only thing to do in the circumstances.'

Both men were, of course, lying their heads off, each trying to out-macho the other. Both of them had been scared stiff that their little rackets had been rumbled, and that they might be either blackmailed in the future, or exposed to the authorities, neither option suiting either of them. And neither of them had destroyed their letters.

Both had the same devious instinct that, if they kept the original letters, there may be an opportunity in the future to turn the tables on whoever had sent them, maybe to their own personal profit. Birds of a feather really do flock together, for

Charles had concealed his anonymous letter in a secret drawer in the desk in his study, and Vernon had hidden his between the pages of a King James Bible, which was deeply buried in his personal bookshelves at home.

And both were to be disappointed in their hopes for a future revenge, as Hermione had now been identified as the author of the cutting and accusatory missives, and both were finding the information hard to swallow.

'I just can't believe it was Hermione!' exclaimed Charles. 'She was in and out of here all the time, and although she may have noticed a little clue here and a little clue there and put two and two together there was something she didn't say in the letter which could have blown my life apart. I don't know. Maybe that is evidence that she sent them, not using the most devastating thing she knew.'

'It may all have been an elaborate piece of research for a new book,' Vernon suggested. 'You know, actually send some of these letters, then watch first-hand to see what various people's reactions are.'

'What, and risk prosecution? I don't think so. Hermione was generally risk-averse.'

'Unless she was stealing plots from me,' Vernon mumbled under his breath, and was then glad that Charles did not appear to have heard him. That was an old grudge – very old – and it would not be particularly clever to air it at the moment.

His innocence was quite touching, as he did not know the contents of the letter that had been found and taken away in Hermione's typewriter. He might not be mentioned by name, but the police were capable of working things out for themselves, given a large enough circle of people to talk to, some of whom had known her for decades.

Both men felt secure, after their little consultation, that they were safe, having admitted to burning their respective letters but both actually having preserved and concealed them. The contents of both were obscure, and unlikely to be in the public domain. With this newly found feeling of security, they raised their glasses to each other, and Charles proposed a toast to the late Hermione Grayling, may God rest her soul.

'Hey, I wonder who gets all the money?' queried Vernon, after a quick sip of his whisky.

'Don't push it, old son,' advised Charles. 'Just be grateful for small mercies.'

Back at The Spinney earlier that afternoon, before the mortal remains of the householder had been removed, Dr Pierce was not making himself popular. He was the new-kid-on-the-block in the house, Falconer, Carmichael, and Dr Christmas having worked together before, and established, as it were, friendly relations.

Dr Pierce, turning up out of duty, as Hermione was, or had been, his patient, made his first faux pas when he was introduced to Carmichael. Used to respect from his patients due to his position in the village, he thought himself a bit of a wag. No one, so far, had had either the inclination or the guts, to inform him that he was just downright rude, and not in the least amusing.

'What have we got here, then?' he asked, as the introductions were made, looking the sergeant up and down, as if he were a specimen in an exhibition. 'How long have you been working with Ronald MacDonald, Inspector Falconer? Or should I call him Coco the Clown?'

There was a deathly silence. Dr Christmas looked at Falconer, Carmichael looked down at his cherry-red trainers, and Dr Pierce looked smug, as if he were expecting a pat on the back for his wit and observation.

There was a minute or two of absolute silence, which is a very long time in those kinds of circumstances. During this time Falconer's face drained slightly of colour, and his jaw set as he clenched his teeth. Finally his brows drew together, and he said,

'I believe Dr Christmas will concur with me when I say that, having known Detective Sergeant Carmichael for some time and knowing what an excellent officer he is, we believe that his abilities as a serving police officer far outweigh anyone's opinions on his dress sense. Personally, I think that Detective

Sergeant Carmichael's appearance is a celebration of his personality, which is colourful, exuberant, generous, and kind. I think that covers it, don't you Philip?' he concluded, looking towards Dr Christmas.

'It certainly does, Harry,' and he ignored the comments made by Dr Pierce as if they had never been spoken. 'Now, as to the body, we'll never get it out lying on a stretcher, because of the way the handle of the billhook sticks out at the back of the head. We're going to have to move it in a sideways position, and I'll remove the murder weapon at the mortuary. Cause of death appears to be perfectly obvious, but the PM report will confirm, and if I do find anything iffy, I'll ring it straight through to you, OK?'

'Perfect!'

Throughout this short exchange Carmichael's face had been a picture of wonder and confusion. He had just heard the inspector defend the way he dressed, after having a go at him in the office for his appearance. Whatever was going on?

Harry Falconer looked similarly confused. He, too, could not believe what he had just said in defence of his partner, and wondered whether he was just getting used to Carmichael and his 'Technicolor-dream-coat' outfits, or whether he was defending the man for whom he was gaining respect every time they worked together against the harsh judgement of an outsider, although Dr Pierce had said nothing that he, Falconer, would not say, and probably had said regularly, during the cases on which they had worked together the previous year.

Dr Pierce merely looked sulky at being thus snubbed, and only took a brief look into Hermione's 'bookery nook' as the mortuary van arrived to collect its slowly stiffening cargo.

Many people in Steynham St Michael were destined to sleep uneasily in their beds that night, due to a guilty conscience over one thing and another, but only one had the stain of murder on their heart.

116

Chapter Ten
A Penny A Point

Saturday 9th January

As Falconer headed for his car the following morning, his neighbour on the drive side of the house, called out to him over the dividing fence, 'That cat of yours is very protective of your property, isn't he?'

'Which cat?' Falconer asked, more out of politeness than interest. 'I've got three now.'

'That dark brown Siamese one: the one you've always had.'

'What about him?' If this was about Mycroft, Falconer wanted to know if he'd been involved in any more criminal activities.

'I saw that big black one of yours high-tailing it out of the cat flap the other day, with a raw salmon steak in his mouth.'

'The black one? Tar Baby?' Falconer had believed that Mycroft had stolen the salmon he had defrosted for his own supper.

'That's the one. Then the other Siamese-y one came haring out of the cat flap after him, and bopped him round the head with a paw so that he dropped the salmon. Then the Siamese one picked it up and took it back through the cat flap again. I just thought you ought to know how honest and loyal he was, bringing your supper back like that, as that's what I presume it was.'

'Thanks. I caught him having a chew at it, and thought he was the one who'd taken it.'

'Nah! It was that big black one. Your other one was probably just having a little bite as a well-earned reward,' and at that, his neighbour moved away from the fence with a wave, and got into his own car.

Well, what about that, thought Falconer. So it hadn't been Mycroft after all, and the poor thing had been blamed needlessly for something he hadn't done. He'd set a trap: that's what he'd do, he decided. He'd set up some prawns between two plates when he got home, for he had some in the fridge, and see which of the three of them went a-stealing. If it was Tar Baby again, at least he'd know he had a thief in the house, and exactly who it was, and would leave nothing to chance again. And he'd have to make it up to Mycroft somehow, as he had been rather ignoring him since the incident as a punishment.

He was first to arrive in the office, but Carmichael was only a few minutes behind him, dressed soberly in jeans, a white sweatshirt, and white trainers. At Falconer glanced up at him, the sergeant jumped the gun a bit and said, 'There's no need to look so surprised. Kerry might have suggested dress-down Fridays, but that doesn't apply to the weekend. She expects me to turn up to work on a Saturday or Sunday respectably, if not formally, dressed.'

'I wasn't going to criticise, Carmichael. I was just surprised, that's all. I had no idea until yesterday afternoon how used to your – um – bright garb I had become. When you came in yesterday morning, it was like seeing an old friend again, that's all.'

'Well, I really appreciated the way you defended me to that Dr Pierce. He made me feel about six inches tall, after what he said, and the way he looked at me. I felt like a half-wit.'

Falconer tried to imagine anyone cutting Carmichael's height by six feet, failed, and replied anyway. 'He had no right to criticise you in front of me, or Dr Christmas. You're ten times the man he is, and don't you forget it!'

'Thank you very much, sir.' Carmichael was well-nigh speechless.

'That's quite all right, although I think I may be coming down with something: maybe a severe case of nice-itis, but I expect I'll soon be cured, so don't get used to it, OK?'

'Don't worry, sir. I'm in full agreement with you. It'll soon wear off.'

'I hope so,' Falconer agreed. 'I don't like it.' And in fact he had been surprised the previous afternoon, when he had rushed so quickly and vehemently to Carmichael's aid, when Dr Pierce had been so scathing about Carmichael's dress sense.

After a bit of a think, he decided that either he had become immune to the colour combinations that his partner was capable of, or he was gaining a real respect for the policeman who was gradually emerging from behind the multi-coloured, weirdly dressed exterior. Their partnership was still in its early stages as yet, but Falconer had hopes that in the long run it would prove a successful one. They were very different characters, but they had complementary skills, and were now working well together. Long may it continue, he thought.

Breaking out of his reverie, he looked up to address his partner, who was at that very moment exploring his right nostril with a forefinger, and decided that he might have been a bit heavy on the sentimentality. Carmichael would do, but no more than 'do'. Finding out that Mycroft was not a thief must have so affected him, that he had overdosed on the goodwill a bit towards his colleague. Falconer decided to keep an eye on himself in future, for similar signs of going soft in the head.

'Why do murders always seem to happen on a Friday?' he asked, as an opening conversational gambit. 'Doesn't Kerry get sick of you having to come in over the weekend?'

'Not really. She knows it's my job.'

'Mine, too. So, let's work out our plan of action. We've got quite a few interviews to do, and probably quite a bit of house-to-house. I'd bet anything you like that there are more of those letters out there, and I want to know where they were sent. Who got one of those little stinkers and is keeping quiet about it? Who's got something to hide that their local author knew about? Or, to put it another way, who guessed that it was Hermione Grayling who was writing those poison pen letters, and decided to silence her permanently, so that she couldn't do any further damage?'

'If we find that out, sir, I reckon we'll have found our

murderer,' Carmichael opined.

'I do believe you're right, Sergeant. It's not a large village, and the gossip must circulate like wildfire, along with its friends, Rumour and Conjecture. We need to plug into that, see if we can't get some of the residents to play a game of Grass Thy Neighbour, eh, Carmichael? Do you remember that little game from our other cases?'

'Definitely, sir, and most effective it proved on those occasions. Now, when will the PM report be through? Any idea, sir?'

'Not just yet, but it's more or less immaterial, isn't it? I mean, there she was, with this bloody great billhook sticking out of her head. I doubt she was poisoned as well.'

At that moment the phone rang, and Falconer answered it, to find Dr Christmas on the line. 'How funny,' he commented to the mouthpiece. 'I was just thinking about you. What have you got for me?'

'I'm afraid the old duck was chock-full of Valium, Harry, so it's a bit more complicated than we originally thought.'

'I don't believe it! Carmichael and I were just joking around about her being poisoned as well. Surely you're having me on?'

'No. I wish I were: but if it makes you feel any better, look on it as her being relaxed to death.'

'How big was the dose?'

'Enough to fell an elephant. There was actually no need for the billhook. She must have been at death's door when that entered her skull, maybe even actually dead. I really am sorry about this. It leaves you in a bit of a cleft stick, doesn't it?'

'It does, rather,' answered Falconer, his mind racing. If the sedative had been administered by a different person than the one that had cleaved her skull open, who exactly would be the murderer? 'Any idea which of the attempts actually killed her?'

'I'm waiting for some test results, but in the meantime, yer pays yer money and yer takes yer chance, Harry.'

'Thanks a bleedin' bunch, Philip. You've really made my day.'

'Oh, by the way, before I go, can you tell Carmichael, 'well done – a brilliant idea,' and he hung up, leaving Falconer looking confused.

'What's up, sir?' asked Carmichael, noticing the puzzled expression on the inspector's face.

'Nothing, Carmichael. Nothing at all. By the way, Dr Christmas said to congratulate you, and tell you it was a brilliant idea.' This should be the opportunity for the sergeant to enlighten him. He certainly wasn't going to ask.

'Ta, sir,' was Carmichael's only reply, followed by a complete change of subject. 'Where are we going to start today?'

'Mmmm?' Falconer was still bemused, and had to make an effort to concentrate his mind. No doubt everything would be made clear later. 'We've got the list of the members of that card club she ran from her desk. We could do worse than start with them, as they seem to be a fairly tight bunch, meeting every week like that.

'The properties we need to visit are almost all in the north-west quarter of the village, but we'll take Merv Green with us. He can call at the properties in the south west quarter – do a house-to-house, see if anyone was out shopping and saw something that they don't realise is important. He can also go back to two and four Barleycorn Crescent and speak to Mr Pryor's neighbours again. I know it's a straightforward suicide, but you can never be too careful, and I don't want to be hauled over the coals by old Jelly because I missed something obvious.'

'Old Jelly' referred to their aggressive and very tetchy superior officer, Superintendent Chivers. He was known for not suffering fools gladly – in fact, he didn't often suffer geniuses gladly either. Everyone, to him, was either an 'idiot' or a 'bleedin' smart-arse': he recognised no happy medium.

'I'll get Bob Bryant to rustle up Merv Green – he's on secondment to us at the moment, and we'll meet him in the foyer in, say, five minutes. You should have brought your rainbow hat, Carmichael, it's brass monkeys out there.'

'I did, sir,' answered Carmichael, drawing the hat from the

121

pocket of his coat, which hung up near the door. 'The boys bought it for me special, 'cos I'm always complaining about cold ears.'

The look on Falconer's face said it all.

As they descended the stairs, Bob Bryant, the desk sergeant, caught sight of them and shouted, 'Nice one, son,' to Carmichael, giving him a double thumbs-up sign, and once more Falconer kept schtum. He would *not* be tempted. He would *not* let Carmichael get one over on him. He'd work it out for himself eventually, and without looking like the only one who wasn't in on the big secret, for they had found Merv Green as arranged, by the desk, and his first words had been, 'Fantastic, DS Carmichael! You're a dark horse, aren't you?'

Having briefed PC Green using a section of a large scale map, pointing out the roads and properties they wanted him to call on, he left them to get a patrol car and another constable, for it was better, especially in a murder enquiry, that they hunted in pairs. Even without a murderer on the loose, one never knew what was behind closed doors, and working in pairs was station policy.

Falconer and Carmichael travelled in Falconer's car, as Carmichael still had the Skoda dustbin he had owned when they first worked together, and the addition of two step-children had done nothing to deplete the vast collection of crisp packets, chocolate bar wrappers, and fizzy drink containers scattered around its inside, like an entry for the Turner Prize. Falconer would actually have entered it for the prize, if he didn't think Carmichael would notice its loss: one heap of rubbish is much like any other heap of rubbish, and in this respect, he felt it stood a fair chance of winning. He'd made his decision to use his own Boxster whenever possible after his trip in Carmichael's car on Wednesday. It was like being jolted around in a refuse truck.

On their drive to Steynham St Michael, Falconer drove home his theory that there must be more poison pen letters than they knew about. Someone with that much poison to share

122

would not stop at just two, and he wanted their questioning that morning to be as probing as possible, to see if they could get anyone else to admit to having received one.

Policemen travel in pairs for safety, because of what could lie behind closed doors for the unwary. This also applied to the victims of anonymous letters. All these nice, respectable people they were going to interview today could have God knows what buried in their pasts. After all, some murderers, once deemed to be extremely dangerous, were let out on licence with a new identity, and managed to start and maintain a totally new life without any one of their new friends or neighbours suspecting a thing.

On a less dramatic note, most people had something in their past that it would be shameful for them to admit to, even if it would be no big deal to anyone else. Everyone had an Achilles heel of some sort, even if it was just stealing a chocolate bar or taking a pound from their mother's purse when they were kids. It was amazing how touchy some people could be about even the most innocuous of offences.

As it was a Saturday, some of the residents would, no doubt, be at work, but they could track them down easily enough through information gained from friends and neighbours; if necessary, they could make an appointment to speak to them during their lunch break, if they were reluctant to speak in a public place.

Hermione's address book, diary, and calendar had been very informative, and had given them quite a list of local people to speak to. What they needed to find out was who was really a friend and who might have been an enemy in false colours. She had at least one enemy, otherwise she wouldn't have been murdered. And, as they had found an unfinished poison pen letter in her typewriter, she may have had many who were, literally, out for her blood.

Falconer became more and more convinced as he drove that finding out who the recipients of the – at present only imagined – letters were, would be the key to this case. Parking the car in the car park of the Ox and Plough with this thought still in his

123

mind, he decided out loud that they should start with Dimity Pryor. *Pryor*! *Again*! The people in these villages were all connected in so many ways, and it made him a bit uncomfortable.

Dimity answered the door of Spinning Wheel Cottage *(which did, indeed, have a small spinning wheel in its front window)*, with bloodshot eyes, her face red and puffy from crying. 'I'm so sorry,' she apologised after the necessary introductions had taken place, and warrant cards displayed. 'I really am terribly upset,' she explained, ushering them into her sitting room.

'I've known Hermione for such a long time: in fact, we were at school together, and have remained close friends ever since, and she's going to leave such a hole in my life. She was my little bit of glamour, as well as being such a good friend. With her writing, she met so many famous people, and she always told me about those whom she'd met, and the functions she'd been to. It made me feel special, that she told me about that side of her life, and it made me feel a little as if I were sharing in it too, if that doesn't sound too silly.'

'Not at all,' Falconer said in a soothing voice, while thinking just the opposite – it was pathetic in his opinion.

'And once,' Dimity continued, 'she took me with her to Barbados. That was just after she'd bought her house there, and she said she'd like some familiar company, as she didn't know how she'd feel with all those darkies – oh, I'm so sorry! – I mean those dark-skinned people, around her.'

'Was that the only time you went away together?' Falconer was merely being polite, before going in for the kill.

'Oh, yes, but it was very colourful and exciting, although I don't really feel comfortable in a hot climate.'

Right, so Hermione had dipped her toe in the Caribbean Sea, found the water to be to her liking, and not needed her little lap dog around any more. She'd obviously acclimatised herself to the local residents very quickly, thus making her future trips rather cheaper, with only one fare to find. That might be worth making a note of, in case jealousy was the motive, Falconer

124

thought, noticing, with approval, that Carmichael had got out his notebook and was busy scribbling in it at a ferocious pace.

'Have you any idea if Miss Grayling has any family hereabouts? We haven't located an address for any next-of-kin yet.'

'Not to my knowledge. She never married, although she had plenty of boyfriends when we were younger. She never went short of admirers. In fact, at one time – oh, so very long ago – she and Charles Rainbird dated. He's got the little antique shop in the High Street: lives in Mill Cottage, round the back of here, in Farriers Lane.'

'And was it serious?' the inspector enquired, wondering if he could close this case in a day, having already found what he considered to be two motives.

'Oh, no; nothing like that. I think they only went out a few times, then it just fizzled out, but they've always remained good friends.'

'Did you and Miss Grayling ever fall out?' he asked, abruptly changing the subject, in the hope that he might surprise some information out of her.

'Inspector, I can tell you honestly that Hermione and I have not 'fallen out,' as you so delicately put it, since we were sixteen or so, and a lot of water has flowed under the bridge since then.'

'Would you mind telling me what it was about, Miss Pryor, even though it was so long ago?' he asked, with little hope from a disagreement or argument that happened forty years ago.

'It was all over a boy, if you can believe it,' Dimity explained, allowing a coy smile to cross her countenance. 'I can't even remember his name now, but he was my first – and, I must admit, only – boyfriend. Oh, of course, it was Barry Barker – however could I have forgotten that? It's not as if I were Mata Hari, is it? We'd been dating for about a month, when Hermione seemed to get it into her head that he was the best thing since sliced bread, and proceeded to lure him away from me with her superior charms.'

'That must have been very hurtful, Miss Pryor.'

'Not really, Inspector. She explained to me later that she knew he was two-timing me, and I was so smitten that she didn't think I'd believe her, I'd just think it was sour grapes. So she stole him, treated him like dirt for a couple of weeks, and then dumped him. It was only then, that another friend told me about him going out with another girl while he was going out with me. Of course, Hermione only did it to protect me, and she's been like that ever since. If I've ever needed help or guidance, I've always gone to her. In fact, I don't know what I'm going to do without her. How can she possibly be dead? Everybody *loved* Hermione!'

At this point, Dimity dissolved into tears, and reached into her cardigan pocket for her handkerchief.

'I'm sorry to have upset you again. I've only got a couple more questions, then we'll leave you in peace. Did Miss Grayling, to your knowledge, have any enemies?'

'Certainly not, Inspector. The very idea! I've just told you that everybody loved her, and they did. She was just so kind and generous.'

'I'm sorry, Miss Pryor, but I had to ask. And my last question is about the card club that you belong to. I believe you had a meeting a few days ago.'

'That's right. We met on Tuesday evening.'

'Where did you hold your meetings? At the Ox and Plough?' Falconer suggested, as it was so conveniently placed.

'Sort of, only it was more complicated than that. Neither pub had a room large enough for us to use all together. They wouldn't let us use their function rooms, as we didn't want to have to pay and they didn't want us losing them any bookings. Anyway, enough of this rambling. I do apologise. I don't think I'm over the shock of it all, yet.

'Both pubs: we used both pubs. Do you know the Fox and Hounds on the High Street? Much trendier and more up-to-date than the good old Ox and Plough. Both pubs said they could let us have a small room, so we split into two groups for playing. Hermione and I were in the Ox and Plough group, along with Vernon Warlock, Charles Rainbird that I mentioned before –

126

I'm sorry Sergeant ... Carmichael, is it? – am I going too fast for you?'

So she *had* been aware of Carmichael writing everything in his notebook. Either she was a very observant lady, or she was not as upset as she seemed to be by her friend's death.

'Now let me see, where was I? Oh, yes, there were Monica and Quentin Raynor the estate agents, Craig Crawford, he works from home at Cedars, and poor, poor Gabriel.'

'And who was in the other group?' It would be easy enough to check from Hermione's stuff, but he wanted it from the horse's mouth, as it were, to see how she reacted to each name.

'Tilly and Tommy Gifford – she's the receptionist at the doctor's surgery. Roma and Rodney Kerr – they have a little ladies' fashion shop in the High Street. Bryony Buckleigh, she lives at Honeysuckle, on Dairy Lane – turn right when you leave here, and take the first right, and it's on your right. Buffy Sinden –'

'We know where Ms Sinden lives, thank you, Miss Pryor.'

'And that just leaves Amy and Malcolm Littlemore who ...'

'It's all right. We've got an address for them, too. Now, absolutely last question. Can you think of anyone you saw on Tuesday night, who may have been acting a bit strangely, a bit out of character because, maybe, they'd received an anonymous letter? By the way, have you had one?'

'Ooh!' This had certainly rattled her. 'Of course I haven't. Hermione was my friend. But let me see ... Vernon was a bit odd – Vernon Warlock, that is. He, Hermione, and Charles Rainbird had volunteered to sit-out, because Gabriel Pryor hadn't turned up – for obvious reasons, as it happens. With him missing, it was a choice of playing with two packs and only three people, with some of the cards removed, or sitting-out and having a drink, which was what they opted for.

'I had to take a quick break to go to the ladies, and when I went through I ... well, I heard something and I stayed to listen for a little bit. Charles was at the bar getting drinks, and I scooted off when I saw him approaching, but when he got back to the table, I heard Vernon say something like 'sod off' or 'bugger off', and he stormed out of the bar, and didn't even come back later to play.'

'Do you have any idea what had annoyed him so much?'

'As a matter of fact I do, because the self-same thing came up on Thursday night, and it was Vernon who raised it, but he was in a high good humour, then. I couldn't believe the way his attitude had done a complete *volte face*.'

'I think you'd better explain, Miss Pryor. It might be important,' Falconer prompted her, although she'd not really needed any prompting thus far, and seemed willing just to babble on about any subject he suggested to her.

'I'm afraid it's another thing that goes back into ancient history. Hermione, Vernon, Charles, and I go back a very long way – to long before Hermione was a writer. It was Vernon who wanted to write, and he started really young. Unfortunately he didn't seem to have any talent and, unknown to him, Hermione had 'borrowed' one of his plots, and then went on to write an absolute blockbuster of a book. It set her on the road to fame and fortune, really.

'Vernon, of course, was furious when he found out what she'd done, but he did have to admit that she had a natural flair for the written word, while his efforts, frankly, stank. They made up, of course, but Vernon always said she should have dedicated at least one of her books to him, as, technically, he was the one who really got her started, by providing her first plot. It turned into a sort of joke between the four of us, and has been ever since.

'That was why I was so surprised, when he got all bent out of shape about it on Tuesday night, then just went along with it on Friday, as if his outburst had never happened. Still, Hermione had just splashed out – do pardon my little pun – on six bottles of champagne for us, and asked the landlord to put some more on ice, so I suppose he couldn't be too churlish, could he?'

'And what exactly did happen on Friday night? You haven't made that clear.'

'It was all about Hermione finishing her book. She'd phoned

everyone, and invited us for a drink at the Ox and Plough, and in the meantime, booked her trip to Barbados. She was last to arrive in the pub, but when she did, it was champagne all round, so that we could share in her celebration at finishing her book. She really was so generous I can't believe anyone would do her any harm!'

'Thank you very much, Miss Pryor. I'll have to get you to sign a statement, and you'll have to have your fingerprints taken – just for elimination purposes, you understand – and I'll probably need to speak to you again, but that's all for today. Thank you for your help,' Falconer concluded, but was halted on his way to the front door.

'Hold on just a second. I just wanted to say something to your sergeant,' Dimity explained, and craned her gaze upwards to the face of Mount Carmichael. 'Excellent work, Sergeant! The world would be a better place, if there were more people like you in it. Good-bye.'

As they made their way to the next house in silence, Falconer ground his teeth and cudgelled his brain, trying to work out what Carmichael had done, that everybody but him seemed to know about and applaud. He'd just have to brazen it out: there was no way he was going to ask about it at this late stage of the game.

There was no one else at home in the terrace, but Dimity Pryor had provided them with enough information to find most of the residents, so they crossed the road to Cedars. As she had mentioned that Craig Crawford worked from home, there was a fair bet he'd be available to talk to them.

And he was. Craig Crawford proved to be a tallish man, his hair worn *en brosse*, his age about the same as Falconer's, although he looked younger, as if life had never dealt him a rough blow and left its mark. He recognised immediately who they were, or rather what they represented, and invited them straight in, offering a choice of either tea or coffee as he showed them into his sitting room.

Cedars was a large house, possibly the largest in the village, and was furnished with impeccable taste in the Art Deco style, all the pieces original and in superb condition. Money might not buy anyone happiness, but it sure gave them a swanky pad to be miserable in.

Art Deco figurines, both in bronze and porcelain, adorned a circular display unit, cut across by shelves at various heights, and looking too nineteen thirties-glamorous for words. A glass-fronted display cabinet, also reeking of its decade of origin, held pieces of Lalique glass alongside the brash and bold colours of Clarice Cliff, and an exquisitely hand-painted tea service by a name that Falconer knew but could not bring to mind at that moment, so bowled over was he by the perfection of the illusion of living in another age.

Their host returned with a tea tray with somewhat more everyday crockery on it, apologising for its nondescript origins, but admitting that he did not use his 'finds' on an everyday basis. They were soul food and eye-candy only – not for general use.

Accepting a cup of tea and a bourbon cream, Falconer started his investigation with a trawl for information that was of personal interest to him. 'This is a big house,' he stated baldly. 'Do you find you rattle around in it, or have you uses for all the rooms?'

Crawford was not at all offended at this bald question, and rose from his chair to beckon the two of them out of the room, across the hall, and up the stairs. Apart from the master suite on the first floor, the other bedrooms had been knocked into one room, and re-enforced with beams where necessary. The huge open-plan space was a model-railway enthusiast's dream.

A whole countryside opened out in front of them, with stations, signal-boxes, trees, roads, model villages, and model villagers too, little rises for hills, and even the impression of a large pond or small lake was achieved, with the use of a cunningly shaped piece of looking glass. There were even model animals in the fields. The whole county seemed to be there, all in pocket-sized order, and beautifully tidy.

'Wow!' Carmichael gasped in wonder. 'This is absolutely

fantastic! How long did it take you to put this together?' There was a yearning, hungry look in the sergeant's eyes, of which Falconer did not like the look.

'Just about all my life,' Crawford answered. 'I started when I was about seven or eight years old, and I just got hooked, and went on and on collecting. I took it all with me when I left home, but it's outgrown everywhere I've lived. It's even getting too big for here, so I'll probably move it up to the attic floor, where my bedroom and bathroom won't take up any space, and give it a bit more room to grow.'

'Don't you ever have visitors who need somewhere to sleep?' Falconer asked, genuinely curious.

'They use the attic bedrooms at the moment, but when I move my little world up there, I can re-instate some of the rooms down here, so that it looks like a regular first floor again.'

After a few more minutes of silent admiration, not only for the layout, but for the dedication involved in collecting and creating it in the first place, they returned to the sitting room, and Falconer began to ask him about his friends and neighbours, with particular reference to Hermione and the card club, but he got little joy from that vein of questioning.

The card club was, in fact, Craig Crawford's only social contact with his fellow villagers. He was a loner by nature, and his needs were met by acquiring his collection for his home, and his creation of a world of miniature railways on its first floor. He had adequate work to keep him at his desk during the day, with only the occasional meeting to disrupt his normal pattern of life.

He had only joined the card club because Hermione had made it her business to badger him into doing so, when he had first moved to Steynham St Michael, and without her tenacious stubbornness, he would not have bothered. But she had pushed and cajoled, persuaded, begged, and pleaded until he could resist no more, and finally gave in after about three months of trying to find somewhere to hide whenever he caught sight of her figure in the distance. The assault upon his doorbell and telephone had been equally as ruthless. He realised now, in retrospect, that he had never really stood a chance.

But he had enjoyed his evenings with the others, partly because the present game was so challenging and unpredictable, never falling victim to the whims of tactics or other subtle plans. He was reasonably happy with his life in general, and he looked it.

He admitted to attending the drinks gathering in the Ox and Plough on Thursday night to celebrate the completion of Hermione's latest tome, and one of the reasons he had gone was because he knew there would be champagne – there always was – and he had a particular fondness for free champagne.

He had not received an anonymous letter, and could think of no reason why he would, try as he might to remember anything in his past which would bring a blush to his cheek, if made public, and no, he didn't take any medication, and had never been prescribed Valium, by any doctor anywhere or any-when: and that seemed to be it for Craig Crawford.

He led a very quiet, private life; he bothered no one, and no one bothered him. He appeared to be absolutely what he was – a blameless citizen, and Falconer and Carmichael saw no reason to bother him any longer.

As they reached the front door, however, he stopped Carmichael and shook him warmly by the hand. 'A splendid idea!' he said. 'You should be really proud of yourself.' Neither Craig Crawford nor Carmichael uttered another word, and the two policemen left in silence, Falconer feeling a right old stew coming on.

It seemed that the whole world knew something about his sergeant that he didn't, and it was really starting to get on his nerves. If he didn't find out what it was soon, he would burst; but he mustn't give in, and give Carmichael the satisfaction of being asked. It just wouldn't do, for him to have to yield like that.

Falconer decided that their next call would be at Clematis Cottage, to see Buffy Sinden. She, at least, had admitted to

132

having received a letter, and he wondered if she, too, knew whatever it was about Carmichael, that he, his inspector, and therefore his superior, didn't. He wouldn't put it past her; she had seemed like a very persuasive young (*or not quite so young. – Meow!*) lady, and probably knew everything that was going on in Steynham St Michael.

They hardly recognised the Buffy who opened the door to them, though. Since they had last seen her, she had worked a miracle on the first impression she made on people. Her hair, roots freshly attended to, was scraped back in a tidy bun and her make-up was discreet, but the biggest change of all was in her mode of dress.

Unbeknownst to anyone but Roma Kerr, she had made a visit to the village's ladies' fashion shop, and kitted herself out with a few mix-and-match items which totally changed her appearance. Today she wore a respectable knee-length wool skirt, a white silk blouse and, as a concession to the season of the year, an emerald green cardigan with a ruffle round the front, which dipped on both sides to give a very flattering but discreet line. The sleeves were also ruffled, she wore black hose and a pair of flat-heeled black patent shoes. The overall effect was stunning.

Gone was the ageing tart they had previously met, to be replaced with this eye-wateringly lovely figure of a woman, and Falconer wondered that she had never thought of dressing like this before. If one-night stands were no longer to be a part of her life, she would still attract men like bees round a honeypot, but in a more sophisticated and mature way. She could probably not have chosen a better transformation in order to net herself a decent lifetime partner – a husband even – and not some low-life, who was only after one thing.

Here was a woman any man would feel proud to have on his arm at a cocktail party, or at dinner with colleagues. She had done well, and he silently wished her the best of luck in her future hunting. Mr Right was bound to spot her in her new colours. The low-lives she had previously 'consorted' with wouldn't even see her in this incarnation.

All these thoughts passed through Falconer's head in a matter of seconds, as they were invited in and settled in her sitting room. Even that had undergone a transformation. It was as neat as a new pin, to coin yet another cliché, and every surface sparkled.

Seeing their surprised expressions, she took pity on them, and explained that she had managed to persuade Hilda Pounce to come back and 'do' for her. 'She used to come round before,' she told them, 'but I got embarrassed by the number of gentleman friends who hadn't left from the night before – I don't start work till ten – so I decided I'd be better off managing on my own. But I wasn't. Of course, I wasn't, and everything went to blazes. That awful letter I received made me look at my life in a totally new light, so what you see is the new Buffy Sinden – in fact I think I'll go back to my full forename, and start asking to be known as Elizabeth again. I also got dear old Hilda to come in and give me a damned good blitz, and she's promised to come back once a week, to keep it this way for me. Do you like the new image, by the way?'

For a moment she looked coy and vulnerable, but soon cheered up when Falconer smiled and said, 'Very much!' and Carmichael wolf-whistled his whole-hearted approval, simultaneously giving her a double thumbs-up sign.

'I was expecting you,' she said, producing a tray of coffee in record time. 'It's not just about my letter now, is it? It's much more serious. Do you think the letters had anything to do with Hermione's murder? Everyone knows they were the cause of Gabriel's suicide.'

'We do, Ms Sinden, and that's why we're trying to find out who else received one of these cruel, cowardly communications.'

Carmichael, on the ball as usual, had his notepad out, had placed himself just out of Buffy's field of vision and, with his tongue protruding slightly from the corner of his mouth, was scribbling away furiously.

'Well, I can help you with that one, anyway. I had lunch the other day with Monica Raynor – she and her husband have the

134

estate agency on the Market Darley Road – and she said she'd had one, when we had lunch together on Thursday. Oh, and so did Tilly Gifford. I bumped into her yesterday, and I don't think she meant to mention it, but she really can't keep anything to herself. She's her own worst enemy.

'She just runs off at the mouth. I always say, if you want anything spread abroad in this village, tell Tilly Gifford 'in confidence', and absolutely everyone will know about it by the next day. If she's not talking to people face-to-face, and she does a lot of that in her job at the surgery, she's on the phone to her cronies: in fact I think she spends most of her free time on the phone. She and Tommy don't have a lot in common, apart from the cards club, and he's usually out in the garage, tinkering with something or other. And here I go, doing exactly the same thing as Tilly, with a bad case of verbal diarrhoea. I'm so sorry. I'll shut up now and let you get on with your questions.'

Falconer smiled at her last remarks, thinking what a very nice woman she was, when she wasn't being mutton trying to dress as lamb. 'There're only a couple of questions. Where were you on Friday – yesterday – morning, and do you, or have you ever been prescribed Valium?'

'Ooh, they're easy ones,' she answered coquettishly. 'Yesterday morning, I spent in the back of Roma's shop, trying on outfits in her stock room, so no one would see what I was doing. And it's a big fat 'no' to the second question. Now, I don't want to be rude, but if there's nothing else, I've really got to go. I've arranged to meet a cousin of mine in Market Darley for a bit of retail therapy – see if I can't re-enforce this new image of mine with a few more outfits.'

'We were just on our way, Ms Sinden,' Falconer replied, already rising from his seat.

'Oh, please call me Elizabeth' she asked plaintively. 'You'll be the first people to do that since I was at school.'

'I'd be honoured … Elizabeth,' Falconer replied, smiling, as she smiled at hearing her full name used again, after such a long time.

'Thank you so much, Inspector. I think it's time I acted more like an Elizabeth than like a Buffy, don't you?'

'I think you make an excellent Elizabeth,' was his considered opinion, and nodding towards Carmichael to indicate that they were leaving, he made his way towards the door, as the newly minted Elizabeth Sinden grabbed her coat and car keys, to follow them through the door.

Falconer had decided that they would make their way along the High Street, to see those from the terrace in the Market Darley Road who had businesses there, but they'd go on foot, as it would mean a great deal of stopping and starting of his car, and he didn't want to tax the battery too much in this cold weather. They therefore headed for the car park that was next to the Co-op, and held the village's recycling bins, but as he entered it, he gave a groan.

'What's up, sir? You feeling ill?' Carmichael asked him, with concern.

'No, Carmichael, nothing like that. It's more of a bursting feeling. Do you realise how many cups of tea and coffee we've drunk so far this morning?'

'Too many!' Carmichael replied, as he became aware of the same sensation, and a look of anguish crossed his face.

'Well, we can't just burst in at our next interview, and rush straight off to the dunny for a slash, can we? We'd look like a right pair of comedy policemen, and nobody would take us seriously once word got round. I wish Elizabeth hadn't been in such a hurry to get out. It wouldn't have seemed so bad, asking her if we could use her convenience. The pressure's really getting to me now.'

'Me too, sir. Trees! Just over there!' Carmichael was pointing towards a small copse of trees that disappeared behind the village garage.

'I can see they're trees Carmichael. What about them?'

'We could 'go' behind them, sir, and nobody would know but us.'

'You're a genius, Sergeant,' replied the inspector with

(mental) relief, and they both exited the vehicle and walked towards the copse, two minds with but a single thought.

'Sir?'

'Yes, Carmichael?'

'Shall we use the same tree?'

'Certainly not! The very idea,' Falconer snorted indignantly, placing himself behind a magnificent but bare-branched oak, where he would not be visible from the road. 'You find your own tree!'

Back in the car, and once more at their ease, Falconer proposed that they visit Vernon Warlock's bookshop first, then move on to Charles Rainbird's antique shop. That would leave them just two doors from the Littlemores' craft shop, and they could finish for lunch there, then just nip across the road to the Fox and Hounds for a bite of lunch. They could mop up any stragglers from their list of card players to be interviewed, after they'd eaten.

They left the car in the car park, as there seemed no other convenient place to leave it for access to the village shops. There might not be any double yellow lines in Steynham St Michael, but there were parked cars as far as the eye could see along the High Street.

Vernon Warlock's new and second-hand bookshop was, conveniently, only a few steps away, but seemed to be empty and unattended when they entered it. The bell of the shop door having summoned no one, Carmichael gave a couple of hearty bangs to the hotel-style bell on the counter, and Falconer called loudly, 'Shop! Anybody there?'

After about a minute, there was a scuffling noise from the depths of the densely shelved interior, and a relatively elderly man in carpet slippers shuffled towards them, clutching a handful of what proved to be stock lists.

'Yes? Can I help you?' he asked, sounding as if that was the last thing in the world he wanted to do. 'What time is it? I should probably be closed for lunch!'

'It's only eleven-thirty, Mr Warlock, and we just wanted a

137

quick word with you about the murder' – he made this word sound particularly chilling – 'of one of your oldest friends,' and accompanied his words with the offering of his warrant card.

'Oh yes, dreadful business, dreadful.' Vernon had dismounted from his high-horse, and re-joined the rest of his species on planet earth. 'Never heard of anything so shocking in my entire life. Anything I can do, don't hesitate.'

'There are a few questions we'd like you to answer, if you don't mind, sir. Can you tell me where you were on Friday morning?'

'Let me see. I opened up as usual, but there wasn't a lot of business. I was feeling a bit cheesed off, actually, and I was just wandering home, thinking of having a bite and a bit of a read, when I bumped into poor old Dim toddling weakly back home, after her shock discovery.'

'It was the time *before* that that I was actually interested in,' Falconer directed him.

'I was just in the shop, trying to tidy up the absolute chaos that the second-hand section has become since Christmas – books just shoved back anywhere – not even in their correct genre. It's shocking when you consider how organised it was before. People really don't care these days, do they? They just do what they want, put anything where they want, and … I … simply … don't … know …'

As his rambling speech slowed to a halt, like the mechanism of a musical box running down, he pulled a not very fresh, and very crumpled handkerchief, from his cardigan pocket, and pushed it under his glasses, to catch the tears that had formed in his eyes, and now threatened to fall. 'I'm … so … sorry.'

'Don't worry about it, Mr Warlock. It's quite natural in the circumstances. Look, there's a chair over there – oh, thank you,' he finished, as Carmichael swung the chair over towards him, ever ready to be of use.

Vernon sat down, but instead of recovering his composure, he let his head hang down, and his shoulders began to shake, as the sobs wracked his body. 'Known her … so … long,' he stuttered. 'Can't … cope. No! Not … dead. *No!*' This last word, raising his voice to a shout, took the last of his energy, and Falconer caught him, his body as light as a bird's, as he tumbled towards the floor.

Carmichael swooped down, and caught the little man up like a child, in his arms, and stood there waiting for Falconer to decide what to do. 'We'll put him in the car and take him home.'

'We've got your car, though, sir. There's only two seats.'

'Look, you're simply better at this sort of thing than I am. Hang on a minute, while I see if his house keys are in his coat pocket, then *you* can drive him home and get him settled. I'll come with you to the car park and open up the car for you. Oh, and these look like the shop keys in his coat as well, so we'll be able to leave everything secure when we go. I think we'll take our lunch break early today. I'll walk down to the Fox and Hounds, and I'll meet you there when you get back. And thank you, Carmichael.'

'No probs, sir!'

Chapter Eleven
No Trumps

Saturday 9th January

As Falconer and Carmichael were eating their shepherd's pies, a woman sat down at the table next to them with a large glass of white wine and a plate of ham salad. Opening her handbag, she extracted a small leather folder from it, put her handbag on the floor between her feet, and opened the A5-sized folder. This action led to peals of laughter from her, and a helpless look from her in their direction, which they interpreted as a 'Sorry, I just can't help it'.

Her merriment brought smiles to their own lips, and when she finally had herself under control again, she leaned over towards them in a companionable manner to explain what had amused her so much.

'I've just opened my crochet hook set to read with my lunch, and my Kindle is obviously, at this very moment, sitting in my work basket, and not the slightest use to me at present. I really should have gone for a brighter-coloured cover. Still, I made a detour on my way to work – I'm Roma Kerr, by the way, from the ladies' fashion shop – and picked up the local rag, so at least I've got that to amuse me while I eat my lunch.'

Falconer introduced himself and Carmichael, and was just explaining that they had been planning to come and see her that afternoon, when she unfolded the *Market Darley Courier*, took one look at its front page story, did a double-take, and whipped her head round to stare unashamedly at Carmichael. As if watching a tennis match, she whipped her head back and forth twice more, then said, 'That's you, isn't it?' to the sergeant, her face now a mask of incredulity and disbelief.

'You never!' she said.

'We did!' Carmichael answered.

'Bloody marvellous idea!'

'Thank you!'

'People should do something like that a bit more often.'

Falconer could take it no longer. There had been a plethora of cryptic comments which had gone straight over his head, since first thing that morning, and his pride would have to go to hell in a handcart, because he *would* ask what was going on – find out what other people knew about Carmichael that he obviously didn't – or he'd lose his reason. It would cost him a lot to swallow that pride, but he had to know, and know before any more people got one over on him, or at least, that's how it felt to him.

In answer, Roma Kerr merely passed the newspaper to him, and there was Carmichael's face, smiling out at him from beneath his pantomime hat, beneath the headline 'Local Copper Collects More Than Small Change for Charity', with a sub-heading of 'Pantomime-Themed Wedding Boosts Local Charity'.

He read on: *Big-hearted Detective Sergeant Davey Carmichael, who is currently based in Market Darley and lives in Castle Farthing, got married on New Year's Eve to Ms Kerry Long, also of Castle Farthing. As they already have a cosy home in which to start their married life, and Ms Long has two young sons from a previous marriage, DS Carmichael's natural sense of fun and his generosity led him to suggest that they have a pantomime-themed wedding, getting all the guests to dress as pantomime characters.*

It was not only fitting at this time of year, but the theme would make the wedding unforgettable, especially for his two new stepsons. This unique idea also inspired him to realise that, as they had everything they needed for a comfortable life thereafter, that it would be an even better event if he asked people not to buy them presents, but to make a donation to The Market Darley Children's Hospice. Final figures are not in yet for the total donations, but a statement from the hospice said that the sum had already exceeded four figures, and was still rising.

In the Courier*'s opinion society could do with a lot more people like this open-hearted couple, and we wish them every happiness in their married life.*

Should you also like to make a donation to mark the occasion of probably the most unusual wedding the Market Darley Register Office has ever witnessed, please send cheques to ...

Falconer was stunned, and puzzled as to why everyone but him had been in on the plan, and didn't know whether to pump Carmichael's hand in congratulation at this completely selfless plan, or ask why he had been excluded from all knowledge of it.

In the event, Carmichael had realised his dilemma, and explained. 'I asked you to be my best man one morning as soon as I got to the station, and you came back to work after lunch with that flash, trendy coffee-maker for us. I felt that you'd spent enough already when we decided to go ahead with it, so I didn't tell you then.

'Everything after that seemed to happen at a hundred miles an hour, and when I thought of telling you, it was out of work hours, and a convenient opportunity never arose when we were together. The phone always rang, or someone came in who had to be seen to, or we had to go out to a crime scene, or to interview someone. And suddenly it was only a few days away, and I'd still said nothing.

'That's why I asked to look through your wardrobe, and I selected that Indian top because I thought that if you wore that, it would look as if you had decided to go along with the idea, and were wearing something fitting, but discreet. I didn't know what to say about it afterwards, and as you never asked why there was no display of wedding presents at the reception, I've been in a cleft stick ever since.

'So anyway, I'm sorry, sir. But the coffee from that machine's absolutely gorgeous, and Kerry wouldn't be without it now. Thank you very much for your generous gift.'

After a silence that lasted about ten seconds, Roma Kerr got

143

up from her seat, came over to their table and gave Carmichael a warm hug. 'You're my hero!' she declared simply. 'May your days be many, and your home a happy one,' she concluded, moving back to her own table, taking her substitute reading matter with her, to resume her lunch.

'And may I echo that thought – without the embrace, of course,' said Falconer, now holding out his hand for that overdue shake of congratulations. 'Nobody but you could have come up with that idea, Carmichael. I think you're probably unique, and Kerry is a very lucky young woman.'

'That's enough, sir. You'll make me blush,' replied the sergeant, his actions matching his words, and looking away in embarrassment. 'I just try to keep the inner child alive, that's all. It's all very well having to be a grown-up at work, but in my own time, I can be as daft as I like, and the best thing is, that nobody in my new family minds one little bit.'

'Good for you, Carmichael,' Falconer replied, and really meaning it. It seemed that his sergeant had, indeed, found his soul-mate in Kerry Long. 'Now, if you don't mind, Ms Kerr,' he called across to the next table, 'I'd like to ask you a few questions when you've finished your meal,' and with that, he resumed the consumption of his now distinctly lukewarm shepherd's pie.

They resumed their conversation with Roma Kerr about fifteen minutes later, she moving to their table, so that they didn't have to raise their voices against the general hubbub of the bar. 'I suppose it's about what happened to Hermione Grayling, isn't it?' she asked, saving them the trouble of an explanation.

'That's perfectly correct, Ms Kerr.' Falconer referred to all but the most obviously married women as *Ms* these days, and only altered his terminology if they corrected him. It saved him a lot of indignant contradictions, and as many dirty looks, generally getting him off on a better footing than trying to guess the marital status and titular preferences of the lady in question.

'The first question I need to ask you is a very simple one, and I'd be glad if you'd just give me a yes or no answer. Have

144

you at any time been prescribed Valium?'

'Absolutely not. No. I'm simply not the nervy, tense type. Next?'

'Have you received a poison pen letter in the recent past, or has anyone you know had one?'

'Well, I haven't had one, but I know Buffy – Buffy Sinden – has. She told me the other day, when she was in my shop looking for some clothes for a makeover. In fact, it was yesterday morning,' she concluded, pleased with the accuracy of her memory.

Although Falconer already had this information from Buffy – no, *Elizabeth*! – Sinden, he knew when praise was necessary. 'Well done,' he said. 'It's always useful to have a witness with a good memory.'

Roma visibly preened herself at this blatant praise, then added. 'I say! That's when the old girl bought it, wasn't it? That means that Buffy and I can alibi each other. Gosh, this is just like on the telly, isn't it? Well, not for you, I mean. It's your job. But for me, it's the most exciting thing that's happened for – I don't know – like forever.'

'I'm sure it is, Ms Kerr, and thank you for your time. It's saved us a visit to your shop.'

'No trouble, Inspector.'

'Oh, by the way, we know where you were yesterday morning, but where was your husband, if you don't mind me asking?' Falconer enquired, almost as if he had added the question as an afterthought.

'He was up in town ordering stock. London. He got the eight o'clock with Tommy Gifford, as a matter of fact.'

'Thank you very much, Ms Kerr. We won't detain you any further.'

'Yes, I must be off. Fantastic to have bumped into you, Sergeant – you're a real hero.' With which remark she picked up her newspaper and handbag, and sashayed out of the pub.

The craft shop opposite the Fox and Hounds had a large *Closed* sign on its door, and Falconer winced as he read the shop's name on its fascia board. 'I don't believe it!' he exclaimed, unconsciously doing a passable impression of Victor Meldrew. It's called 'Knitty-Gritty'. How absolutely ghastly! Maybe 'Drinky-Winky' or 'Boozy-Woozy' – yes, definitely that last one – would be a better name for those two to work under. What do you think, Carmichael?'

'How about 'Drunky-Skunky'?' the sergeant suggested, demonstrating that his sense of humour was alive and well, and concentrating on the subject at hand.

In the light of this insurmountable barrier to speaking to the Littlemores, it was decided that they'd start at the antique shop. 'Come along, Superman,' Falconer remarked, sarcastically, still smarting that he'd known nothing about Carmichael's charity stunt. 'We've got work to do. Let's pay a visit to Mr Charles Rainbird – see what he has to say about our three hot topics.'

'If I were you, sir, I'd go for the envelope, rather than the letter,' Carmichael suggested.

After a few seconds of deep thought, Falconer replied, 'I think you might be right. None of them wants to show us a letter that highlights something unpleasant in their past, but the envelope is a different matter. It means a house-point from the police for co-operation, and it still keeps the contents of the poison pen letter private. Well done, Carmichael. We'll make a chief constable of you yet.'

'Yes, sir. I believe there's a blue moon forecast for tonight,' the sergeant replied with good humour, as they strolled down to the antique shop.

Charles Rainbird was sitting at the counter finishing a phone call when they arrived. He had no customers, but Falconer assumed that this was because anyone wanting to view a shop of this sort would be having lunch, and would probably call in later, when they had been fed and watered.

'Good morning, Mr Rainbird.' Falconer commenced with the introductions, both of them displaying their warrant cards, so there would be no misunderstanding, and went straight for the jugular. 'A little bird has told us that you have received a letter that wasn't too pleasant. Now, don't deny it, or pretend you don't understand, because it'll just waste my time, and I

146

don't take kindly to people who do that.'

Carmichael swallowed his surprise, but managed to retain a poker face. If this worked, it could save them a lot of verbal gymnastics, but it was, in his opinion, a bit like cheating.

'And what little bird would that be, Inspector Falconer?' Rainbird enquired, playing for time.

'I've just had a word with Mr Warlock,' he replied innocently, as if in explanation.

'Oh well, it's a fair cop then, Inspector.' The fish had risen to the bait. 'I did get a rather unpleasant epistle recently, but I'm afraid I burnt it. Sorry and all that, but it can't be helped.'

'As you say, no problem, sir,' the inspector concurred unexpectedly. 'I'd be more interested in the envelope, if you still have it.'

'Now that I *can* oblige with,' Charles admitted with relief. He hadn't in fact destroyed the letter, but if this policeman was only interested in the envelope, he could have that, with pleasure, and then perhaps he'd be left alone. He still couldn't believe his old friend Vernon would be so spiteful. Removing the letter from the envelope, and replacing the former in the safe in his office at the rear of the shop, he returned to his two visitors, holding out the envelope as if it were a holy offering.

'That really is very useful, Mr Rainbird,' commented Falconer as he indicated for Charles to slip the envelope into the proffered plastic evidence bag. 'It means we have at least the chance to trace the publications from which the individual letters were cut, and that information can assist us in confirming the sender.'

'I just can't believe it was Hermione, though.' Charles suddenly looked both hurt and puzzled. 'We'd known each other almost all our lives. If she's had any beef with me in the past she's just come out with it. Why resort to spiteful little letters, now? Everyone loved Hermione. And she seemed to love us all back in return. This has really shaken my confidence in my ability to judge character, and to know what's going on in people's minds.'

'Maybe it was just her age, Mr Rainbird. Hormones can be

tricksy little devils, they can play merry hell with a woman's emotions and behaviour.'

Charles sighed heavily. 'I suppose so, but it's so out of character, and very hurtful.'

'Well, we must be on our way after a couple more questions.' Falconer felt uneasy around visible displays of emotion, and was keen to change the subject if he could. Charles answered in the negative to the question about Valium, and pleaded attendance in his shop during the previous morning, and that was that. There was nothing more to be gained, and the dynamic duo bade him goodbye after only ten minutes.

Charles' production of the envelope from his poison pen letter, however, had prompted Falconer to suggest that they call on Vernon Warlock. He had a feeling that those two had found themselves in similar circumstances, and had colluded, and decided on the same story.

As they exited the antiques shop, Falconer indicated for them to turn left into the Market Darley Road, explaining as they walked. 'We're going to try a similar little ploy about envelopes with Mr Warlock, if that doesn't offend your conscience too much, Carmichael.'

'If you're the one that asks, it'll be on your conscience rather than mine,' replied Carmichael, whose mind worked very simplistically in regard to some subjects, honesty being one of them.

'Then we're going to stroll up to the estate agent's and see what's what. It's almost dead opposite The Spinney, and someone might have seen something – you never know your luck. Then we'll hang a right down Tuppenny Lane, see if the library's open, which'll leave us right opposite Forge Cottage, straining at the leash to question the Littlemores. What boundless joy!'

'I wouldn't put it quite so strongly, sir.'

'Then down Dairy Lane to see Ms Bryony Buckleigh,' Falconer continued, oblivious to Carmichael's remark, 'and finally back round in a "P" shape, to the Market Darley Road. I haven't checked to see whether there's a surgery today, but if there isn't, it'll be better to catch Ms Gifford at home, where she might be a bit more forthcoming than she would at work.'

Vernon fell for the old 'a little bird *(Rainbird!)* told me' ploy as easily as Charles had done, leaving Falconer to reflect that these two definitely didn't watch enough police programmes on the television, or they'd never have been so naïve, but it had worked to his advantage and saved time. He was now in possession of two more envelopes, and didn't really give a tinker's cuss about the letters for the moment.

Both Monica and Quentin were in their office when the two policemen arrived. Quentin was on the phone to what sounded like a potential client, giving brief details of property after property, and scoring out addresses as he talked. Monica was sitting at a computer keyboard updating their records: deleting clients' details for those who had bought from another agency, sold through another agency or – and this was their main problem – had decided not to move in the current economic climate.

Monica's professional smile faded as they introduced themselves, and answered in the negative to Falconer's first question, which was the Valium one. In answer to his second question concerning their activities on Friday morning, it would seem that they both alibied each other, both having been in the office. A diary provided a meagre list of appointments and phone calls, which helped give veracity to their claim to have been at work. His third question, however, produced a very interesting and unexpected reaction. At the mention of an anonymous letter, Monica blushed a bright but attractive pink, and Quentin gave a hastily suppressed, but nevertheless recognisable, harsh bark of laughter.

'Have I said something amusing, sir?' Falconer was reluctant to let this opportunity pass. 'Do you find something funny at the thought of someone receiving a distressing letter?'

Now it was Quentin who was red with embarrassment. 'I'm sorry, Inspector, it was nothing to do with the seriousness of the subject – more of a private joke really, and only connected with the letters in a very tenuous way.' He was clearly flustered, and glanced over at his wife who was, at that very moment, blatantly lighting a cigarette before his very eyes – again! At least she'd identified the humour in the situation, but had reacted by kicking him in the balls – metaphorically, of course – with that accursed filthy habit of hers, which she was supposed to have ceased on the first of this month.

'You know this is a non-smoking office, Monica,' he declared, with some pomposity, but she kicked again, and a little harder this time.

'My name is on the lease of this establishment, and my name is over the door. If I want to smoke in here, I will. In fact, if I choose to smoke anywhere else, I will!'

Falconer detected an undercurrent – a sub-text he could not hope to read – and hastily returned to his questions, negating to mention the government's smoking ban. 'Did you, in fact, receive such a letter? Either of you? At all?'

His embarrassment showed, but Monica piped up, 'Yes, as a matter of fact *we* did, but I destroyed it.' This drew a glance of puzzlement from Quentin, but he let it go, evidently leaving it to her to decide what to admit to, and what to deny.

'I don't suppose you kept the envelope, did you?' the inspector asked, a hint of a twinkle in his eye, to which Monica immediately responded.

'Yes. I did keep the envelope, as a matter of fact, though I've no idea why I should do such a thing.'

Falconer glared furiously at Carmichael whose mouth he had detected in a minute movement, indicating that he was about to speak, and the sergeant settled down again, a silent mountain with a notebook. Falconer knew what the man was about to say: he really was too honest for the job, but he didn't want him saying a word that suggested, or even hinted, that Monica was telling anything but the unvarnished truth.

'Do you have it here?' he asked, trying for a normal tone of voice, after his little scare about Carmichael.

'I'm afraid not. It's at home, but I could go and get it for you, if you like. It won't take more than five minutes with the car.

Falconer and Carmichael spent the short interval reading the details of the properties displayed on the various boards in the office, both silently marvelling at how prices had tumbled over the last eighteen months. If a cash buyer were in the market for a nice country property with all amenities, including swimming pool, he or she could pick up a veritable bargain at the moment. Those that could not take advantage of this were, of course, the people who had something to sell, who were having to offer their properties at very depressed *(and depressing)* prices.

Monica was as good as her word, and within ten minutes, they were walking down Tuppenny Lane, to discover that the library was still closed. They had been told that the couple who worked there, Noah and Patience Buttery, had gone away after Gabriel Pryor's suicide, but the County Council would have to sort out temporary staff in the very near future.

A village library was a popular and much-used amenity, and the recent talk of closing small branches of the library service had caused uproar in the countryside. Even the promise of being included on the mobile library van's rounds hadn't sufficed to calm angry residents. They were used to going to *their* library, when *they* wanted to, and not waiting for *it* to visit them when it saw fit.

Turning their backs on the dark, locked building, a 1960s monstrosity completely out of keeping with the rest of the village, they looked across the road to the Littlemores' house, and became aware of the sound of loud music, escaping from any nook or cranny it could find. '*Led Zeppelin IV*, I believe,' Carmichael identified, giving an insight into another part of his character that had hitherto been undetected.

'You like this old stuff?' Falconer asked, wrinkling his nose at the noise.

'This one's a classic, sir – 'Stairway to Heaven'. Fantastic few years round about then. 'Soft Machine, The Strawbs, Genesis, Jethro Tull ...' he recited, a broad smile on his face as he remembered the music.

151

'How come you know about all this stuff? You're much younger than me!'

'Me mum and dad, sir. They were always playing stuff from this era when I was growing up,' he explained. 'Recapturing their youth, they used to say.'

Falconer merely looked bemused. His mother was more likely to have played renaissance dance music or opera when he was a child. If there existed two things that were even more opposite than chalk and cheese, then they would surely be his and Carmichael's backgrounds. It would seem that the only thing they had in common from their respective childhoods was that they had both been children at the time!

They could not make themselves heard with either the door knocker or the bell, and eventually went round to the back of Forge Cottage, where they found the kitchen door unlocked. Stepping inside, the music grew even louder, declaring itself to come from the sitting room of the property.

Opening the sitting room door allowed a wave of sound to buffet them in a way that felt almost physical, and they both reeled from it, Falconer detecting the source of the racket, and moving over to stop it before his ear-drums burst.

Amy and Malcolm Littlemore were both sprawled in armchairs, oblivious to their visitors, as loud snores replaced the hideous cacophony that had prevailed just a few moments ago. 'Come along, sir, madam. Wake up, do! I'm Detective Inspector Falconer and this is Detective Sergeant Carmichael. You must remember us. We met just the other day.'

Malcolm Littlemore was returning to consciousness, and squinted at the two intruders with one eye closed, the other like a blood-shot blue marble. 'And that gave yer the right just to stroll on in here, without a by-you-leave nor nuffink?' he challenged them, pulling himself up to a sitting position and nudging his wife rather roughly in the ribs, to stop her snoring and wake her up. 'Come on, old girl. Sit up and take notice.'

'You're lucky it was us that called round, sir. Your back door was unlocked, and both of you were 'deeply asleep'.' The inspector was being diplomatic.

'Yer could've rung the doorbell like any other Christian gentleman, instead of just bursting in on us like that.' Malcolm wasn't going down that easily.

'We did knock, sir,' Falconer informed him, 'and we did ring. In fact we did both several times, but it would have been impossible for you to hear us, because of the volume of the 'music' that was playing. I have turned that off, although you didn't seem to notice my action at the time. And may I point out that you were lucky it was us that let ourselves in. It could've been anybody. You could've had your throats slit as you slept, and not known a thing about it! This may be a rural area with little crime, but don't forget too quickly what happened to Hermione Grayling just yesterday morning. Take precautions! You can never be too safe!'

'Point taken, old boy. You're perfectly right, o' course. We just didn't think. 'aven't really taken in just what did 'appen yesterday.' As he spoke, Malcolm Littlemore ran his hands over his face and the fuzz of short hair covering his head, in an effort to re-establish contact with sobriety, no matter how tenuous the connection.

Amy Littlemore began to babble incoherently, and then to giggle like a schoolgirl, still in a state of near-unconsciousness, but Malcolm soon brought her back to the here and now by grabbing her by the shoulders, and shaking her until her eyes opened, and she began to protest, at which point he indicated that they had company, and propped her upright in the chair as if she were a doll.

It was all a waste of time anyway. Neither of them had ever been prescribed Valium, which wasn't surprising given the circumstances. The only way they could have been more relaxed was if they had been in a coma. Neither of them had received a letter, and for some reason Falconer believed them. Maybe it was because their shortcomings were so obvious that it would be impossible for anyone to drag anything up that would actually embarrass them.

As for as whereabouts on the previous morning, they claimed that they had been stock-taking at the shop, an activity

153

to which there were, inevitably, no witnesses, so they would have to alibi each other for the time being.

Carmichael, being his usual thoughtful self, went into the kitchen when the inspector was questioning them, still able to hear enough because of the open-plan nature of the layout to make notes, and made a pot of coffee, which he brought in and put down in front of the Littlemores, before they departed. 'Drink that!' was all he said as he straightened up, and followed Falconer out through the door.

Walking to their next destination, Falconer pondered how the Littlemores had managed to penetrate the inner social circle of Steynham St Michael. Their roots were a long way away from the roots of the other members of the cards club, and others that those members socialised with.

Had he but known it, the explanation was simple. Before moving to the countryside, they had run an exceptionally successful business, allowing them access to circles closed to normal, everyday folk. Malcolm had been a member of the Round Table and an enthusiastic Mason, belying his lowly East End birth. The moving force behind welcoming them into the gang, rather than ostracising them, had of course been Hermione, who found it amusing to have such cuckoos in the nest. In fact, in one moment of enthusiasm she had declared them better than television, to the amusement of all who heard her. They were, however, very much square pegs in round holes, and it is to be considered whether they would continue to be tolerated now that Hermione was no longer there to make pets of them and be their champion.

Turning right into Dairy Lane, they saw a sign that read 'Honeysuckle', and knew that they had reached Bryony Buckleigh's cottage. The exterior was chocolate-box pretty, without a thing out of place, and it proved to be matched by its owner in its perfect appearance.

She answered the door to them, warmly but elegantly dressed, not a grey hair out of place, her make-up subtle and discreet, with no effort made to disguise her age, which was in the lower sixties. Her eyes were bright, and her voice, when she invited them in, was warm, with an accent that hinted at a good education. Pleasantness, however, didn't solve cases, and they found that she had nothing material to add to what they already knew.

When they left the cottage, a mere ten minutes after they had entered it, a difference in desires split the pair up. They were far too early to visit Tilly Gifford at home and Falconer, chilled to the bone in his elegant and fashionable attire, wanted nothing more than to settle down in 'Goldfinches' and drink a cup or two of hot coffee.

Carmichael, on the other hand, had a yen to explore the churchyard and chapel of the Strict and Particulars, so they went their separate ways, the sergeant pulling his colourful but warm hat further down round his ears, and heading back up Farriers Lane the way they had come.

The churchyard's gravestones were, in the main, fairly old, or very old, many of them weather-worn into illegibility, others lichen-covered and leaning at odd angles, like mouthfuls of neglected teeth. One thing that was obvious, though, was the proliferation of the surnames Pryor and Buttery. Along with three or four other surnames, these formed the bulk of those now at rest beneath the untended and weed-bedraggled ground.

Hearing the crack of a breaking twig, Carmichael turned round to find Dimity Pryor leaning on the wall that surrounded the churchyard. 'I'm sorry if I startled you, Sergeant,' she apologised prettily, and he walked over to her, to see if, sharing one of the names of many of the graveyard's occupants, she could provide him with a little information about the chapel and its past.

She certainly could!

One of the strangest stories she told him was of the Steynham St Michael cross. It was kept in the locked chapel, from whence it had not exited in many a year, was about ten feet in height and made of wood. In days gone by, it had been traditional that male members of the congregation, on Good Friday, would take it in turns to drag this object round the village, balanced over a shoulder the way the real Christ may have dragged his own cross nearly two thousand years ago.

No one knew when the practice had begun and no one remembered now when exactly it had been discontinued, but it was within living memory, for Dimity could remember witnessing it when a tiny child, the memory almost a short snap-shot of a memory, but vivid nevertheless.

After a few minutes more of his local history lesson, Dimity and Carmichael parted, she to return to the Market Darley Road to check up on Vernon, who had been so upset that morning, he back down Farriers Lane to the High Street, to meet his superior officer.

By coincidence, Falconer had also come in search of Carmichael, having satisfied his caffeine craving and staved off a low blood sugar attack *(any excuse!)* with a Danish pastry. They met at the junction of the Market Darley Road and the High Street and, noting that it was now half-past four – and dark – they set off for Foxes' Run, in the sure and certain knowledge that they would catch Tilly Gifford at home, and available for a word in private.

'If she hasn't gone into Market Darley to do her shopping,' Carmichael offered, pessimistically.

'That's a risk we'll just have to take, Sergeant,' Falconer replied, pulling his collar up and shoving his hands deep into his pockets, for with the darkness had come a biting cold, and a wicked little wind that was too lazy to blow round you, so blew right through you instead. Carmichael adjusted his rainbow hat for maximum cosiness and produced, one from each pocket of his coat, a pair of matching mittens.

Falconer was aghast. 'Dear God, Carmichael!' he exclaimed. They're not on strings in case you drop them, are they?'

'No, sir, but they're very warm. Just the thing for a day like this. You ought to get some,' and he smiled as he said it.

Falconer smiled back, sensing another small step forward in their partnership. 'If I do, you'd better be wearing black, Sergeant.'

'Why's that, sir?'

'Because it'll be over my dead body. OMDB, Carmichael. OMDB!'

'Understood, sir, but they really are very cosy.'

'Enough, already!'

By now they had reached Foxes' Run, and Falconer rang the bell and followed this with a swift tattoo on the fox-shaped door knocker. He was freezing and wanted to get inside with as little delay as possible.

Tilly answered the door, still unwinding her scarf, her coat not yet removed, so she had obviously just got in. In daylight, they would have seen her car pass them on the way, but in the dark that was more or less an impossibility, unless one knew the vehicle very well.

It took a few minutes for introductions, invitations to sit, and the production of the inevitable tray of, in this case, tea, the warmth of which Falconer found very welcoming after their cold trek here on foot, even after his recent caffeine-fest in the restaurant. As Tilly was fetching in the teapot, the inspector shivered and looked at Carmichael, who seemed unmoved by the outside temperature. The sergeant mouthed one word, as Tilly returned to the room, but in that one word, all was revealed.

'Thermals.'

She was another resident of Steynham St Michael who had never been prescribed Valium. What a very naturally relaxed village this was proving to be, thought Falconer, hardly daring to think the word 'chilled' lest he start shivering again.

Her reaction, however, to their certain knowledge that she had received an anonymous letter, was a little less than relaxed. 'Who told you that? It's all lies, wicked lies – what was in the letter that is. I don't deny that I've had one – but it's all lies, not a word of truth in it at all: I'd never be so irresponsible. I've no idea who could have insinuated such a wicked thing. I've never been so insulted in my life …' Tilly finally ground to a halt, mainly because she needed to draw breath.

'I'm not concerned with what was in the letter,' Falconer

157

inserted, while he had the chance. 'I just want you to confirm that you received one, and whether you still have it.'

'No, I certainly do not,' Tilly almost shouted in her own defence and, as it happened, quite untruthfully.

'Do you still have the envelope?'

'I might have.'

'Do you think you could take a look for us?'

'I might do.'

'Now …?'

'Oh, all right. Just give me a minute,' she requested, and disappeared into what the two detectives assumed was the dining room.

She was back in less than two minutes, holding out an envelope at arm's length. 'Here you are. Take the filthy thing. I certainly don't want it: in fact, I can't understand why I haven't burnt it already.'

'I'm glad you haven't, Mrs Gifford. Every little bit helps.'

'That's true,' Tilly mused, looking immediately happier, now that it appeared she had done the right thing, even if it was for all the wrong reasons.

'And finally,' Falconer said, placing his now empty cup back in its saucer, 'may I ask you where you were on Friday morning? And your husband, of course,' he added, to ascertain that she would confirm Roma Kerr's story.

'Tommy took the eight o'clock train to town. He works there, you know, and I know he caught it, because he phoned me at half-past, just as I was getting ready to leave for work, to ask me to pick up his suits from the dry cleaner's.'

'And did Mr Gifford happen to be with him at the time?' Falconer asked – cunningly, in Carmichael's opinion.

'Now how on earth did you know that? You've been checking up on us, haven't you, Inspector?' she asked, with a twinkle in her eye, before deciding that flirting with an investigating officer was definitely not the done thing, so she had better can that idea *tout de suite*.

Picking up the dry cleaning? thought Falconer. So that was why she had been a bit late getting home from work. 'And I was at the surgery,' she continued, the twinkle definitely quashed. 'I start at nine, so I'm always there at a quarter-to, and I don't finish until four. I usually take a packed lunch with me, and catch up on the filing over the lunch break. It's not a very long break, and it doesn't seem worth going home just to eat a sandwich.'

'I know the feeling,' concurred Falconer, and out of the corner of his eye, he could see Carmichael nodding his agreement.

'And you really don't want to know what was in the letter?' Tilly asked, incredulous that she should be let off the hook so lightly.

'I haven't the faintest interest in its contents, Mrs Gifford. We know who wrote it, and we're more concerned with finding her murderer than plumbing the depths of what must have been a very dark mind.'

'I still can't believe it! Everyone loved, or at least liked Hermione, and we all thought she was our friend, while all the time she had all this spiteful stuff in her head about us. I still can't believe it. It's just too bizarre.'

'Bizarre or not, I'm afraid it's true. And now, Mrs Gifford, we will leave you in peace. Thank you so much for your co-operation and help.'

The two of them walked very briskly indeed back to the car park outside the Co-op where they had left Falconer's car. What with walking instead of driving, and the temperature dropping even lower, it had seemed like a very long afternoon, though it was not over yet. They still had to return to the station and rendezvous with PC Green, to see if he had come up with anything at the other end of the village.

PC Merv Green was on secondment from Carsfold, and the three of them had met on a case in the village of Stoney Cross a few months ago. Out of uniform, Merv looked a very scary character, being of a muscular build, darkly tanned due to being out on the beat so much, and with a totally bald head, but he was actually a very civilised young man, who could discuss the merits of fine wine with Falconer and the music of the seventies with Carmichael with equal ease.

He was waiting for them in Falconer's office, his helmet resting on the inspector's desk, his feet up beside it, totally at ease, until he caught sight of them, at which point he was up on to his feet in a flash, to greet those in the position he hoped, one day, to find himself in.

'Anything to report, Green?' Falconer asked, hoping that Carsfold wouldn't snatch him back too soon. He saved them so much legwork, and was keen and intelligent to boot.

'Not a lot going on down there, sir. I spoke to that Pounce woman you mentioned – the cleaning lady. Cor, don't she rattle on? It seems she works just about everywhere. If anything happened to her, she gives the impression that the whole of the village would disappear under a thick layer of dirt.

'Nothing to report really, though, except for a few people mentioned the previous tenant of number six Prince Albert Terrace – a woman called Marilyn Slade. It seems that she cleared out rather suddenly, and you know how people like to call on their two old friends, Rumour and Gossip.'

'Go on, Green,' Falconer encouraged him. The constable had a nice turn of phrase, sometimes, that he appreciated.

'In the end, it seems that she has neither been foully murdered, nor been abducted by either aliens or sinister foreign agents. Word is, she left to nurse her mother, who was suffering from early onset Alzheimer's – poor cow!'

'Which one?' Carmichael asked, entering the conversation with what seemed a totally unrelated question.

'Both!' was Green's cryptic reply, which he gave without batting an eyelid. 'I'm surprised you haven't heard about her already, sir. It seems she used to do a few hours for that craft shop on the High Street – Knitty-Gritty it's called.'

'I know!' exclaimed Falconer with a vehemence that surprised the constable. 'Oh, it's not you, it's the name, and the couple that runs – if that's the right word – the craft shop. They're a couple of drunks who are never sober for long enough to know which way is up. I'd be surprised if they even

160

remember her if she's been gone longer than a week.'

'Like that, is it?'

'Very like that, Constable. I wouldn't be surprised to find either or both of them dead or in rehab by Easter, they're that bad. Still, I'll soon be shot of them, when this case gets solved.'

His optimistic statement belied his lack of confidence. He intended to do a summary of everything they had learnt so far when he got home, and he wasn't feeling confident that the solution would be staring him in the face, at the end of it. But first things first – he had a little experiment to conduct when he got home, concerning the honesty of a certain bunch of pussycats.

Chapter Twelve
Find the Lady (Or Other Culprit)

Saturday 9th January – evening

The first thing Falconer did when he got home, after pouring himself a gin and tonic, was to remove three fat prawns from his fridge and sandwich them between two plates, which he placed on the work surface where he could observe them from his second-favourite chair in the sitting room. He'd sit and sip his chilled reward, in his pleasantly warm room, and solve a domestic crime before he did anything else. He still could not believe that his beloved Mycroft was a thief, not after all the time they had been together.

After all, Tar Baby and Ruby were fairly recent additions to his household, only tolerated because they had belonged to someone he had recently fallen for. It would never have worked out for them, but when the cats had found themselves abandoned he had felt obliged to step into the breach and give them a home in remembrance of what might have been.

When they had first moved in he had been an emotional mess and their demands – no, their simple needs – and their mere presence, had driven him to distraction, so set in his ways with his 'only cat' was he, but he was gradually getting used to seeing them around, and even developing a grudging affection for them. But he would not tolerate them stealing his food – even if he should have stood his salmon steak in the microwave for safety, a little demon voice taunted him from the depths of his thoughts.

After only ten minutes, while he was still sunk in thoughts about his feelings towards the two cats who had invaded his home, not to mention disturbed his well-ordered routine, there was a definite sound of plate upon plate, and he started, and turned his head towards the kitchen doorway.

And there was the culprit, caught, red-pawed, in the act of attempted theft – no, of actual theft! Tar Baby had managed to slide one plate across the other with a deft paw and, at this very moment, had a succulent prawn in his jaws, and was preparing to flee through the cat-flap with his booty.

Falconer's rise from the chair hastened the cat on his way into the garden and, mystery solved, he rewarded Ruby and Mycroft *(who were sitting innocently on the kitchen floor looking upwards hopefully)* with the other two fishy morsels. His neighbour had been perfectly correct when he had identified Tar Baby as the thief, but now he knew for certain a feeling of guilt crept over him.

It was his own fault, really. Maybe Mycroft would never have done such a thing, but to leave such tempting seafood items out on the work surface, and not expect them to be touched when he came home from work, with three cats in and out of the house all day, really was expecting too much. He would make sure that he defrosted any future temptations behind a closed glass door, and would not put his felines under so much pressure not to behave the way a cat behaves naturally, in the future.

Putting a coquille St Jacques and a couple of small potatoes in the oven, he fetched his briefcase from the hall, began to spread papers across the kitchen table and, grabbing a spiral notepad and pen, began to collate what he had learnt so far.

First, he divided his suspects – the members of the cards club, for he had decided that the culprit lay in that membership – into two groups: the Fox and Hounds group, which he thought of as the slightly younger and trendier group, for no better reason than that same description applied to the pub, and the Ox and Plough group, slightly older in the main, and a little old-fashioned – again, like the pub they met in.

Of the Fox and Hounds group, only two members – Tilly Gifford and Elizabeth (formerly Buffy) Sinden had received poison pen letters. Four members of the group from the Ox and Plough, however, had received letters, and Hermione had one to herself in her typewriter, unfinished, when she was murdered. That letter was obviously her cover. If she received one too, how could she be responsible for the others?

But everyone had seemed so fond of her. It seemed difficult to believe that someone who was regarded with universal affection should harbour such darkness in her heart towards those who regarded her as a friend. If she really felt like that, would she actually stroll into the Ox and Plough and casually order six bottles of champagne to share with them? Would that make her the kind of person who had instructed the landlord always to keep half-a-dozen of her favourite brand on ice, just in case she had something to celebrate with her friends? Was she the sort of person who would write a note that would drive one of her *(so-called)* friends to suicide?

This approach was obviously getting him nowhere, and Falconer tore a sheet from his notepad, threw it in the general direction of the rubbish bin, and decided to approach things from a different angle, and examine everyone's alibis, starting with Tilly and Tommy Gifford. Well, they were a complete washout. He knew that Tommy had been at work that day, and had caught the eight o'clock train to London. And Tilly had been at the doctor's surgery at a quarter to nine.

What about Roma and Rodney Kerr? He'd learnt from more than one source that Rodney Kerr was on the same train as Tommy Gifford, bound for the capital on a buying – or at least, ordering – trip. Roma had apparently spent the morning helping Elizabeth Sinden undergo a complete change of sartorial image, so that was two more from that group accounted for.

Bryony Buckleigh claimed to have been doing her shopping in Market Darley and, having met the lady, he was sure that, if asked, she could produce a string of shop assistants who had spoken to or seen her yesterday morning.

The only people left in the Fox and Hounds group were the Littlemores, who claimed to have been stocktaking. This might even be true, for the only other alternative Falconer could think of was that they had been pissed out of their heads again. Anyway, if one of them had tried to sneak up on Hermione Grayling in the state he had found them in on two occasions, it would sound like an elephant approaching through thick undergrowth. No way could one of that pair have caught as astute a woman as Hermione Grayling off her guard to that extent.

But he was forgetting – she had been sedated with Valium, and was probably deeply asleep when she was attacked with such murderous force. She would have been incapable of reacting to a real elephant charging through thick undergrowth, with her in its sights. Whoever had administered that sedative had done so to make her, literally, a sitting target, unable to move, cry out, or fight back in any way to save herself. That really had been evil!

Sedation aside, however, he still didn't think it had anything to do with the Littlemores. Even if one of them had been in a drunken rage with her, they wouldn't have had the nous to have gone in earlier and slip her a sedative, then returned later to sink a billhook into her skull: that was a non-starter of an idea.

And that was the whole of the Fox and Hounds group accounted for. Two poison pen letters between them, and each and every one of them with an alibi for the time of the murder. Damn! He'd have to move on to the group that met at the Ox and Plough, but at least this group looked a little more promising, at first glance. Four members had received unpleasant epistles, and one, only half-born, had awaited him, in the clutches of the ancient Underwood in Hermione's 'author-torium' – what a truly ghastly word that was!

This group really consisted of Hermione's chosen few, and her relationships with them were much more deeply rooted than with the members of the other group. Three of them, in fact, she had known since schooldays, or shortly afterwards, if his memory served him correctly. Were there any old grudges to be unearthed, there?

Yes, indeed there were.

At this point he left the table, took a bowl of salad out of the fridge, and removed the rest of his meal from the oven. Got to feed the inner man, he thought, or the brain will seize up. As he ate, he pondered the main items being examined for fingerprints. He had little hope they would find any, but he thought that someone may recognise the billhook. He must take it a-visiting when it had finished its sojourn in the laboratory.

The letters too probably had nothing to offer in the way of fingerprints corroborating that they were sent by Hermione Grayling – the general public was just too well-informed these days. It must have been great, he speculated, to have been a policeman when fingerprints were first recognised as evidence, but their existence and importance were not a matter of public knowledge.

The envelopes were a different matter. They would give up the titles of the publications from which the letters that constructed their contents had been cut. That in itself should confirm that it was Hermione behind them. And there was the fact that they had not been posted, but delivered by hand, so it was obviously someone local.

Here he pulled himself up short. They knew that Hermione Grayling was responsible for the poison pen letters: they had found one half-finished in front of her dead body. Shaking his head to clear his thoughts, he continued with his meal, ignoring the mews of the cats, who were pleading that they hadn't had anything to eat for days and were dying of starvation. Little liars!

Returning to his notebook after he had rinsed off his plate and put it in the dishwasher, he was aware that somewhere in the far distance – in the farthest regions of his mind – there was an alarm bell ringing, trying to warn him that he had missed something: something that he had not realised the significance of; something small and obvious that was right under his nose. But it was no use chasing it, for it would slide away and hide from him. He would just have to wait for it to swim into his conscious mind in its own time, for it wouldn't be hurried.

Falconer recalled very well a conversation during the course of which he had learnt that Hermione, like Tar Baby, had been a bit of a 'tea leaf', back in her younger days. There were four in that group who had known each other since youth – Hermione Grayling, Dimity Pryor, Charles Rainbird, and Vernon Warlock.

Vernon had been the one at that time so distantly past who had wanted to write, and who had developed his first plot, confiding the details, maybe to all of them, but certainly to Hermione. Falconer suffered a rare moment of insight, imagining Vernon Warlock as a young man, full of plans for his career as a writer, sure of where his future lay, and full of hopes and dreams.

Then the unthinkable happened. Hermione – his dear friend Hermione – had stolen his plot, written it as a book herself, duly got it published and, from there, had metamorphosed into the writer that he should have been, getting the praise and plaudits that should have been his by rights. She had stolen not only his thunder, but his entire life, when looked at like this.

Suddenly the whole situation became real for Falconer: the depth of feeling, the sense of betrayal – the whole devastating incident, brutal, dishonest; the act of a traitor or an enemy, not a friend. He'd looked at it previously as something that had happened a long time ago, but old sins have long shadows, and maybe Vernon Warlock still cherished revenge in his heart. She'd become a well-known writer, with holiday homes all over the place: he'd become a dealer in second-hand books – a nobody, in short.

Vernon had claimed to be at work when Hermione was murdered, but there were no witnesses to this. He could easily have put a notice on the door stating that he had popped out for five minutes and would be back soon, and got himself up to The Spinney. If he'd gone up Farriers Lane and down Tuppenny Lane, he would have passed only three houses, and once out on the Market Darley Road, would have needed only to cross the road to enter the grounds of The Spinney. There was little likelihood of him being seen and, if he was, he could always have made his excuses, and tried again another day. Vernon

Warlock was a definite possibility as a suspect.

Who next? He decided to take a look at Charles Rainbird. What had he heard about him and Hermione? Yes, that they had gone out together – were an item for a short time in their youth, although no one had mentioned why they had ceased to be an item.

Having met Charlie Rainbird, Falconer had a fair idea. The man was gay, in Falconer's opinion, although not in any overt way, but it was obvious to a policeman who had his 'gaydar' switched on, and that was a piece of mental equipment that one needed in the force. Identifying a person's sexuality at little more than a glance could be the difference between diffusing a situation, and someone getting a knife in the guts, as a homophobe with a bellyful of beer and his dander well and truly up didn't care who got it, so long as it dissipated his own anger and hatred. He realised that he may, of course, be judging Rainbird wrongly; the man may, in fact, be bisexual, but that would have made no difference to Hermione. It would not have been compatible with her plans for life and, in fact, nobody had matched up to her expectations in the end, and she had spent the rest of her life as a spinster.

As the evidence of Rainbird's sexuality was not something that had been spread abroad for public consumption, he assumed that this was a secret that Hermione had held in trust for him all these years. Yes, it may just be an assumption on his part, but his gut instinct told him that he had made the right call. Now, what was Mr Charles Rainbird up to yesterday morning? Why, he too was at work. Apparently.

How simple, again, to place a note on the door, and walk openly up the Market Darley Road to the general store to buy his copy of the local newspaper. No one would even notice him doing that, or make a note of it, it was such an innocent action. The Spinney was only a few yards further along the road on the opposite side. How simple it would have been to cross over and, if anyone saw him or spoke to him, to just call in and say hello, and leave it till another time.

He probably hated the fact that Hermione held the secret of

his sexuality in the palm of her hand, and could change everyone's opinion of him in just one sentence. Rainbird, like Vernon Warlock, had motive and opportunity. Falconer would work on the means later. And give forensics a jog. He'd still had no information as to fingerprints, or about the publications mutilated to produce the letters.

He had a muse about Dimity Pryor next. She had said that she and Hermione had been best friends, even at school. From what Miss Pryor had said, Hermione was a bit of a one for the boys back then, but she, Dimity, had only ever had one boyfriend. And Hermione had stolen him from right under her very nose. How that must have rankled, that her best friend, who had the pick of the boys, should steal the only one that Dimity was ever interested in. Then, apparently Hermione had cast him aside, saying she'd only stolen him to prove that he was a two-timer.

That must have been cold comfort to the young Dimity, who had no idea that the two of them would be life-long maiden ladies. She must have felt that her world was at an end, the way young people always over-dramatise things, thinking that they will actually die if such-and-such a thing does, or doesn't, happen. Magnify that through a lifetime of spinsterhood, and you had a jolly good motive for murder. Gosh, he was going great guns on this group. Now, who was left?

Monica and Quentin Raynor were practically on the spot, and Monica had received a letter. He had a fair idea of the subject matter for Vernon and Quentin's letters, but no idea about Monica's. He assumed, estate agency being a dirty business sometimes, that it could have been about dodgy dealings sometime in the past, or about her fidelity. He knew a flirt when he saw one, and was particularly susceptible to spotting marital tension.

The latter, though, he dismissed out of hand. The tension between them didn't seem the sort that existed due to the discovery of an affair, so he was going to plump for dodgy dealings on the property market in the past, something he might have to examine more closely, if he found no culprit elsewhere.

That left him with Gabriel Pryor, who had committed suicide, and Craig Crawford, who was obviously a social inadequate, unable to deal with relationships with real people, and hiding instead in his toy railways and pretend landscapes. He appeared to have no close friends. Crawford had not received a letter but, rather like Gabriel Pryor, his only social outlet was the cards club. Falconer considered him a non-starter in the role as first murderer.

Chapter Thirteen
Time Out

Sunday 10th January

Harry Falconer had anticipated Sunday as being a quiet day, empty, for him to fill with a whole lot of doing nothing. All the interviews in Steynham St Michael had been carried out, and the forensics department was unlikely to have anything for them on a Sunday *(heaven forbid!)*.

He was, therefore, surprised to receive a call from a very excited Carmichael, just before lunch. 'You've got to come over, sir,' he bellowed with no preamble whatsoever. 'You've just got to see this. It's unbelievable. It's absolutely fantastic, and I want you to come and see it for yourself, 'cos I could never, ever describe it to you as good as it is. Please come over, sir. Kerry and the boys want you to, too.'

'Come over and see what, Carmichael? Whatever could be that marvellous or that important that I have to see it immediately?' Really, Carmichael's inner child must have escaped again, Falconer thought, with a superior grin.

'It's dogs, sir, dogs! You know I said, on that case in Stoney Cross where there were all them dogs, that I'd like to get one and ...' Here, his voice trailed off as he realised what that particular case had meant to Falconer.

After a couple of seconds given over to a loud inhalation of breath to get his enthusiasm re-inflated, Carmichael continued. 'We decided in the end, me and Kerry, that is, to get two dogs – puppies; one each for the boys to look after. They can feed them, and change their water, and walk them twice a day, and start to understand what it is to be responsible for another life. What do you think, sir?'

'I think it's risky, Carmichael. You know the poor record kids have for looking after pets when the novelty wears off. They just abandon them to their parents' care, and move on to the next enthusiasm of childhood. Have you thought about that?'

'I've done a bit of bribery, sir, and promised them they can take their pets to obedience classes, once they've settled in. And I've promised that, if they look after them well, and keep them bathed, washed, and looking nice, that they can enter them in the pet shows at the village fetes, in the summer.'

'Actually, that's quite a clever ploy,' Falconer had to admit. Carmichael wasn't just an intimidating presence. There was 'summat to 'im,' as someone's old granny must have said at some time or other. 'So why, exactly do you want me to come over right now?'

'Because I've picked them up this morning, and they're just so good with the boys, and I wanted to share it with you, because I'm so excited, and because you haven't got anything like this in your own life ...' Again Carmichael trailed off. He'd said too much; spoken his mind, instead of obscuring his motives with polite waffle. He just couldn't help telling the truth. It was one of the traits that his new wife loved so much about him.

Again, Falconer decided to ignore his sergeant's *faux pas*. If Carmichael were a puppy – admittedly a huge one – at the moment, he'd have widdled all over the floor in his excitement. 'OK, I'll be right over,' he promised, not wishing to give his sergeant even more imaginary rope with which, metaphorically, to hang himself. 'Just let me get changed first.'

Falconer had a picture forming in his mind of a pair of Labradors, bouncing all over the place and just waiting to have a good old wrestle with the ankles of his trousers. And knowing Carmichael, the 'puppies' would probably have been the last of a litter, and be just about full-grown. His old jeans would suit his purpose for this visit, he decided, heading upstairs to his bedroom.

This was Falconer's first visit to Castle Farthing since Carmichael had moved into the marital home, although his sergeant's new wife Kerry had lived there for some years. In fact, it was in response to a murder in said village of Castle Farthing that Carmichael had first been assigned as Falconer's partner, albeit as an acting detective sergeant.[1]

They had worked together on that unfortunate business at Stoney Cross as well,[2] with Carmichael still an acting DS, and Falconer would never forget the day that his partner had been informed that he had passed his sergeant's exams and was being transferred to CID, to work permanently in partnership with the inspector.

The first he had known that there was something on the cards, had been when Carmichael was summoned to 'Jelly' Chivers' office – upstairs, in more than one way. A small smile of nostalgia, of which he was totally unaware, appeared on his face, as he remembered that polite knock on the door, twenty minutes or so later.

Answering the summons, he had discovered a red-faced Carmichael standing there, with an expression that threatened that his head might explode, if something wasn't done fairly rapidly. 'Would you mind opening the door very wide, sir, and standing well back?' he had asked, with a curious little splutter in his voice.

Falconer had done as he was asked without question, taking a mere peek round the door, to see if he could figure out what the young man was up to. Carmichael had retreated down the long corridor, at the end of which Falconer's office lay and, with a little bounce on the balls of his feet, commenced to cartwheel towards the office door like a giant runaway wagon wheel.

Falconer's head had retreated in self-defence, and he held tight to the door, lest it try to close on what was approaching, at what he considered was a reckless speed. Carmichael knew

---

[1] See *Death of an Old Git.*
[2] See *Choked Off*

what he was about, though, and completed his last tumble, just short of the window, regaining an upright position with a huge grin on his face and looking as if he had won the lottery.

And, in his opinion, he *was* a winner in life's lottery. In just a few short months he had investigated his first case of murder, met the girl of his dreams, got engaged to be married, gained two stepsons-to-be, passed his sergeant's exams, and now been promoted to full sergeant and transferred to plain clothes. What more could he possibly want? The newly appointed Detective Sergeant Carmichael wasn't much of a one for money, but he always counted his blessings, and he seemed to have so very many more of them these days that, today, he was fit-to-burst-happy.

His mood had been highly infectious, and Falconer had found himself grinning inanely back at him, and pumping his hand as if he expected water to spurt from his mouth. And all the time there had been a faint voice at the back of his mind, screaming, 'He'll be with you on every case now. There's no escape! There's no way back! You'll be together for ever!'

He was beginning to learn, however, that Carmichael may be as weird as he appeared to be at first glance, but he wasn't so green *(or orange, or purple, or yellow, or blue ...)* as he was cabbage-looking. He knew his onions, even if he'd learnt them in a very odd way. Superintendent 'Jelly' Chivers had spotted it, and Falconer was coming to realise that he was right. Carmichael would more than do, even if he was sometimes *(often!)* a bit weird – or *unexpected.*

At this point in his musings, he had arrived at the village green in Castle Farthing, beside which Carmichael *et famille* lived in two cottages knocked into one, though still retaining the outward appearance of two dwellings, due to local planning regulations. They had been allowed to join the two back gardens, however, to give the boys (and now presumably the puppies as well) plenty of room to run around, and expend all that abundant energy that youth held in its gift.

Locking his beloved car, more by habit than necessity in this quiet backwater, he knocked at the first front door he came to, expecting his knock to be answered with the deep baying of two no doubt enormous dogs. Instead, the other door opened, revealing his sergeant with a couple of balls of fluff in his arms.

Falconer, wrong-footed yet again, approached the other door, staring at what Carmichael held dubiously. What on earth were they? And then one of them yapped, which started the other ball of fluff off, and they went inside with Carmichael's delighted laughter mingling with the high-pitched yap of two minute scraps of dog.

'Whatever have you got there, Carmichael?' Falconer asked him, still trying to work out exactly what his sergeant was carrying.

'May I introduce you to Fang,' Carmichael said with a perfectly straight face, holding out a Chihuahua puppy in the palm of one hand, 'and this little scrap here is going to learn to answer to the name of Mr Knuckles,' he concluded, offering up a tiny Yorkshire terrier in his other spade-like hand, and before Falconer could get a word in, he added, 'The boys were allowed to choose their names, and I think they've done a very good job, don't you, sir?'

'Yes,' agreed Falconer flatly, with a bland expression, catching sight of two little faces standing behind their new stepfather almost bursting with pride. 'They're, um, lovely. I'm sure you'll all have a lot of fun together,' he added, while hoping that Carmichael didn't sit or step on one, and unwillingly become responsible for a family tragedy.

Anything that small, with Carmichael around, ought to have a fluorescent collar and a proximity sensor if it wanted to grow to adulthood, and even then, they wouldn't be much bigger, would they? They were hardly breeds that would be useful as guard dogs, unless they could yap an intruder to death. Playing rough-and-tumble between the two boys the furry participants, being very young, fell asleep side-by-side sharing the same cushion, looking more like a couple of over-large dust bunnies than anything canine. Identifying this as an opportunity, and not wishing to seem rude by leaving so soon after he had arrived, Falconer asked them if, as it was Sunday, they would like to join him at The Fisherman's Flies for a spot of Sunday lunch? It would be his treat.

There were no noticeable smells of cooking in the house, so he assumed that he would not be upsetting any already in-progress plans for food. He was proved right in his assumption by the whole-hearted agreement of all four of them, and they donned coats, hats, and scarves, hands being stuffed in pockets, for their short trip across the village green, for the temperature was still bitter, and could prove very uncomfortable even on very short trips outdoors.

George and Paula Covington, the couple that ran the pub, greeted Falconer like an old friend, and settled all five of them at a table, close to a very welcoming roaring log fire, informing them that the choice of roasts today was between pork and beef, and requesting their orders for drinks.

When all was in hand, George skewered Falconer with a gimlet eye and said, 'We're all very proud of this young man here, not just for that charity stunt he pulled for the wedding, but also for what he's done in his job. I hope you're treating him right, for if you're not, and I get to hear about it, there'll be trouble.'

It was said in a jovial way and accompanied by a sly wink, and Falconer took it in good part, assuring George that he was nurturing Carmichael as he would a son of his own, glad that his sergeant was appreciated in his community, and attributing a small part of this to the fact that his first case had been here, in Castle Farthing itself.

As they ate, Kerry brought their host up to date with the latest news from the village. They had no vicar, at present, to replace Rev. Swainton-Smythe, and Castle Farthing was in the same position as Steynham St Michael in that it was just on a rota now for a peripatetic vicar who only held services on one Sunday in the month.

Her godparents, the Warren-Brownes, had retired from their duties at the post office only the month before – at Christmas, to be precise – and were busy settling in at The Beehive, a property that they had snapped up as soon as it had come on the housing market. It was a lovely place, with plenty of garden, and the added bonus of what had been a studio for the previous owner, and which would soon be a super-duper playroom for Dean and Kyle, Kerry's two sons. And it hadn't been the only property to be put up for sale, either, as the little cottage in Sheepwash Lane was still looking for a new owner.

Not much seemed to happen in a village, and then, there was a cataclysmic event, and the effect moved out through everyone's lives, like the ripples on a pond where a stone has been thrown in the water. The changes in this case, though, sounded as if they were for the better. A young couple had taken on the post office, and the garage had re-opened after a closure of only a couple of months, so the Castle Farthing motorists no longer had to make the trip to Steynham St Michael for their petrol supplies.

The very convivial lunch was followed by coffee back at the Carmichaels' and, of course, another session of admiring the miniature mutts, who cavorted around the sofa as if it were a continent. It wasn't until half-past five that Falconer made a move to leave, refusing all offers to stay on for his 'tea'. He left them with a very contented feeling – you might say that he was 'heart-warmed' by his visit, and he drove home with a rare smile on his usually serious face. Carmichael was, indeed, a very lucky young man, and Falconer hoped he realised how blessed he really was.

Chapter Fourteen
The Final Trick

Monday 11th January

Monday morning brought with it three pieces of news relating to the murder of Hermione Grayling. The first was from the forensics department, to inform Falconer that the only thing they could detect on the bill-hook was a very expensive brand of bleach called 'Blanche-issimo'. There had, of course, been no evidence of fingerprints, and the only other things found on it had been blood, hair, both real and of the wigged variety, and brain matter, which wasn't exactly a surprise result.

The typewriter keys, strangely enough, had also shown no sign of fingerprints, not even of Hermione's, which was very odd considering that it was Hermione's typewriter, that she had been found dead in front of it, and that it had had a half-typed letter on its roller.

The cut-out letters, from which the letters had been constructed, were identified as coming from the *Daily Telegraph* and old copies of *The Lady*. It seemed fairly obvious to Falconer that these were likely to have originated from Hermione Grayling herself, in keeping with all the other evidence, but they would have to check with the general store, which functioned also as a newsagents, and which provided the Steynham St Michael residents with their daily dose of news, and their weekly or monthly copies of a variety of periodicals.

Falconer also received a phone call just after nine o'clock, only fifteen minutes after he had sat down at his desk, from Noah and Patience Buttery, who had returned the night before to Pear Tree Cottage. They explained that they had gone away for a few days after Gabriel Pryor, their cousin, had hanged himself, because they had been so shocked and upset. They had been brought up to consider suicide to be a sin, as had Gabriel, and the news had knocked them sideways.

They realised, though, that they could not just leave the library in the lurch like that, and had come home, only to learn of Hermione's death from Dimity, their next door neighbour, and to a poison pen letter waiting for them on their hall floor.

Falconer said that he would be there as soon as he could, and he would be grateful if one of them could remain at the cottage, so that they could speak privately. Speaking in a slightly louder voice than was usual for the telephone, he fixed Carmichael with a 'death-ray' stare, and found his sergeant not only on his feet when he hung up the telephone but already in his coat and hat.

'Oh, Carmichael! What's with the hat again?' he asked in despair.

'It's still January, sir, and it's still cold. Until it warms up again, you'd better get used to Mr Hat, because he's not going anywhere without me. Sir,' he added, in case Falconer misinterpreted the tone of what he had just said, but of course he hadn't.

'Good grief!' he thought. 'Carmichael has just made a joke!'

'What's going down, sir?' the sergeant asked as they drove out of the police station car park.

'Well, I've just had a call from Noah and Patience Buttery, to say they're back in the fold of village life, and it would seem that they had a poison pen letter waiting for them when they arrived home yesterday evening. They didn't even know about the murder, so I think they were pretty shocked at the news. They may not have been in Miss Grayling's cards club, but they knew her well enough to be horrified at her murder, and the manner in which it was carried out.

'In fact, that's a bit odd, when you come to think of it, isn't it, Sergeant? Everyone else who has received a letter has been in this blasted club, to the point where we've only concentrated on its members. And now the Butterys have got a letter. I mean, is it random, or does it mean something? Me, I haven't the faintest idea at the moment.

'And we've got to check everyone's home for signs of some fancy-pants bleach called Blanche-issimo, and check with the newsagent what deliveries everyone had in the way of newspapers and periodicals. What do you think of that for a morning's work, Carmichael?'

'What was that, sir?'

'Oh, never mind. I'm certainly not going to repeat it all. Just follow my lead, and you won't go far wrong.'

'Aye aye, sir,' was Carmichael's last comment, as they once more pulled into the car park shared by the Co-op and the village's re-cycling bins.

Carmichael had been right about Mr Hat, thought Falconer as he locked the car doors and felt his ears already beginning to tingle with cold. He'd have to find out if Mr Hat had a brother, or perhaps a slightly less exotic cousin, before he himself became a martyr to frost bite, and his ears fell off.

It was Patience Buttery who answered the door to them, an expression of anxiety and distaste on her face. Noah was waiting for them in the sitting room, staring at the letter which was on the dining table.

Falconer dealt with the introductions, then asked, as tactfully as he could, if they might see the letter. Other recipients had been reluctant to let him read or even look at their letters in case he learnt something about them that they did not want made public, and he could perfectly understand their reticence. Why, if he received a letter threatening to expose his 'guilty secret,' of enjoying baked beans on toast with lashings of brown sauce, he wouldn't want to bandy the letter around either.

She handed the letter to him without faltering, explaining that, as what it said was true, and that most of the older residents knew about it anyway, they didn't mind him seeing it. It was just the sheer spite of it that had upset them, and they really couldn't believe that Hermione had written it. It seemed so out of character, as she had always been perfectly friendly towards them, whenever they had met.

183

Falconer took the letter and read:

You have only one living child, but how many monstrosities have you buried over the years, you freaks? Close relatives should NOT marry.

Know this: that you shall not go unpunished!

The look of puzzlement on his face was quenched immediately, as she explained, 'Noah and I are first cousins, and there is no ban on us marrying in the Church. I have had three miscarriages over the years, but we have accepted that these things can happen. It is God's will. But there is nothing wrong with our relationship, and there's nothing wrong with us either. We're not freaks! And we were a perfectly happy little family until Gabriel killed himself because of one of these filthy letters, and then we opened this.'

'If this was Hermione Grayling's handiwork, then she was an instrument of the Devil, and deserves to burn in Hell.' Noah's opinion harked back to their Strict and Particular roots, but Falconer didn't even notice it. He was standing staring at the letter, as if he had never seen anything like it before, his eyes protruding from their sockets, in his surprise.

At the back of his mind, a penny dropped, and the palm of his free hand actually slapped his forehead, as the truth finally revealed itself to him. Yes, he'd have to confirm his revelation, but he already had an idea of how he was going to do that, and he was already looking forward to it, at this very moment.

Everything was suddenly crystal clear. It was, literally, staring him in the face; it had been there in open view, since he had first arrived at the scene of the murder, like Poe's 'purloined letter'. And because it was so blatant, he hadn't, like anyone else, consciously acknowledged it. He had merely retained that tiny niggling little warning bell at the back of his mind, which was at that very moment signalling 'told you so' to him and blowing silent raspberries inside his head.

Pulling himself together, Falconer put both letter and envelope in an evidence bag, and asked, 'Just one final thing before we leave. Do you mind if I have a look inside your cleaning cupboard?'

Both Patience and Noah looked at him with startled expressions, as if he had gone mad. 'I assure you, I'm perfectly serious, and it does have relevance to the case. It has become necessary that I check to see which cleaning products anyone who knew Hermione uses,' he explained, his target of course being the Blanche-issimo bleach.

'Please, be our guest, Inspector,' replied Patience, actually summoning a weak smile. 'Is there a new criminal offence, using the wrong type of bleach?'

'There just might be in this case, Mrs Buttery.' He smiled back at her, and followed her into the kitchen, to poke his nose into the cupboard under her sink.

Having come to an abrupt decision, before they left he asked, 'Would you be so kind as to tell me what time the library shuts tonight?'

'Seven o'clock, Inspector; same as always. It allows people who work during the week to change their books in the early evening, instead of having to wait until the weekend.'

'Thank you very much. I wonder if you would be good enough to remain there after work tonight. There are a number of people I need to talk to *en masse*, and the library would be a very convenient place to do it, having, as it does, sufficient floor space for me to address a number of people without having recourse to use a public house – most unsuitable – or a private sitting room.'

'That's no problem at all, Inspector. I'll put up the 'closed' sign at the usual time, and you can admit whoever you've invited.'

'What a practical and helpful woman you are, Mrs Buttery. Thank you again for your co-operation and help.'

Outside once more, Carmichael asked him, politely of course, what the hell he was up to, only to receive the uninformative and maddening response, 'You'll see, Sergeant. You'll just have to wait a little, like everyone else, although *they* don't know that yet.'

It proved to be a tedious morning, and cold, walking from house

185

to house and inspecting the cleaning products of all their suspects, in search of the Blanche-issimo. Although they knew they would not be able to catch everyone at home, they were kept in Steynham St Michael even longer, due to the appointments they had to make to visit people in their lunch breaks, for the necessary nose into their cupboards, but it did give them sufficient time to return to The Spinney to have a final look at 'The House of Death', as the press would no doubt refer to it.

The kitchen was really the only room they needed to check – and, indeed, they did find two bottles of the product in question, along with furniture polish, glass cleaner, floor polish, and all the other liquids, gels, and creams necessary to keep a house dirt-free – but they had time on their hands, and Falconer fancied a final wander around. At least it kept them indoors and out of that biting wind. His glances at Mr Hat were more intensely envious today, although Carmichael, fortunately, didn't notice them.

Falconer was at his most observant, having felt such a fool at their first visit of the day, and babbled away, as they made a slow circuit of the accommodation. 'Well, anyone but a fool could see that this wasn't a burglary gone horribly wrong, couldn't they, Carmichael? There are a couple of nice Victorian oils in the hall, along with at least two signed Lowry prints.

'And look over there,' he pointed to a display cabinet on the opposite wall. 'In the cabinet next to the Davenport. That's as mouth-watering display of Austrian cold-painted bronzes as you could wish to find, and if I'm not mistaken, I caught sight of a pair of Sevres pieces in the dining room. No one intent on theft would leave things like that behind.

'I'll bet you anything you like that old Rainbird's mouth is watering at the chance of getting back in here to make a ridiculously 'conservative' bid for some of the choicer items.' The very thought made rub his hands together, and he looked at his sergeant for a response to his mini-inventory.

'Yes, sir,' Carmichael replied on cue, but the inspector had lost him way back in the hall, and he had switched off at that point, to wonder what he was going to eat for his tea that evening. Old and fussy things didn't interest him in the slightest, and he couldn't wait to get back into the fresh air again and away from all this clutter.

Their final call on what had proved to be a very long morning was to Hilda Pounce, the finder of Gabriel Pryor's body, and considered a very unlucky woman by her fellow residents. Both she and Dimity Pryor received a dose of silent sympathy from all who knew them, for having to cope with the memories their experiences must have created for them.

She braked to a squeaky halt on her bicycle as they approached her house, fumbling in a pocket for her door key, and screwing up her face into a mask of disapproval. 'You again!' she almost spat at them.

'I'm afraid needs must where the devil drives, Mrs Pounce. And it's only a quick question we want answered. It won't take more than a minute or two.'

'It'd better not had. I've got to get some lunch down me, and get back to work for two o'clock, and the likes of you comin' along and wasting my time don't 'elp.' she stated baldly, standing aside so that they could enter.

When Falconer asked his standard question for the day, specifically mentioning the elusive brand this time, she exploded like a tuppenny squib. 'Blanche-issimo!' she almost shouted. 'Do you know how much that stuff costs? It's like gold, and much too rich for the likes of my purse. I'm just a poor cleaner. Elbow grease is my product – of necessity.'

This was probably a bit rich, but both detectives got the point, and left her in peace as they walked back to the car. They had to get back to Market Darley for the inquest this afternoon, and they were now running behind. 'Fresh air sandwich again,' commented Carmichael on their lack of lunch, his mind returning once more to food. 'Getting sick of them, I am. Tasteless, and not a lot of substance.' And those were his final words on the matter.

The outcome of the inquest was a foregone conclusion: death by person or persons unknown, and of course an adjournment was announced, the Coroner expressing his dismay at the violence of the attack on a defenceless woman.

The occasion did, however, give Falconer a chance to meet Hermione's publisher and agent, both of whom looked like they'd lost a shilling and found sixpence, which they had, metaphorically. There would be no more Victorian sagas from Hermione Grayling with which to line their wallets and waft them abroad on luxury holidays.

Falconer reckoned from the expressions on their faces that if the murderer were revealed to these two gentlemen now they would tear that person limb from limb and stamp on the results, so much financial damage had that person done.

He had found their contact numbers in Hermione's address book, phoning them himself with the news, and both had reacted in exactly the same way, going from being jolly, 'hail-fellow-well-met' types to down-in-the-mouth glumness in the space of a few sentences. It had irritated him at the time that neither had expressed any personal regret for the murdered woman, their prime concern being their own cut of the deal and their own loss of income, rather than the loss of a well-respected client or friend.

He had had little time for them on the phone, and had even less now, in person, pausing only long enough to learn that Hermione had left a will, and that everything of which she died possessed was to be used to set up a writing prize for new, young authors. That would be one in the eye for everyone who knew her, and it made him smile, as he made his way back to his office, to prepare himself for what was to come that evening, and then to get something to eat before he passed out with hunger.

Chapter Fifteen
Game Over

Monday 11th January – evening

Both Falconer and Carmichael had gone home to eat before setting out for that evening's meeting, in their separate cars, as Carmichael now lived in Castle Farthing. Falconer had made his arrangements for later, before he had left the office. PC Green, accompanied by PC Linda Starr from Carsfold, was to take a patrol car and arrive in Tuppenny Lane about seven forty-five, parking on the piece of waste ground to the east of the library so as not to cause alarm.

He and Carmichael would also park there, leaving their cars sufficiently towards the front of this unused piece of land, to allow PC Green to use them as a screen, by parking behind them. 'Softly softly, catchee monkey', as Falconer was fond of saying, to Carmichael's continued bewilderment.

They arrived within a minute of each other at ten past seven and, on entering the library, began setting the scene. Two trolleys of returned books were relocated between the stacks, and as many chairs as they could find were set in a semi-circle in the large open space between the doors and the returns desk.

Falconer had invited fifteen 'guests' for the evening, and he intended to give them value for money for the inconvenience he was causing them.

Dimity Pryor and Vernon Warlock were the first to arrive, at a quarter-past as the chairs were still being arranged. They amused themselves, in the meantime, by scanning the books on the abandoned trolleys to see if there was anything worth reserving for their next visit, Vernon snorting audibly at what he described as 'romantic women's nonsense'.

Charles Rainbird was next to arrive, with Bryony Buckleigh on one arm and Roma Kerr on the other, Rodney Kerr not being included in the invitation, and they were followed next by Elizabeth (Buffy) Sinden and Tilly Gifford, Tommy Gifford also being excluded from attending. At twenty-two minutes past, Craig Crawford strolled in, closely followed at twenty-five past by Monica and Quentin Raynor, the latter commenting on how crowded the parking was on the waste ground.

'Oh, God,' thought Falconer. 'Surely they haven't all come by car for that small distance. I know it's cold, but this is ridiculous. At this rate, there won't be any room for the patrol car,' and he hoped that PC Green had the nous not to come into the library to ask where he should go for alternative parking. There was no point at all in him setting this up if he was going to have a 'beater' go berserk and alert the prey before he was ready to take his shot. Everything about this evening's performance was about stealth, cunning, and timing, and he didn't want his chance blown by a PC with no initiative.

At twenty-nine minutes past seven, the Littlemores entered, slightly unsteadily, complaining about having to go out in the cold, and causing those they greeted by name to lean backwards as the fumes of alcohol hit them.

That was everyone there, and he could call his meeting to order and get things going. He was really looking forward to his performance, but more of that later. Clearing his throat loudly and pointedly, he fixed his eyes about a foot above the heads of those in front of him, and began a process, the like of which he had longed to be involved in since the age of about thirteen.

'I'm sorry to put you to the trouble of coming out on such a cold evening,' he began, 'but I felt it was necessary, in the circumstances, to clear up this whole business of poison pen letters and murder.

'First of all, let me say that I have examined all your alibis, finding some of them dubious, and others reliant on the word of only one other person, so I have had to consider your various relationships with the deceased very carefully.'

'I say, old man! That's not really cricket. We all loved

190

Hermione,' interjected Charles Rainbird at this point.

'It is necessary, sir, no matter how unpleasant it appears to you. Now, to continue, most of you, I believed, were telling the truth about your whereabouts, but I did take a very good look at three of you – namely you, Mr Rainbird, and also you two. Mr Warlock, and Miss Pryor.'

At this point a babble of disapproval echoed round the high-ceilinged atrium, which Falconer quelled with a lift of his hand, in the instantly recognisable symbol for 'stop'. 'I know this is unpleasant, but please have the courtesy to hear me out.

'It would have been simplicity itself for either Mr Warlock or Mr Rainbird to have closed their shops for a few minutes – a small sign on the door would have sufficed to inform customers that they would be back in ten minutes or so.' In a corner, Carmichael scribbled furiously in his notebook in his 'not-Pitman's' shorthand (*or whatever the current fad for such things is, and if it even now exists*).

'Mr Warlock could have snuck up by the roundabout route of Farriers Lane, hardly passing a dwelling on the way, fully ready to abandon his plan should anyone see him, then nipped down Tuppenny Lane, with only the Market Darley Road to cross, before reaching The Spinney.'

'And why exactly would he want to do that?' interrupted Quentin Raynor, his hackles up, at the thought of people he regarded as his friends having to put up with this sort of treatment.

Vernon Warlock made an inarticulate noise in his throat, but Falconer was too quick for him, and cut in with, 'I don't think we need to discuss that at the moment, Mr Raynor. I'm merely putting it forward as a possibility.

'And a damned impertinent one, at that!' was Charles Rainbird's contribution to the conversation.

'Ah, yes, Mr Rainbird. It must be perfectly obvious to everyone here present, that you could have used exactly the same ploy.'

'And just marched up the Market Darley Road, informing anyone I met that I was off to murder my very dear, old friend

Hermione Grayling, I suppose?'

'Absolutely not, sir. I would have expected you to have made your way up the road, citing your intention to collect your copy of the local newspaper from the general store, and if you had been stopped, and had needed to give this explanation, you too, would have abandoned your plan for that day, and tried another time.'

'Preposterous!'

'Well, leaving that for the moment, I must now inform Miss Dimity Pryor that, as a very old friend too of Miss Grayling's, it was obvious to us that you were closest to the scene of the murder, and had only to cross the road, ostensibly for a quick word or a cup of tea, to be at The Spinney, probably noticed by no one.'

Dimity wasn't taking this sitting down, and she physically rose to her feet, matching her actions to her state of mind and asked, 'Do you really expect anyone to believe that I had the strength to wield that dreadful implement? Hermione was twice my size.'

'She was, however, sedated, as I'm sure you all guessed from my questioning about Valium,' Falconer countered. He was really enjoying himself now. It was proving to be worth the twenty-seven year wait, to realise his ambition.

'Did you ever feel the weight of a billhook, Inspector? Do you imagine I would have the physical strength to bring that down on Hermione's skull and cleave it open?' Dimity asked again, shuddered, and closed her eyes, as her words brought a dreadful picture to her mind. 'Hermione was my best friend since we were at school together, and although we may have had minor differences of opinion over the years ...'

'Including Barry Barker?' asked Falconer, on a whim, well into his stride now, his mental state one huge grin.

'Including Barry Barker, Inspector. She was quite right about him: he was a two-timer, and would have ended up breaking my heart – something that Hermione could foresee, but I couldn't, being so smitten with him. Anyway, as I was saying, we were best friends since schooldays, and I don't think there's a thing in this world that could have made me feel towards her as did the person who struck that devastating blow. So there!'

As Dimity made her defiant statement, those gathered there heard a faint electrical humming noise at the back of the library, which was gradually increasing in volume as it moved closer to them.

'As I said before, yours were the three alibis I looked most closely at, but there was no reason at all why some of the others who alibied another person should be telling the truth. What if Amy Littlemore,' here,' he skewered that lady with his eye, defying her to protest, 'had not been stocktaking with her husband all Friday morning, but had covered for him while he left the stock room at the back of the shop, and nipped up to The Spinney for a spot of murder?'

'I say, old son, that's a bit strong, isn't it? I may be a bit of a lush, but I wouldn't lie about something this serious!'

'Which is exactly what a congenital liar would say in the circumstances! That's enough, for now Mr Littlemore,' the inspector shot out, noticing that Malcolm Littlemore was gathering all the alcohol in his bloodstream for a good old 'frank and explicit exchange of views'.

The sound of the vacuum cleaner grew louder as it approached ever nearer, yet not too loud to drown out what was being said. A few heads turned, concerned that Falconer had not silenced it, not stopped it interrupting them and intruding on what felt like the privacy of an almost secret meeting, but he ignored it, and continued.

'You, Mr Crawford: you intrigued us for a while, and we spent some time considering you in the part of murderer. No! Don't speak! We gave up that idea fairly quickly, having decided that you were much too much of a cold fish to let anyone get under your skin enough to do what was done to Hermione Grayling.

'We looked at all of you, wondering if you were strong enough, both physically and mentally, to commit such a horrific crime, but I won't dwell on that any longer, as there was one person we had not considered, and whom we should have taken more seriously …'

He broke off, as the droning noise became loud enough to make continuing, an impossibility, and looked to Carmichael to get up and turn the machine off, indicating to its operator that he could do without the noise.

'Ladies and gentlemen, may I present to you my fifteenth guest for this evening, and the murderess of Miss Hermione Grayling: Mrs Hilda Pounce.'

There was a chorus of 'noes', and 'nevers', and Hilda Pounce assumed the expression of a rabbit caught in the headlights of a car. But this didn't last for long, as she made a bolt for the door, her face suddenly screwed into a grimace of rage.

Carmichael was ready for her and sprang after her, to be aided at the door by PC Green, who had been keeping an eye on things standing well-obscured by the darkness outside. They both made a grab for her, It still needed the two of them to subdue her and get the hand cuffs on, the honours being done by PC Starr, who was there for form's sake, as it was a woman who was being arrested.

'Take her round to the car, Green, and caution her. Oh, and thanks for being on the ball,' said Falconer, after cautioning the furious Hilda Pounce.

'There's no 'round to the car', sir. Most of this lot must've come by car, and there was nowhere for us to park on the waste ground. We've had to leave the car outside the chippy. Sorry about that, but there was nowhere closer,' explained PC Green, with a rueful smile.

Falconer sighed. Would nothing in this damned rural area ever go right for him? Instead of the discreet arrest, there would now be a right song and dance – for Hilda was not going to go quietly down to the chip shop which, at this time of night, would no doubt be full of people back from work and wanting their cod and chips double-quick.

He'd be a laughing stock when this got out.

It was very late before they had Hilda Pounce processed and locked up for the night, but Carmichael did not have the patience to wait until the morning for an explanation. Falconer had been singing from his own personal hymn sheet, and Carmichael, when the moment came, had known neither the words nor the tune. He made a quick phone call to Kerry before they left the station, to tell her not to wait up for him, and they drove in their separate cars to Falconer's house, lights already on for security purposes, courtesy of a couple of timer devices.

The three cats welcomed them both ecstatically, as if they had not seen a living soul for months (*cats and dogs are such liars when it comes to embarrassing their owners*), and they had to fight their way through a furry barrier before they could settle down with a glass of beer each, and actually discuss what had happened at the library that evening.

'What on earth was going on there, sir? You never said you had a soul in mind as the culprit, yet you went ahead and organised that meeting. What did you think you were going to do? Bluff the murderer out into the open?'

'I might tell you, Carmichael, that tonight I was realising an ambition I have cherished since I was a mere stripling. I started to read the books of one Mrs Christie, Agatha that is, when I was about thirteen, and developed a longing to conduct the denouement of a murder case in a library, just the way Hercule Poirot did in fiction. Tonight, I got the opportunity. Yes, it may have been a public library, and not in a vast old country house, but it did it for me. I can file tonight's experience away with ambitions achieved. Now, what did you ask me? Did I mean to bluff the murderer out into the open? Not at all, Carmichael: not at all. The solution came to me in a flash, when we were at the Butterys' this morning,' Falconer replied, putting down his glass on a table, so that Mycroft could curl up in his lap. 'The poison pen letter they received was typed, like the one in Hermione Grayling's Underwood.'

'And?' Carmichael still wasn't any the wiser.

'Just because it was in her typewriter, doesn't mean she typed it, does it?'

195

'And you think that the Pounce woman typed it?'

'I do, Carmichael. The doctor's given her a sedative for tonight, but we'll do a taped interview tomorrow, and it'll all come out.'

'Do you mean she typed it after the woman was dead? But why? Hermione Grayling was responsible for all the other letters.'

'No she wasn't, Carmichael. Let me start at the beginning, and then tell the story the way I see it. Hilda Pounce has never achieved anything, done anything, or made anything of her life. She was one of life's underdogs, just a cleaner, who wasn't always treated with the respect that she thought she deserved, and the resentment must have built up in her mind to bursting point.

'Bursting point for her being an explosion of poison pen letters, which she delivered herself, having constructed them from old publications that she had cleared out of Hermione Grayling's house. If we'd suspected her earlier, we could have searched her property from top to bottom, and we'd still never have found any evidence, because it's winter, and she could simply burn all the magazines and newspapers she'd cut out letters from on her open fire.

'But surely someone would have seen her going to people's houses.' Carmichael was not convinced.

'Yes, they probably did see her, and what did it mean to them? Nothing, Carmichael! Absolutely nothing! She was the cleaning lady. She went to people's houses to work. That was what she did. As a cleaner, she was completely invisible, like the postman, the milkman, and the paperboy. We see them all the time, but if we didn't see one of them on a particular day, we wouldn't really remember, because they're just part of the everyday scenery to us.

'Her husband was an agricultural worker, and used to do a little gardening after he retired, so no doubt she has quite a collection of what we would consider to be dangerous weapons in her shed at the back of her house.

'I must admit I had a bit of a chat with her while we were

going through all the paperwork, and I managed to learn a bit about the things I didn't understand and, even though it was off the record, I have no doubt that she'll cough the lot tomorrow. That woman has worked like a slave all her life, and I think she's actually looking forward to a rest in prison.

'She was out seven days a week sometimes, doing stuff for others who had so much more than her, and over the years she'd picked up all these little titbits to their discredit. She'd been brought up in the Strict and Particular ways, but it seemed so unfair that she should graft so hard, while all these sinners lived the life of Riley. Then one day she just snapped. She thought she'd teach the lot of them to feel a mite of guilt for their past misdeeds, and a little bit of fear, knowing that someone else knew their secrets.

'You know how she reacted, just to bringing her library books back a little late. She thought it would go down in writing that she had done wrong. When she twigged that the typeface could point the finger at her, and that she'd be marked down as a blackmailer, that would be her finished. Not only would she never get work again, or get a reference worth a light, but she'd probably go to prison as well, and have a criminal record for the rest of her days.

'I think that's where her logic blew her mind. She reasoned that if she killed Hermione Grayling and left a part-finished letter in the machine to Hermione herself, then it could prove to be the perfect murder. She believed there was no way of tracing her to the deed, as she wasn't timetabled to go there that day, and that Hermione would take the blame for the letters, and she could just forget it all, and get on with life as normal – almost as if she could wipe it from her mind and it wouldn't, therefore, count. It does have a sort of mad logic to it, when you consider it.

'I found out that the Valium she used to sedate Hermione Grayling was originally prescribed for her husband when he was having episodes with his 'glass back', and she actually typed the letter in the machine while Hermione was out for the count, and then gave her that radical centre parting.'

197

'Sir!' exclaimed Carmichael, giving his boss a glare. 'That was in very bad taste!'

'It was, wasn't it? Now, where was I? Oh, yes: she wasn't supposed to go to The Spinney that day, as I just said, so that's why she went, if you see what I mean – to avoid us suspecting her. She just bluffed her way in, saying she'd left her scarf there, and then offered to make a cup of tea while she was there. She did this in her rubber gloves, and Hermione didn't suspect a thing, being used to seeing her in the things all the time.'

'Why did she give her the Valium, sir? I don't understand that bit. It's hard enough to think of someone other than Miss Grayling being responsible for the letters, without being all confused with sedatives and the like.' Carmichael was struggling.

'Because she said she couldn't face doing it while Hermione Grayling was conscious, which makes sense of a sort, but she nevertheless cold-bloodedly sat down at the same table as her comatose employer, put a sheet of paper into the woman's typewriter, and wrote the final poison pen letter, just to shake us off the scent.

'She said she only did for Hermione because she – Hilda – had used the typewriter for the letter she'd posted through the Butterys' door. That tiny action sealed Miss Grayling's fate. The Butterys' letter was typewritten because she was fed up with all the fiddling around with cutting out letters, and using tweezers and the like, to construct them, then she had second thoughts when it was much too late. As I said just now, if the typeface was traced to Miss Grayling's machine, it would soon become obvious that the owner of that machine was not responsible for any of the letters, and that would leave old Pounce in the frame.'

'Why wasn't she splattered with blood, sir? A blow like that wouldn't leave her squeaky clean, as we can both witness, having gone into that room.'

'Simple, Sergeant. She brought an extra set of clothes with her – her very oldest, I should imagine – for she's not a woman to waste anything useful. She changed into them, whacked Miss

Grayling, having wiped the keys of the typewriter clean after her decoy epistle, took the clothes home in the big canvas bag she always has in her bicycle basket, and then burnt the evidence on her open fire. Job done! And she almost got away with it, because I was too thick to see a clue right out in the open.

'Everyone calls her Potty Pounce, you know. Well, sometimes there can be more truth in a nickname than one realises. And she was always there. She works for, or has done, in the past, for most of them, and she was even in the pub the night of Hermione's champagne celebration, giving the cellar a good going over, Thursday being a slack night usually. She managed, by judicial timing of going up and down stairs, to overhear the bulk of their conversation, and not one of them even noticed her. She really was invisible, like domestic staff in Victorian times.'

'And what about the people who *didn't* get letters? Was there a reason for that, or was it something she intended to get round to, when she had time?'

'They were people who had been kind to her in the past, and she didn't want to appear ungrateful. Dimity Pryor, for instance, would make occasional gifts from the charity shop to her, no doubt paid for out of her own pocket, but carefully chosen, good-quality things that Hilda would not have ordinarily have been able to afford.

'It was something similar with Roma Kerr, as well. She often passed new garments on to Hilda if they were a little shop-soiled, and couldn't be returned to the wholesaler.

'The Littlemores occasionally got her to 'blitz' their place – it was all extra money – and she never left their house without a generous payment for her time and effort, and a bottle of sherry or port.

'Craig Crawford had foiled a bag-snatcher in Market Darley where she was shopping one day, and returned her bag to her intact, with nothing stolen. I think she sees him as a bit of a hero.

'And Bryony Buckleigh, a really sympathetic soul, used to

sit with Hilda's Bert when his glass back was playing up, keeping him company sometimes, when Hilda had a particularly full schedule, and would have had to leave him on his own all day.

'She only sent letters to people who had slighted her in some way, or dispensed with her services in the past. And apart from the letters and the murder, she really was a very honest woman. Patience Buttery mentioned that when Mrs Pounce returned her library books late and had to pay a fine, she was truly mortified, and even returned later in the day, sort of hoping that something could be done about it.'

'That doesn't alter the fact that she killed one of the country's most popular authors,' Carmichael commented in a disapproving voice.

'Yes, she did indeed. And she even gave the kitchen what she called 'a lick and a promise' before she left the scene of the crime.'

'Yet they do say that the pen is mightier than the sword, sir,' offered Carmichael with a little smile.

'Not in this case,' replied Falconer.

'And hardly a sword.'

'Or a pen.'

'But it's certainly inkier.'

'I think that should be 'more inky', Carmichael.'

'No, sir. Inkier. Definitely!'

Epilogue
Change In The Air

Spring

The entire police staff of the station were crammed in to Superintendent 'Jelly' Chivers' office, there being no room for the civilian staff, in whom Chivers took little interest. Whatever this was about, they would be the last to know. His expression, as he surveyed them all from behind his desk, was one of hard-nosed determination, thinly disguised by a veneer of concern.

Clearing his throat at a volume which would silence the hubbub of speculation that filled the room at the moment, he fixed them with an 'I don't like this any more than you do' glare, and began to address them.

'I know there has been a lot of speculation and general talk, both here and at Carsfold, and you would be perfectly correct if you assumed that there was change in the air. We live in difficult times, financially, and sacrifices have to be made, at all levels, in our lives.

'I'm sure you've all had to make cuts in your housekeeping budgets, as food prices have risen, as has Mrs Chivers, with much GBH of the earhole for me.' He paused to allow a little chuckle of concurrence, going for a jokey approach, with a bit of 'we're all in this together, lads' for good measure.

'The police force, along with everything else that is funded by the public purse, also has to pull in its horns, so there will be changes in the near future. The intention is to reorganise and streamline the force, to make it more effective: to cut budgets without cutting services.

'Now, the Chief Constable and I, along with a number of other senior and experienced officers, have considered long and hard about how we can achieve the goals we have been set by the government, and we think we have come up with a plan that will satisfy not only our Westminster masters, but you, as well as Joe Public.

'What we are proposing to do is to practically dorm the station at Carsfold. It has few staff and quite a lot of under-used space, and most of the work in the district filters through this station. It has, therefore, been suggested that Carsfold operate with a skeleton staff, and during office hours only. Outside of these times, the public will be expected to contact us here.

'The unused rooms in the Carsfold station will be taken over to be used as a paper archive for the area, as so many of our records have not yet been digitised. We have far too much paper stored here, taking up far too much room. Carsfold has its own stock of old paper records, and so do all of the other tiny rural stations. These will now be combined in one archive, in one place, easy to access, and easy to use.' (*Who did he think he was kidding?*) 'The extra space created here will give us extra office space for those personnel to be transferred.

'Details have not been finalised for who goes where, but what is certain, is that PC Green and PC Starr will both be joining us, and very welcome additions they will be.' Here, he smiled, to show that he wasn't really the big bad wolf. 'There should be a few more additions to our number from other rural locations, and CID will, after the builders have finished the alterations, have its own room. It's possible that there could be an addition to its number.

'As for existing staff, please let me assure you that everything possible will be done to retain those who wish to continue on the payroll. Until final decisions are made, however, no one's future is certain, not even my own.

'Now, I'm not going to ask you if you have any questions, because you probably have dozens, but I won't be able to answer them until the whole plan is finalised. Thank you very much for your time. Now off you go to serve your public, and thank you for your patience. Mind how you go.'

As they trooped out, Falconer turned to Carmichael with a

question on his lips, and Carmichael was interested to hear what the inspector's first question would be after that bombshell.

'Where did the boys get Mr Hat?' he asked, drawing an incredulous look from his sergeant. 'I could do with one myself, although perhaps in rather more muted colours.'

THE END

A Sidecar Named Expire

A Falconer Files Brief Case: #2

Andrea Frazer

Chapter One

'Now, my cocktail starts with one-and-a-half measures of gin.' There was a short glugging sound from around the corner of the L-shaped room, as Chelsea Fairfield began to mix the drinks with which they were going to celebrate their first St Valentine's Day together.

They had only been an item for three weeks or so, but Malcolm Standing had been captivated by her since their first meeting, and had gladly accepted her invitation to spend this evening at her house, drinking cocktails together. He had high hopes of not going home at all tonight, and sprawled on the sofa in an ecstasy of expectation. Tonight would probably be the night!

'One and a half measures of Cointreau,' her voice purred on, 'and one and a half measures of lemon juice. Shake,' he discerned the quiet sloshing of the cocktail shaker being agitated, 'and strain into a frosted glass, over ice. There! That's my White Lady sorted. Now for your Sidecar.'

'How come I don't get to choose my own cocktail?' he called out to her.

'You can after the first one. I just thought a Sidecar was rather appropriate, as you ride a motorbike,' she called in answer, and Malcolm could feel his whole body tingling in anticipation of the evening to come.

'Right! A Sidecar. Bit of information for you here, my dear. This cocktail was originally created after the First

World War, in 'Harry's Bar' – the one in Paris, not the one in Venice, and was named after an officer who used to go there by chauffeur-ridden motorcycle sidecar. See what I mean?

'And now for the ingredients. One measure of cognac, one measure of Cointreau, and one measure of lemon juice.' As she shook the cocktail, he raised his voice to give his opinion of the two recipes.

'Yours seems to be half as strong again as mine. Why's that? It doesn't seem fair to me.'

'Just think about it, sweetie,' she answered, and he heard her speaking in a slightly quieter voice. 'There we go! And strain, garnish with a slice of lemon, over crushed ice. I'm on my way.'

In less than a minute, she came round the 'L', carrying a small silver tray with the two glasses on it.

'Hand it over, then,' Malcolm said, holding out his hand.

'Not just yet, big boy. I want the occasion to be just right, so, just before we drink our cocktails, I want us to enjoy a black Russian cigarette.'

'But I don't smoke!' he protested.

'Neither do I,' she replied, 'but trust me, this is definitely the best way to enjoy these cocktails,' and in so saying, she removed a small black box from a drawer in a wall unit, opened it, and held it out for him to take a cigarette, took one herself, and produced a lighter to light them. 'Now, she ordered, 'a couple of puffs on that, and we can have our glasses. Happy Valentine's Day, darling.'

'And the same to you … darling.' He hesitated over the last word, as this was the first time that they had used it, but he got over his surprise by gazing at the huge bouquet of flowers that he had brought with him, and thought that they had been worth the money, if this was the effect they had on her.

While all this was going through his mind, he was having difficulty not to succumb to a fit of coughing from the cigarette smoke. He had tried smoking when he was about nine or ten, but it had made him throw up, and he just hoped that this unfortunate consequence did not recur this evening. How that would ruin things for him!

Asking for an ashtray, he took a token puff on the cigarette and put it down in the corner of the receptacle, looking pleadingly towards the two glasses on the tray.

'You can have your drink, now,' Chelsea purred, and placed the tray under his nose with a flourish. 'Enjoy!' she said, taking her own glass, and setting the tray down on the wall unit where it had sat in the meantime.

Only a few minutes later, Chelsea stood up and announced that she was going to mix them another drink. 'What, already?' he asked.

'Yes! Come along, slowcoach. Get that down your neck, and we can have another one before seeing how events develop.' Eager at the promise in her words, he downed the last of the liquid in the cocktail glass and watched as she disappeared behind the 'L' again.

'That seemed awfully strong,' he said, raising his voice a little so that she could hear him, and realised that his head was beginning to spin.

'I'll cut down on the measures this time, if it's a problem for you,' she called back. 'And don't forget to have a couple of puffs on your cigarette. They're dead expensive, they are, and if I don't see you smoking it when I get back round there, I'm going to be very cross with you.'

'But I don't like 'em,' he replied, realising that his voice was beginning to slur.

'I don't care! I'm educating you in the finer things in life, and you'll do as I say, or else!'

When she came back to him this time, she put down the tray, extracted two more cigarettes from the box, and lit them both, handing one to him, but when he reached for it reluctantly, he seemed to have two hands on the end of his arm. 'Blimey!' he thought. 'The things that blokes do, just to get a leg-over.'

Putting the slightly smoked cigarette down in the ashtray, he held his hand out for his glass containing his second Sidecar of the night.

As he supped the cold liquid, he took a moment to protest. 'I thought you 'ere goin' to le' me cock my own choose-tail, af'er the firs' one,' he complained, listening to the deterioration in his speech with puzzlement.

'You can choose the next one, my darling,' she soothed him, holding up her glass in salutation to encourage him to drink more of his.

Malcolm had no idea of the time, but it seemed to be a lot later, and he was incapable of moving, and barely capable of thinking. Chelsea was telling him something, but he couldn't understand what she was saying. It seemed to be in a foreign language; one that he had never heard before.

He was aware of her tucking his feet up on the sofa, and removing his shoes and the cocktail glass, which his right hand had still been clutching. How many had he had? He had no idea. His memory was a blank. Slowly his eyelids closed over his reluctant eyes, and he slept.

Chapter Two

Monday 15th February

The voice on the phone was breathless with urgency. 'But he's dead, and he's on my sofa, and I don't know what to do about it. Please send someone as quick as you can. It's so horrible, looking at him just lolling there and … well, being dead, I suppose.

'I've given you the address, but I can't bear to sit here looking at him any longer, so I'm going round to my next door neighbour's. I'll watch for the car from there. Please be quick. This is doing my head in. Oh, I know that sounds awful, but it's just not *him* anymore, it's an 'it', and it's really giving me the willies.

'God knows what happened. He must have had a weak heart, or something. All I know, as I told you, is that he's dead, and in my house, and I simply can't cope with that a moment longer than I have to. Goodbye.'

Desk Sergeant Bob Bryant put down the telephone receiver and made a quick decision to alert Detective Inspector Harry Falconer and his partner, Detective Sergeant Davey Carmichael. This one sounded right up their street, and shouldn't take too long to wrap up once Dr Christmas had got the poor gentleman on the table and opened him up.

Using the internal phone service, he rang through to Falconer to send him and his sergeant on their way, then went back to an external line to contact Dr Philip Christmas to attend the scene as well. As it was an unexpected death, he decided to send a small SOCO team as well. It was better to be safe than sorry, he'd always found, and if things didn't turn out as simply, as he was almost sure they would, it would be in his favour if he had dotted all the i's and crossed all the t's.

Following that flurry of activity, he called one of the uniformed PCs, who had just wandered in, to take over at the desk for ten minutes while he went for a cup of coffee. It was thirsty work, holding the fort at Market Darley Police Station, and he needed a break after that sudden burst of activity.

'It's not far, so we'll take my car,' DI Falconer decided as he and DS Carmichael exited the station, noticing that Bob Bryant was no longer on the desk. 'What was that address again, Carmichael?'

'Twelve Coronation Terrace – built just after the coronation of our present Queen,' he observed, displaying, as usual, more local knowledge than Falconer would have believed could exist in the young man's head. He had recently got married, and seemed, if possible, even happier than he had been when he was first partnered with Falconer the previous summer.

In fact, it was during the previous summer, on their first case together, that Carmichael had met the young woman who had recently become his wife, and he lived with her and her two sons from a previous marriage in the village of Castle Farthing, the locus for said first case.

It only took ten minutes to reach Coronation Terrace, and as they slowed to read the numbers of the houses, a woman came out of one of them stepped over the low dividing front garden wall to the house next door and beckoned to them to stop.

'I've got 'er in 'ere,' she informed them, indicating her own house by the bending of her head in the direction of her front door. 'She's in a terrible state, poor little thing. Such a dreadful thing to 'appen, when you're as young as she is. She can 'ardly take it in, nor neither can I. I'm Ida Jenkins – Mrs – by the way.'

The woman was in her late sixties, and had a motherly look about her. A comfortably round figure with an apron tied over the front of it was presented between sensible carpet slippers and wrinkled stockings at the bottom, and a mop of greying curls and a sympathetic face at the top. She looked kind; just the sort of neighbour one would want to have in an emergency.

'You come on in,' she exhorted them, stepping back over the wall on to her own path. 'She's inside, with a small glass of brandy to perk 'er up. You go in an' see 'er, and I'll make us all a nice cup of tea. I reckon I've got an unopened packet of chocolate digestives in my kitchen cupboard as well. Nothin' like tea to raise the spirits, my old ma used to say, and she was right, too.'

She led them into her living room, which had not been knocked through in the way that many of the houses had, and they found a young woman sitting on the only sofa, quietly crying into a handful of tissues. 'Chelsea Fairfield?' enquired Falconer.

At the sound of his voice she looked up, displaying red eyes and a face made puffy by weeping. Unable to manage a spoken answer, she just nodded her head in acknowledgement of her identity.

'I'm Detective Inspector Falconer from Market Darley CID, and this is my partner, Detective Sergeant Carmichael,' the inspector said by way of introduction. 'We've come in response to your 999 call.'

Miss Fairfield began to cry again, her body wracked by great hiccoughing sobs, as she remembered afresh what had happened. 'I-I'm s-so s-sorry. I just d-don't seem t-to be able t-to t-take it in,' she stuttered, between waves of tears. 'It all s-seems s-so unreal – like a d-dream – a n-nightmare.'

Carmichael immediately sat down beside her on the sofa, his giant frame dwarfing hers, and put a hand round her shoulders. 'Just let it all out,' he advised her, 'and then you'll feel a little better, and we can talk to you, and start to investigate what took place.'

At that juncture, Mrs Jenkins re-entered the room carrying a large, old-fashioned tray, and set it down on a low table that sat so conveniently for the sofa, and the two armchairs that comprised Mrs Jenkins' three-piece-suite, a dazzling affair in red, orange, and yellow velour.

As Mrs Jenkins poured tea for everyone, solicitously asking whether they took milk and sugar, Falconer gazed around him at the room in which they sat. Mrs Jenkins was evidently fond of bright colours, her three-piece-suite being a sufficient example of this to confirm such a belief. Just to add even more evidence to his surmise, the walls were hung with bright prints, and the two rugs on the floor also glowed with jewel-bright colours.

'Very nice, bright room,' he complimented her. Although he preferred more muted shades himself, he needed her on his side if he were to question Miss Fairfield without undue interruption and opposition. She must become an ally, not an enemy.

With the chocolate biscuits being handed round on a pretty porcelain plate, Carmichael removed himself from the sofa, Mrs Jenkins sat down comfortably beside Chelsea Fairfield, and Falconer took the spare armchair. There! That was them all settled now. He'd give it a couple more minutes for the tea and biscuits to do their job of soothing, then the questioning could begin.

Miss Fairfield was calmer now, and had accepted a cup of tea and a couple of biscuits with admirable dignity. Carmichael, without a shred of dignity at all, shoved a chocolate biscuit, whole, into his mouth, to free his hands to extract his notebook from his jacket pocket. To see his sergeant's mouth dealing with such a large offering was an experience Falconer rather wished he had not been witness to. The faces he was making made him look totally alien, and not a little half-witted.

Fortunately, neither of the women noticed, and Falconer only stared because he could not avert his fascinated eyes. They were glued to the spectacle, and there was not a thing he could do about it. Swallowing mightily, Carmichael smiled across at the inspector, and helped himself to another biscuit.

As the whole of it disappeared into his mouth again, Falconer pretended to be interested in the knick-knacks on the mantelpiece, to save himself a repeat of what he had witnessed before.

Chelsea Fairfield finally put down her cup and saucer, blew her nose quietly into the bundle of tissues she still had in her hand, and pulled herself into a bolt-upright sitting position, thus indicating that she was composed now and ready to talk.

Carmichael jammed a final biscuit into his gaping maw and sat with notepad and pen at the ready, but turned slightly away from the group, so that his activity would not be too intrusive and interrupt the natural flow of questioning.

Falconer opened the proceedings. 'Mr Standing – I believe that's the name you gave the desk sergeant? – Mr Malcolm Standing was your boyfriend?' he asked gently, starting with the easier-to-ask questions so as not to upset her too early in the process.

'Yes,' she whispered.

'And you had been going out with him for how long?'

'About three weeks.'

'And what were your plans for last night?' Falconer was gently approaching the nub of the matter.

'It was our first Valentine's Day together, and I wanted to make it really special.'

'In what way?' he probed, but he had obviously touched a sensitive spot, because her face crumpled into a grimace of misery.

'I was going to let him spend the night with me.' She spoke so quietly that he could hardly discern the words.

'And that would have been the first time that he had been invited to do so?' Falconer felt like a rat, poking and prying into this very private part of her life, but it was part of the job and had to be carried out and accepted for what it was.

'That's right,' Chelsea confirmed with a small nod of her head.

'So, what had you planned for the evening?'

'We were going to have some cocktails. They're not something I've ever really drunk before, but a couple of weeks ago I went out with a bunch of girls and we went to a club that specialised in them, and I thought it would be really romantic if we had some, to celebrate being together.'

'You're doing very well, Miss Fairfield,' Falconer praised her, then had his attention distracted by Carmichael, who was doubled over in his chair, coughing, biscuit crumbs flying everywhere.

'Sorry, guv,' he said, between coughs. 'Crumbs went down the wrong way.' Honestly, you could only ever take Carmichael anywhere twice; the second time to apologise.

Trying to recreate the intimate atmosphere that Carmichael had so thoroughly shattered, Falconer continued, 'And what cocktails did you drink?' This might have seemed a pointless question to some, but it could produce the key to the young man's death in that he may prove to have had a severe allergy to one of the ingredients.

'I had a White Lady, and he had a Sidecar.'

'And was it just the one drink?'

'Oh, no. We had more than one. It was such a special night, you see,' she explained. 'And we smoked Russian cigarettes. I wanted it to be so exotic and romantic, and as far away as it was possible to get from a night down at the pub.'

'I understand,' Falconer assured her. 'And who mixed the cocktails?'

'I did. I bought a book, so that I could get the recipes right. I even bought a cocktail shaker. No one in my family's ever had one of those before.' So, she was breaking new ground, socially.

'What happened, when you'd had your cocktails?' This was the difficult bit – finding out about how the young man had become ill, deteriorated, and finally lost his life.

'He said he felt funny, but I just thought it was the exotic drinks that he wasn't used to. Then he got sort of dizzy and unwell; said he felt awful, so I thought the best thing to do would be to settle him down on my sofa for the night, and see how he was in the morning. Of course, it ruined our romantic Valentine's night in, but that didn't matter.

'I got a blanket, and made him as comfortable as I could, then I – I went to bed. That sounds terribly callous, but I didn't think there was that much wrong with him. I thought it was just the strength of the cocktails. If I'd have known how serious it was, I'd have called a doctor. I'm so sorry. This is all my fault!'

'Of course it's not, Miss Fairfield. You're not medically trained. How on earth could you have known what the consequences would be?'

'I should have played safe and called for help,' she stated, tears now coursing down her cheeks. 'But I was woozy too. Cocktails seem to be much stronger than you think they're going to be. I just thought he was a bit more of a lightweight than me where alcohol was concerned, and staggered up to bed because my own head was spinning so much. So much for a romantic evening in! 'Oh, why didn't I call a bloody doctor'?' she wailed in despair, and Mrs Jenkins took her in her arms and rocked her like a baby.

'There, there, lovey. Don't take on so. There's no way anyone can turn back the clock, now is there? We just has to put up with what life dishes out to us, and make the best of it, don't we? Come on, lovey, pull yourself together. You were doin' marvellous there, givin' all that information to the nice inspector.

'Get a hold of yourself, now, and just answer the rest of his questions, then I'll put you upstairs in my own spare room, what used to be my Sharon's, and you can have a nice nap while everyone else gets on with finding out what happened to your poor old boyfriend.' Mrs Jenkins patted Chelsea on the back in a maternal fashion, and gently returned her to her upright position. 'There you are, my duck. Won't be long now, and I'll make you a nice cup of cocoa afore you goes up.'

Falconer had judged this neighbour well, for she was proving a tower of strength now, dealing with Chelsea Fairfield's explosions of emotion, and he was grateful to have been spared the job of doing it himself. Of course, Carmichael would have been better at it than he, he acknowledged, and, in reality, he would probably have left it to his sergeant to restore a calm atmosphere.

Chapter Three

Monday 15th February – later

The two detectives left Chelsea Fairfield in Mrs Jenkins'
tender care and went round to take a look inside number
twelve. Red and white crime tape sealed off the house at
the path, and they ducked under it to approach the
policeman on duty at the door, who had stood stoically
silent as Mrs Jenkins had hopped, slightly arthritically,
back and forth across the adjoining wall when they
arrived.

'Good day to you, PC Proudfoot,' Falconer greeted
him. 'Dr Christmas showed up yet?'

'Arrived just after you went in next door, sir,' answered
PC John Proudfoot, drawing up his somewhat portly body
into the best imitation of 'attention' he could manage.
'Photographer's been, and so has the fingerprint jonnie,
sir. There're a couple of SOCOs waiting to see what you'd
like them to do with regards to searching.'

Duty done, the constable lost his grip on his
strenuously maintained upright position and slumped into
a version of 'at ease'. His protruding belly just could not
cope with being held in restraint for longer than a couple
of minutes, and he thought he'd really have to cut down on
the pork pies and Mars bars that he usually had about his
person for emergency snacks.

Falconer and Carmichael entered the house, and
Falconer couldn't help but notice the complete contrast in

decor between this house and the neighbouring property. Where Mrs Jenkins filled her house with chaotic and eye-catching colour, this house was presented in muted shades, highlighted here and there with the addition of a couple of bright cushions or a single picture on a wall.

No bric-a-brac crowded shelves or mantelpiece, and the whole place, knocked through as it was into one large living, dining, and cooking space, was airy, light, and contemporary.

Mrs Jenkins' house looked like it had been furnished by someone who habituated market stalls and went on holiday to the more English resorts in Spain every year. Chelsea Fairfield's home, in contrast, looked as if its interior design had been culled from up-market magazines and such like. Falconer favoured neither look, but was nonetheless impressed with how very different two neighbouring homes with identical floor plans could look.

Fingerprints having been taken, they found Dr Christmas round the other side of the 'L' shape, washing his hands at the kitchen sink. 'Sorry about this,' he apologised, apropos of nothing. 'It's those damned gloves I have to wear. They leave an awful smell on my hands, and I can't wait to wash them as soon as I've taken the damned things off.'

'Hi there, Philip,' Falconer greeted him, having worked with the doctor a few times now, and managed to establish a congenial working relationship with him. 'Anything to tell us?'

'Apart from the fact that you've got a dead 'un, not really. To all intents and purposes, it would appear that he ingested something that disagreed with him, to the point of fatality. What that substance was I can't tell you at the moment.'

'Stomach contents?' queried the inspector.

'You've got it in one. Also, the fingerprints guy waltzed off with a couple of cocktail glasses and a cocktail shaker. I've rung for the meat wagon, to take the body to the mortuary, and I'll get him opened up as soon as I can. Do you want to sit in on this one?' he asked.

'Why not?' Falconer replied. 'We'll both keep you company,' he volunteered, pretending not to notice the greenish tinge that was colouring Carmichael's face at the very thought of attending a post mortem. 'I haven't attended one for ages – must be getting squeamish in my old age. What about you, Carmichael? When did you last attend an autopsy?'

Carmichael had to suppress the impulse to gag, before he managed to squeak, 'Just the once.'

'Well, it's time you widened your experience, my lad,' Dr Christmas commented hard-heartedly, totally unaware that Carmichael had a weak stomach and was liable to lose the contents of his own insides with remarkably little provocation. 'I'll get on with it first thing tomorrow morning, Harry. See you both at the mortuary at nine o'clock, sharp!'

As the doctor made his exit, the two remaining police personnel approached Falconer to receive instructions as to what they should be looking for. One of them took it upon himself, to be the first to speak. 'By the way, sir,' he began, addressing Falconer, 'we found the back door unlocked this morning. Maybe the young lady forgot to lock it, given the circumstances of her boyfriend being unwell, and feeling a little drunk herself.'

'Gadzooks!' Falconer exclaimed. 'The jungle drums round here are damned efficient. I've only just learnt all that myself, but thanks for the information. If it was unlocked all evening, it might not preclude the possibility that someone entered that way and put something in the

221

cocktail shaker, or one of the bottles, because if Miss Fairfield and Mr Standing were round here, drinking, they wouldn't have been able to see the back door. The bottles will all have to go away for testing as well.'

'You don't think this could have been the work of the young lady then, sir?' asked the other officer.

'From what I've seen of her, I don't think so, but we must investigate all possibilities. When we've finished here and got everything nicely recorded at the station, Carmichael and I will go back next door and dig a little deeper into her background, and that of her boyfriend.

'I shall need a fingertip search done of the garden and any pathways. If anything was introduced into something that young man drank, then it had to be contained in something, so you'll be looking for a small discarded container of some kind. If it was glass, then maybe it was even ground underfoot. Pull out all the stops on this one, and don't forget the wheelie-bin's contents. Many a vital clue has been lost because no one fancied scrabbling through the contents of a refuse container. As it is, the local paper will probably lead tomorrow with the story, with a ghastly headline like "St Valentine's Day Massacre".'

With a duet of 'yes, sirs', the two SOCOs went about their business, and the two detectives headed back to the police station to consolidate what they had learnt so far.

Having stopped for a drink, with a cup of coffee for Falconer and a huge mug of tea (with six sugars) for Carmichael, they chatted about matters unrelated to crime to give themselves a proper break.

'How are you finding married life, then, Carmichael?' Falconer asked, for Carmichael had married his sweetheart at New Year. 'I believe I've actually recovered from the wedding hangover now, but it's taken a long while.'

'You're pulling my leg, sir,' retorted Carmichael, more at ease with the inspector now than he had been when they had first been partnered together. 'And it's grand. I felt like I'd won the jackpot before when we were engaged, and I went over to spend the evenings with Kerry and the boys. Sometimes the Warren-Brownes would babysit, and we'd go out on a proper date. But being married? It's absolutely fantastic, sir. I'd recommend it to anyone.'

'So you quite like it, then?'

'Ha ha, sir. Very funny!'

'Any plans to add to the family?'

'!' Carmichael gave the inspector a very old-fashioned look, which was immediately understood.

'Of course, it's none of my business. I apologise for prying, Carmichael.'

'That's all right, sir, but you know how I feel about discussing anything … like that.'

'I should have remembered.'

'How are your three cats getting on, sir? All well?'

'Very well, thank you. And all eating me out of house and home. Their latest little stunt must have been a joint effort, considering the strength needed to accomplish it. I got home one night a couple of weeks ago, and they'd managed to deposit the back half of a dead rabbit in the middle of the kitchen floor.'

'Half a rabbit?' Carmichael was dumbfounded.

'That's what I thought, until I realised it was probably one that had been run over on the main road, and they'd found it, just grabbed the best bit of booty on offer, and brought it home to me as a little present.'

'Makes a lovely stew or a pie,' said Carmichael, a faraway look in his eyes. 'One of my ma's treats for us when I was a nipper was a rabbit pie. One of my uncles used to go out lamping, and bring her back a brace now and again.'

'I don't think we want to pursue that line any further, Carmichael. I'd hate to have to arrest a member of your family for poaching.'

'Much appreciated, sir,' replied the sergeant, only now aware of what he had let slip.

'Well, better get our noses back to the grindstone. We've got to go back to Coronation Terrace before we're finished for the day, and I want to go to see someone from Standing's family too.'

Bob Bryant had managed to trace Malcolm Standing's next-of-kin, and PC Green had been dispatched to break the news of his death, a job Falconer had hated doing in the past, when it had fallen to his lot. It was the worst news you could bring to anyone, and it always made him feel like an absolute heel having to be the one to break it. He and Carmichael therefore had the address of Mr and Mrs David Standing with them, so that they could pay a visit after returning to Coronation Terrace to continue their questioning of Chelsea Fairfield.

She was up and about, having woken about a quarter of an hour before they arrived, and was now having a cup of tea at Mrs Jenkins' kitchen table. She looked less panic-stricken and upset than she had before when she turned to greet them, and Falconer considered that she had only been going out with the young man for three weeks, and they had not yet instigated a physical relationship. Maybe she'd get over it quicker than he'd thought when he saw her earlier.

At their arrival, Ida Jenkins hurriedly produced two more cups and saucers and poured tea for her two new visitors. As Carmichael ladled sugar into his, she remarked, 'I've never seen anyone take his tea that sweet before, Sergeant Carmichael. But then, you do have a big frame to maintain, so I expects you needs it.' Carmichael just smiled at her, and continued to spoon a little more sugar into his already sticky brew.

Falconer courteously finished his cup of tea before announcing that it was time they resumed questioning. 'I need to know a little more about you and the deceased,' (he winced at the harsh reality of the word) 'Miss Fairfield. I know this is painful for you, so soon after the event, but it is necessary, I assure you.'

'I do understand, and once I've told you, it's done, so fire away, Inspector.' replied Chelsea.

'I need to know, and this may seem a little odd, where you work, and where Mr Standing worked. I would also like you to tell me how and where you met, and anything you know about his life before he met you.'

'I work in the pharmacy in the High Street, and Malcolm … worked,' (she had a little trouble using the past tense, in this reference to him) 'as a sous chef in the Italian restaurant, about three doors from the pharmacy. We worked so close together, but never came across each other until recently,' she informed the two detectives, Carmichael huddled over his notebook, his chair pulled to a slight remove from the table so as not to draw attention to his note-taking.

'Did he tell you anything about his past, or his family?'

'Not a lot. He just said he'd worked there for a few years, and that he was estranged from his family. I never met any of them.'

'Did he say why?' This had interested Falconer.

At this question, she flicked her eyes away from the table and took a deep breath. 'We never discussed it,' she answered abruptly.

'What, never?' Falconer was definitely interested.

'He said he didn't want to talk about it: that it had been some silly adolescent squabble, and that it wasn't relevant to his life anymore. I took him at his word.'

'Do you know where his family lives?'

'I'm afraid not,' Chelsea answered, shaking her head to emphasise this negative.

'Did he have brothers and sisters?'

'I've no idea,' she said, again shaking her head.

'You really knew very little about him, then,' Falconer stated.

'People's pasts don't concern me; only their presents and futures,' she stated emphatically, as if this were really important to her.

'But surely what has happened to us makes us who we are today'?' commented the inspector.

Chelsea's answer consisted of just two words, 'Not necessarily,' and then she clamped her mouth shut, and stared down at the table blankly.

'I think we'll leave it there for now, thank you, Miss Fairfield. We'll be in touch when we have any more news or information. Thank you for your time, and thank you again, Mrs Jenkins, for the refreshments.'

They rose to leave but, just as they were passing through the kitchen door, Falconer looked back and caught a sideways glance after them that expressed extreme relief, on Chelsea Fairfield's face. It could just be a normal reaction. It could be that she was concealing something. He didn't know which, but he intended to find out.

Chapter Four

Tuesday 16th February

In the office the next morning, Falconer and Carmichael fell into a casual chat as they waited for various pieces of information to filter through to them which would allow them to continue their investigation.

'Buying that cottage next door to Kerry's was the best thing I ever did,' Carmichael threw out casually.

'It was originally bought by a couple of weekenders, wasn't it, after that first case we worked together?' asked Falconer.

'That's right, sir. With two very noisy dogs. I don't think the Brigadier knew what had hit him when they bought it. He did nothing but complain to them when they were down for the weekend, and even went to the Parish Council to see if anything could be done about it, but they said he'd just have to put up with it or get the noise abatement officer in from the council if he wanted to take it any further.'

'So they didn't settle?' Falconer had never heard the full story, and was in just the right sort of mood to have his mind distracted while he waited. 'They can't have felt very welcome. I've met the Brigadier, and he can be a fearsome character.'

'They only came down for a few weekends. Kerry left it as it was, telling them that she'd been through it, and they could keep anything they thought was of any interest to them, but the state of the place just defeated them.

'Not only was there a tremendous amount of work to do, but they had constant complaints about their dogs barking, and there was nothing to do in the village, and only the village pub and the tea-shop to amuse them.

'They soon got fed up with spending every weekend they came down clearing out and cleaning, and when Kerry and I had a talk about it, and I offered to buy it from them at the price they'd paid for it, they jumped at the chance.

'Kerry and I knew we'd get married even then, so it seemed like an ideal opportunity for me to take out a mortgage and buy the place, so that we could enlarge the living quarters, without all the upheaval of having to move. And with me buying it, it left Kerry's nest-egg intact for anything big that came up in the future. It was a form of being joined together before we actually tied the knot.'

'Smart move, Carmichael. So now *you've* got to do all the clearing out and renovation.'

'No problem, sir. One of my brothers has got a flat-bed truck, so it'll be easy to get all the rubbish to the tip, and everyone in my family's a dab-hand with a paint brush. We'll get there, and it's a bit of an adventure, too, all the funny little personal bits and pieces we come across, and all the old photos.'

'So, life's being good to you at the moment, Carmichael?' asked Falconer.

'It's just got better and better, since we've worked together,' Carmichael stated, without a whit of embarrassment.

'You soppy old sentimentalist, you!' said Falconer, nevertheless feeling pleased. They did work well together, chalk and cheese that they were, and he was beginning to feel proud of the partnership they were forging.

The telephone rang on Falconer's desk, and as he answered the call, Carmichael applied himself to his computer to carry out the check he'd promised himself he'd do first thing this morning, and had then been waylaid from his intended task by his enthusiasm for his new-found happiness.

Placing the telephone to his ear, a voice spoke without preamble. 'Get your lazy-ass butts over here now! You promised me you'd both attend the post-mortem, and I'm not starting it without *both* of you being here in person.'

He realised immediately that it was Dr Christmas, and blushed at being so remiss. Not only had he forgotten all about their agreement the day before, but it seemed, so had Carmichael. 'I'm so sorry. We both seemed to have suffered a crisis in short-term memory. We'll be over as soon as we can,' he apologised, and ended the call, indicating to Carmichael that they were going out.

'Just a minute, sir. I've got something here!'

'Can't it wait?'

'No, I don't think it can. I've just run Malcolm Standing through the records, and although he has no criminal convictions, it would seem he received a police caution in 2005,' Carmichael informed him.

'What for? Anything interesting?' asked Falconer.

'Don't know if it's relevant, sir, but I don't think it shows him up in a very satisfactory light,' said Carmichael. 'He was cautioned for interfering with a little girl – not very edifying – and it would appear that it wasn't just a one-off offence.'

'We'll see what we can dig up later,' offered Falconer, continuing, 'We haven't got time to do anything about it now. That was Christmas on the phone. We've both forgotten about his blasted post mortem. We were supposed to be there first thing, remember?'

'Oh no!' groaned Carmichael, turning pale. 'I'd completely forgotten about that.'

'So had I, but good old Dr Christmas has stayed his scalpel, until we arrive. Aren't we the lucky bunnies then?'

'No, sir,' disagreed the sergeant, reluctantly following the inspector out of the office, and on their way to an event that both of them would rather have been spared.

Market Darley was too small a town to have its own mortuary, so any bodies in need of storage or a post mortem were kept at the hospital mortuary, and it was in this direction that Harry Falconer drove his beloved Boxster now. Carmichael, beside him in the passenger seat, was unusually quiet, and Falconer enquired if he was all right.

'Not really, sir. I've got a rather delicate stomach.'

'What, with a physique like yours?'

'Can't help it. I've always been like it.'

'Well, I expect Dr Christmas will have the odd bowl or bucket lying around, should you need one. He's always got things like that on hand, for the various bits and pieces he removes from the bodies.'

'Gee, thanks, sir! And I had a really good fry-up this morning, too,' replied Carmichael in a sepulchral voice.

At the hospital, Dr Christmas was already scrubbed-up, gowned, and gloved, practically trembling with his eagerness to wield his various knives, saws, and maybe even a chisel or two. He enjoyed a great deal of Schadenfreude from observing others observing him carrying out this routine task.

Their reactions were so different, and he could never predict who would be sick, who would pass out cold, and who would just observe, and take an intelligent interest, without any reaction at all, to the various bits that were usually on the inside of a body, being delivered, like bastard deformed creatures, to the outside. Sometimes he'd have a little bet with himself, but he hardly ever won. There was nowt so queer as folk, in his opinion.

Falconer heartily disliked seeing people sliced and diced, as if they were in some sort of bizarre cannibal kitchen, but he could cope with it, because of what he had experienced on active duty in the army.

Carmichael was not quite so worldly-wise, and was unusually squeamish when it came to a lot of substances – inside things being outside, blood, and bones being three of them. He also could not deal with vomit, but predicted that it would only be his own that upset his stomach today.

It was the great Y-shaped cut that set Carmichael off: that and the cutting of the ribs to reveal the contents of the chest cavity. Taking a few steps back from the proceedings, he bent nearly double and gave an enormous heave. Dr Christmas's assistant was more than prepared, however, and managed to pop a bucket under his mouth just before a great whoosh of breakfast sprayed out of the sergeant's mouth.

'Ups-a-daisy!' this anonymous individual encouraged him, and stood there stolidly until the gauge on Carmichael's stomach was registering 'empty'. This was all carried out as quietly as possible, as Dr Christmas was speaking into a small suspended microphone, as he noted his findings.

Carmichael was led solicitously away, and settled down somewhere where he could not see what was being carried out, before being offered a large mug of heavily sugared tea to settle his stomach.

He was just finishing this, and feeling a shade more human, when Falconer and Dr Christmas entered the room, both of them looking perfectly well and not the slightest bit wobbly. 'Please don't discuss it while I'm here,' he begged them. 'If you want to talk about, I'd rather go outside and get some air, and wait for you there.'

'I'll be there in a few minutes,' Falconer assured him, and he left them to their post-post mortem discussion.

Carmichael sat himself down on the boundary wall of the little mortuary car park, and sucked in mouthful after mouthful of clean, living air, and Falconer, true to his word, joined him within ten minutes. In his hand he held an empty carrier bag, which he handed to Carmichael. 'Here you are!' he said.

'What's that for?' asked Carmichael.

'To keep under your mouth on the drive back to the station. After this start to the day, if we go out again, we'll take your car. I will not tolerate you being sick in my Boxster, and that's that! If you're sick at the wheel of your own car, I'll happily hold the bag over the steering wheel for you, but I will not allow even the chance of you 'chucking up' in my beauty.'

Back at the station, Falconer had a word with Bob Bryant about the information that Carmichael had turned up on the computer before they had been peremptorily summoned to the mortuary. 'This dead chap, Bob,' he explained. 'Name of Malcolm Standing. It seems he received a caution for child abuse in 2005, when he was in his early twenties. I wondered if there was anything you could dig out about it for me.'

'Seems to ring a bell, but I don't know if the details will be on the computer yet,' Bob answered, his expression one of careful thought. 'I'll see what I can dig up – or get dug up – for you. I'll also ask around, see if anyone remembers it, or was involved. I'll send up anything I find to you, 'ASAP.'

'Thanks, Bob. I owe you one.' If you wanted to know anything about past cases, or even police gossip, you consulted Bob Bryant, who seemed to have worked on the desk forever, and knew every little thing that happened, as if it reached out to him from the past out of the ether.

Upstairs in the office, he found Carmichael sprawled backwards in his chair, still an unnatural colour, and insisted his sergeant took an early lunch, as his tank was obviously out of fuel, and he wouldn't be able to think straight without it. Carmichael smiled at him wanly and ambled off, still looking unhappy, in search of nourishment and a happier tummy.

Chapter Five

Tuesday 16th February – afternoon

When Carmichael returned to the office, he looked a lot more like his normal self and, as Falconer had just stopped to eat his own healthy lunch – a box of salad and a wholemeal bap, followed by an apple and a banana – he took the opportunity to find out a little more about Carmichael's family, the members of which he had met at the sergeant's and Kerry's wedding at the very beginning of the year, but had been rather 'blurred' at the time, and he was now unable to recall them very clearly.

'Well, there's six of us,' Carmichael started. 'Four boys and two girls.'

'And where do you come in that order?' Falconer enquired.

'I'm the fourth and last boy, then come my two sisters.'

'And their names – all of them?'

'My oldest brother's called Romeo, but everybody calls him 'Rome'. He's a builder. Gave me a bit of a hand when I built my little hideaway, when I lived at home. Then there's Hamlet – I told you my ma had this Shakespearian thing about names. He's known as Ham, and he works on a farm.

'Number three is Mercutio – just called Merc, like the car. He's a sort of 'man with a van'. He does small removals, house clearance, odd jobs, and gardening. He reckons the variety of jobs is good for him and stops him getting bored. Then it's me, but you know about me,

234

because we work together,' said Carmichael, stating the bleedin' obvious. 'I got the Ralph bit, because my ma was really taken with an actor at the time – some fellow called Richardson.'

'Tell me, Carmichael, is your 'ma'' (Falconer suppressed a wince at this mode of maternal address) 'a great Shakespeare fan, then?'

'Not really. She just liked the names he used in his plays. Said they had a sort of 'ring' to them, like, but I'd better finish my family run-down.

'Next come the two girls. Juliet's the elder, and she's a hairdresser and beautician. Then, finally, there's Imogen, who's a librarian. She's done really well, passing all her exams and everything, and we're all very proud of her.'

'I should think they're all very proud of you, too,' Falconer commented.

'Yes, well, sort of,' replied Carmichael.

'What do you mean, sort of?' asked Falconer, not quite understanding why his family should not be really happy about what he was doing.

'Not everyone likes having a member of 'the fuzz' in their immediate family,' the sergeant stated baldly, turning slightly red, and avoiding Falconer's gaze.

''Nuff said, Carmichael. No further explanation needed or sought,' Falconer added, hoping to dispel the younger man's evident embarrassment, as he remembered the uncle who used to go out 'lamping' for rabbits. That was, no doubt, one of his more innocent pastimes. What he didn't know couldn't hurt him, and he'd pry no further. 'What about your parents? How did they cope with such a large brood?' 'Dad's a lot older than Ma. He's retired now, but he used to be a bus driver, then a coach driver. He always said he liked the long continental coach trips, 'cos at least it gave him the security of knowing that he couldn't get

Ma in pod again while he was away. He swears that most of us kids were conceived just from him kissing her goodbye on the cheek when he went to work in the mornings.

'Ma married him at sixteen, in a bit of a hurry, and she's never had a proper, paid job. She said she always had too much to do just keeping house and home together, and preventing us kids from overthrowing western society, but I think she was joking about that last bit,' he concluded.

'I should hope so!' exclaimed Falconer, trying to digest the plethora of facts he had just been offered. By crikey! He bet their Christmases were good, if Carmichael's wedding had been anything to go by. He just hoped that he was never asked to join their celebrations.

'Ma says that after six kids, her pelvic floor's so riddled with woodworm, that if one more kid trod on it, they'd go right through,' Carmichael added as an afterthought, and Falconer wrinkled his nose in disgust, determined to change the subject at all costs. He had no wish whatsoever to learn anything further about Mrs Carmichael senior's insides, having just had an intimate encounter with those of Malcolm Standing that morning.

'And how are the two little dogs you got last month? I'm sorry, I can't remember their names offhand.'

'Fang and Mr Knuckles,' declaimed Carmichael with pride, suitably distracted. Fang was a Chihuahua puppy, and Mr Knuckles a miniature Yorkshire terrier. When Falconer had first seen them they were tiny balls of fluff, which looked ridiculous cradled by the enormous Carmichael.

'They're getting on great! The boys love them, and they get more walks than they can cope with, poor little things. They slot right into the family, as if a gap has been waiting for them for some time. You must come and visit them sometime, sir.'

'We'll see, Carmichael. Not when we're in the middle of an investigation.'

Later that afternoon, Bob Bryant came upstairs with a dog-eared buff folder for Falconer, this being the file on Malcolm Standing's official caution. 'There were, apparently, some newspaper cuttings supposed to be in here, too, but they seem to have gone missing. I know there was a bit of a fuss about it at the time.

'We don't know who leaked it to the press, but that's the sort of thing that happens when it's a case of interfering with little kids. People get upset and can't bear to see it brushed under the carpet, even if there's no court case or prosecution,' he explained, having handed over the slim folder.

'Thanks for that, Bob. I'll have a little read of this, see if it throws any light on anything.'

There was very little in the case notes to help, but there were references on a separate sheet of paper to local newspaper reports which sensationalised the caution, blowing it out of all proportion and demonising the young Malcolm Standing.

It had all been five years ago now, and the dust must have settled, as Malcolm had been in the last job he was ever to hold for three years. It made him think of something someone had said when he was a child, and which had impressed itself on his memory, although he didn't completely understand it at the time. 'Good times, bad times, all times pass over.'

This sensation of its time had also passed over, and allowed the younger Standing to get whatever it was that had driven him to it out of his system, and try to lead a more normal life thereafter.

Many of Falconer's dealings with the local press in the past had been with the *Carsfold Gazette*, but this had happened in Market Darley and, after checking the telephone number, he put through a call to the *Market Darley Post* – a local newspaper that was more likely to have carried the story – asking for the editor when his call was answered.

'Good morning. I am Detective Inspector Falconer from Market Darley CID, and I was wondering if I could have a rummage through your archives for some information that may be pertinent to a case I'm working on at the moment?' he asked.

'Good morning, Chief Inspector Falconer. My name's Garry Mathers – that's two 'r's in Garry – and I should be delighted to be of assistance to the constabulary, provided, of course, that I get a scoop on whatever story is about to break.'

'Typical press!' thought Falconer, before replying, 'There might not be any case to break, but whatever comes of it, I promise that you will be the first to know. Is it all right if I pop over now? Time is always rather pressing during an investigation.'

'No problemo, squire! I am here to serve my community.'

Oh boy! He had a feeling he wasn't going to like this, but it had to be done.

Half an hour later found Falconer sitting in a back room at the offices of the *Market Darley Post*, scrolling through records of back numbers of the newspaper. Garry Mathers had provided him with the relevant year, and he knew the date of the official caution, so he worked from that date onwards, scrutinising each issue with a view to identifying any and every paragraph about Malcolm Standing's misdemeanour.

It seemed that the local press had made rather a large meal of the event, and headlines proclaimed the presence in the streets of Market Darley of a young and dangerous paedophile, stalking his victims at will, and, as yet, not behind bars. There were follow-up articles about the public outcry, and a special double-page letters section, allowing the town's residents to have their say, and it didn't make pleasant reading.

There was mention of another child being questioned about whether she had been assaulted or approached by Standing, but her (it was made obvious that this was a 'she') name was never mentioned. The identity of the child, concerning whom the caution had been issued, was also not published for legal reasons, so the articles were not a great deal of help to him. All they really did was to clarify the public hostility the young man must have endured at the time, and how difficult it must have been for him to live this down and start afresh, trying to live a more normal life after all the publicity had been superseded by more current events.

He'd rather naively pinned his hopes on learning something from this outdated reportage, forgetting that the young victim of any sort of abuse was guaranteed anonymity, and he supposed he must have hoped that someone would have let a name 'slip' at the time. Even if they had, the newspaper had not had the temerity to print it, no doubt fearing prosecution should they have done so.

Before he left, he even sought out Garry (with two 'r's!) in his office, to see if he could give him a name on the Q.T. but that was no-go, either. He'd only been there a year, and had no knowledge of events in Market Darley that long ago. 'I moved down from Town,' he explained. 'Thought I'd rather be a big fish in a small pond, than a minnow in the shark-infested waters of the capital.'

So, that was that! Dead end! What now? He decided to go back to Bob Bryant, and see what he could winkle out of the darker corners of his memory.

'Anything you can drag up, Bob,' he pleaded with the desk sergeant, as he entered the station, after his abortive treasure hunt.

'Leave it with me, and I'll give you a tinkle as soon as anything comes back to me,' he promised, and Falconer had to be content with that.

When he got back to his own office, he found a message to contact Dr Christmas, an activity he carried out without delay. He might have identified the substance that caused Standing's death, and that might give them a clue as to who had administered it. Although Chelsea Fairfield was the obvious choice, she had not struck him as a murderer, and Malcolm Standing had had a lot of enemies from the past.

He was in luck, as Christmas answered on the third ring. 'Hello there, Harry. I've got some news for you, my boy.' Bingo! And the doctor sounded happy, so it looked like Falconer was finally going to learn something solid about the case.

'The lab's identified what that young chap ingested. You'll never guess what it was.'

'Don't tease me, please. I can hardly stand the suspense,' Falconer pleaded.

'It was a whacking great dose of good old-fashioned valium. If that girl had called for help when he first started feeling strange, they could have saved him, but valium is a muscle relaxant, and it works on the chest muscles as well and suppresses breathing. If she'd have summoned an ambulance, they could have got him pumped out and stabilised him. As it was, he died of suffocation.'

'I don't really know that I want to tell her that,' Falconer replied. 'She's worried enough about whether he would have been all right if she'd called a doctor the night before. This news would probably destroy her.'

'I'll leave that particular moral dilemma with you. My job is just to identify the cause of death, and pass on that information. Good luck!'

'Thanks, Philip. Goodbye.' Falconer put down the telephone, now faced with a new problem: to tell, or not to tell, that was the question.

While he was mulling this over, the internal phone system trilled, and he found Bob Bryant on the other end of the line. 'So soon?' he queried, knowing that Bob would know what he was talking about.

'I just remembered who administered the official caution, and you're not going to believe this, but it was our very own darling Superintendent 'Jelly' Chivers. It was just before he was promoted from detective chief inspector, and he must have frightened seven shades of shite out of that young lad, for he never reoffended, as far as I know.'

'Language, Bob!'

'I know, but put yourself in the lad's position. Yes, you've done something terrible, and now here you are in front of this terrifying monster while he roars the caution at you and delivers a hell-fire and brimstone lecture to you at the same time. I bet he wished the earth would open up and swallow him.'

'That doesn't detract from the seriousness of the matter, though, Bob,' Falconer felt compelled to point out.

'I realise that, but I bet if he was used on young offenders of any sort, he'd be a better deterrent than these soft Youth Detention Centres they put them in nowadays. I'd be willing to bet that anyone who's ever been cautioned by old Jelly has never reoffended, nor even considered it.' This was Bob Bryant's personal opinion, and nothing would sway him from his belief.

'You could be right, at that, Bob,' agreed Falconer, imagining how he'd felt in the past, when Chivers had given him a good bawling-out over something.

'So I've booked an appointment for you to see the great man himself, at 9.30 tomorrow morning.'

'Thanks a bunch, Bob. Do I get a last request before I enter his office, like a man facing a firing squad?'

'I should advise you to step warily. He's going to a golf club dinner tonight, and he's liable to have a sore head.'

'Great! So, not long after I get in tomorrow, I have to enter the den of a bear with a sore head, and try to get him to think back to something that happened five years ago?'

'That's about the size of it, Harry. Good luck! And let me see the wounds afterwards, won't you?'

Falconer finished the call with just one word, 'Rat!' but he heard Bob Bryant's chuckle. before the line went dead.

Chapter Six

Tuesday 16th February

The next morning, having dressed and carried out his daily grooming with especial care, Falconer found himself outside Superintendent Chivers' office with thirty seconds to spare. Counting them down conscientiously on his watch, he mouthed, 'Three, two, one,' and raised his hand to rap on the door when it unexpectedly opened, and he found himself apparently brandishing a fist in the superintendent's face.

'Sorry, sir,' he mumbled in apology, letting his hand drop.

'I was just coming out to see where the devil you'd got to,' snapped Chivers, striding back into his office and throwing himself, like a large sack of potatoes, into his chair. 'What do you want?'

'I need to talk to you about an official caution you delivered about five years ago,' Falconer began, only to be nearly blasted out of his socks by the voice of a volcano.

'Five years ago? How the devil am I supposed to remember something I did five years ago? Are you mad, man?'

'I think you'll remember this one, sir,' Falconer suggested humbly, glad that he hadn't been flattened in the blast. 'It concerns a young man called Malcolm Standing, and you were dealing with a case of interfering with a little girl. The parents didn't want to put their daughter through the trauma of a trial, I presume, but the press got hold of it somehow, and created a nine days' sensation out of it.'

Chivers sat in silence for a few seconds, then, it seemed, from his expression, that light had dawned. 'I do remember that one. Nasty business, very nasty indeed. I gave the little toe-rag a right dressing down, and it left me feeling physically sick to think what he'd done.'

'It's just that I need to know as much as I can about who was involved, with reference to a case I'm working on now. Standing has been murdered, and I wondered if it could have been done by someone connected with his misdemeanour back then.'

'I see,' said Chivers, thoughtfully. 'The child's family name was, I seem to remember, Ifield. She was their only child, Eileen, who was sinned against. She was thirteen when it finally came out. I don't know what the catalyst was, but she suddenly confessed to her mother, and it would seem that the abuse had been going on from when she was just seven years old until the previous year.'

'Is it possible that you still have an address for the Ifields? I'd like to speak to them, and to Eileen, about Standing. I wouldn't normally rake up something like this, but I need to catch whoever murdered him.'

'I'm afraid you're out of luck with all the members of the family. Mr and Mrs Ifield moved away from the area after their daughter committed suicide a couple of years ago.'

'She killed herself?' Falconer asked, aghast.

'That's right, and only sixteen years of age,' replied Superintendent Chivers, a shadow passing across his expression, as he remembered the sad event.

'How did she do it, sir?'

'With tablets. Something the doctor had prescribed for her. It was all that little bastard's doing, you know. She was never the same after that, her parents told me. I went to the funeral. Felt I had to; show some respect, and the support of the police.'

'I don't suppose you know what tablets she used, or who her doctor was at the time, sir?' Falconer was determined that there was a connection, and he wanted to get to the bottom of it.

'That I can't recall, but it was reported in the local paper. It might be worth your while trawling through their back issues for 2008. I seem to remember that they made a bit of a song and dance about it. Poor little abused girl, couldn't forget and get on with her life – you know the sort of melodramatic crap the media churn out. 'Probably hoped to start off the same old witch hunt again, but the general opinion seemed to be to let the past rest in peace. Raking it all up again wouldn't bring her back, or restore her innocence.

'We had a few calls from members of the public, asking us why we hadn't locked him up and thrown away the key, but I put out a press statement, informing them that the poor girl's life would have been even more blighted by having to go through the trauma of a court case. That soon shut them up. Sorry I can't be of more help, Harry.'

'You've been very helpful indeed. I'll drop in at the *Market Darley Post* offices, and have a look at 2008; see what they reported at the time of her suicide.'

'Good man. And good luck!'

Returning once more in the back room of the local newspaper offices, Falconer metaphorically shook himself free of the invisible slime that Garry Mathers had seemed to coat him in when he had first arrived, then set to work to hunt out the articles he was after.

It didn't take him long to find them, for the story had made the front page: the press, as usual, braying for someone's blood, and not caring in this case whether it came from the local constabulary or Malcolm Standing himself.

Reading the articles written at that time, and the statement issued by Chivers himself, he finally, just out of idle curiosity, began to hunt for the death notices of the young girl, or perhaps he should refer to her as a young woman, at sixteen years of age?

These he found without difficulty. Many of her friends and relatives had put separate announcements in, and he scanned the column conscientiously, his eyes widening with surprise as he read the last announcement, hardly able to believe what he was seeing.

With an expression of infinite sadness in his eyes, he packed up his notebook and left the building, towards the inevitable end of this case.

Back at the office once more, he collected Carmichael and requested that PC Linda 'Twinkle' Starr accompany him on his mission. To neither of them did he say anything, just asking them to take their lead from him, and follow standard police procedure.

He drove, and it wasn't long before they stopped outside Coronation Terrace. Number twelve was their destination, and his steps were slow and heavy as he walked up the garden path. PC Starr accompanied him: Carmichael had been instructed to go round to the back of the property, in case there was a last-minute escape attempt.

Chelsea Fairfield answered the door, her face a picture of panic and despair when she saw who was waiting for her. She'd been a great little actress up till now, but she realised the game was up.

'I think you know why we're here, don't you, Miss Fairfield?' Falconer asked, his voice thick with emotion at the waste of another young life.

'You'd better come in,' she said, as if she cared what the neighbours would think!

When Carmichael was alerted that they had gained entrance, he went next door to number ten and asked Mrs Jenkins to join them. She would be support for Chelsea in her hour of need, and she also made exceedingly good tea. If he was lucky, she might even bring some biscuits round with her. No matter how grave the circumstances, Carmichael was always hungry!

Ida Jenkins went one better, and appeared at the front door with a cake tin. 'Just a little something I made yesterday,' she announced. 'Nothing like a bit of sugar to make you feel a bit stronger when times is trying, is there?' she asked of no one in particular.

She bustled around Chelsea's kitchen area, clattering crockery and boiling the kettle, while Falconer got on with what he had come here for.

'Why did you do it?' he asked the young woman, who had not yet shed a tear at their discovery of her crime.

'She told me about what Malcolm had done when she was about eleven,' she said. 'And I told her that she had to do something about it, but she said she couldn't tell her mum. I used to go and stay there for a while, in the summer holidays, because we were both only children and they lived out of town. It didn't matter about the age difference: she was like a little sister to me.

'The next year, when I went back, I found out it was still going on and I was furious. Of course, by then, I wasn't staying there for long in the summer. I was seventeen years old, and I'd discovered boys and parties and I wanted to be with people my own age. Young people can be so selfish,' she finished, not noting the irony that she was still one of those young people. Maybe she'd had to grow up faster than most, though.

'I didn't want to get involved, but I asked her to show me where he lived, and I wrote him an anonymous letter telling him I'd castrate him if he ever laid a finger on her again, and it seemed that he did stop, but it was also me that told her parents she had something disturbing to tell them, and that they'd better get her to talk to them.

'Time went by so fast that we hardly spoke again until just before she took her own life. I think she'd discovered boys, and found that what he'd done to her had changed her. She didn't think she'd ever be able to have a boyfriend like normal girls do. It was all so sad. She'd lost so much weight. She used to be a chubby, laughing little child, but by the end, she looked like a skeleton. *He* did that to her!

'For me, it was over when I sent that letter and he left her alone, but it had haunted her ever since. As soon as I heard what she'd done, I went over there to see Auntie Maureen and Uncle Brian, and that's when I did it.'

'Did what?' Falconer asked her, his voice muted, his face careworn.

'I took the tablets she hadn't taken.'

'So it wasn't something you got from the pharmacy where you work?' Falconer asked.

'No. I took what was available at the time, and just hung on to them, because I decided there and then that I'd hunt that evil bastard down and somehow get even for her. And that's exactly what I did. Of course, I had to get on with my own life. Then I had to find him, and strike up

248

some sort of relationship with him. Perhaps now you'll understand why I kept him waiting for you-know-what.

'I can't tell you how unbearable it felt, to have that creep slobbering all over me, and trying to get into my knickers for those three weeks.

'There was no way I was ever going to go to bed with that evil little pervert, but I was going to deliver justice to him – a life for a life!'

'Did you know what those tablets would do to him?' Falconer interjected at this juncture.

'I knew what they'd done to my cousin, and I just wanted the same thing to happen to him. I ground them up with my pestle and mortar, and dissolved them as best as I could before he arrived, then I split the suspension between two drinks, hurrying him through the first one so that I could get him to drink the second one before he lost consciousness.

'Of course, when I saw the reality of what I'd done, and phoned the station, I really was hysterical. I couldn't believe it! The seriousness of actually taking a life. But later, I remembered all that poor little Eileen had gone through, and I was glad.'

Her voice trailed off into silence, and Mrs Jenkins erupted into that silence, carrying a tray, and carolling, 'Tea and cake for everybody. Just the thing to lift the spirits, that's what I always say.'

THE END

The Falconer Files

by

Andrea Frazer

For more information about **Andrea Frazer**
and other **Accent Press** titles
please visit
www.accentpress.co.uk